SINDER

T0151029

SINDER

KATHLEEN KAUFMAN

TURNER PUBLISHING COMPANY

Turner Publishing Company
Nashville, Tennessee
www.turnerpublishing.com

Cover design: M.S. Corley
Book design: Meg Reid

Library of Congress Cataloging-in-Publication Data Upon Request

9781684423309 Paperback
9781684423316 Hardcover
9781684423323 eBook

Printed in the United States of America
19 20 10 9 8 7 6 5 4 3 2 1

To Terry—our gentle and wise Matrarc. I miss you.

"The world is full of magic things, patiently waiting for our senses to grow sharper."

—W.B. Yeats

1

AINSLEY, 1924

THE STORIES TOLD OF FAE FOLK WHO HID IN THE
shadow of the wood when the sun burned bright in the Irish sky—
creatures that snuck to the River Lee only after the fire and heat
had slipped over the horizon, leaving the waking world in darkness.
There they would fill their tiny buckets and pails, hauling them
back to their fairy mounds and caves so they could boil the herbs
and leaves they had collected from the ancient forest. If a baby was
set to the colic or a fever had risen that brought the sweats and
delirium, then one could sit very quietly on the edge of the wood,
a small dish of black salt and a bit of bread in hand. If the fae were
feeling generous, if you were quiet enough, and if your need was
pure, then they might bring you one of their tiny vials containing a
foul-smelling poultice or a murky elixir in exchange for the tribute.
The elders cautioned you could not trust the fae entirely. They
were as likely to bring you a tea made from the autumn crocus or
nightshade as they were to heal the rash or calm the croup. Still,
especially when a young one lay ill, face waxy with fever and eyes
unfocused, it was not uncommon to take the risk.

Ainsley Robertson wrapped her pale hair up into a knot and pulled her rough wool shawl tighter around her as she perched at the top of the knoll, on the edge of the wood. The sun was setting across the River Lee, and the water was ablaze with the dying fire of late fall. The air was sharp and carried the hint of the freeze of winter. She had no black salt and had eaten the bread. The fae would need to concede that her stomach was more important than their tribute. But she was quiet, and her need was strong if not pure.

The thing she needed was an end, a tea of weaver's broom or strychnine tree—a means to send the spirit that grew inside her womb back to the place it came from. Or, if the fae were made of the same cowling lot as the elders, then Ainsley wished for a draught of hemlock or wormwood so that she would join the night entire. So she sat watching the sun disappear below the horizon, watching the darkness deepen and overtake the hillside. The fae did not appear, and Ainsley pulled herself off the damp heath and walked back up the hill and along the familiar path to a huddle of farmhouses accented only by the sheep and goat paddocks and the field mare milling about in her stall.

Smoke rose from the chimney of her home, and Ainsley could smell mutton stew and fresh bread. Her stomach twisted painfully, reminding her that the last time she ate was several hours ago and that the meal had been intended as tribute to the fae. With a sigh of resignation, she trudged forward to the front door and slid inside, letting as little of the chill night air in as possible. Her mother looked up from the rough wood table, a basket of dried bilberry before her. She was in the process of grinding the dried berries with a stone pestle when she paused to glare at Ainsley.

"Your father set out half an hour ago to see if you were dead and gone," she muttered. "I had no opinion either way on how I hoped he might find ye."

Ainsley said nothing and hung her shawl, damp from the night air, on the hook by the door.

"Eat," her mother commanded as she nodded toward the hearth where the soup pot, still full of a rolling warmth, had been moved from the fire. Ainsley ladled herself a bowl of the thick stew and sat across from her mother as she commenced with the task of pulverizing the dried berries. Ainsley inhaled the food, the warmth of it spreading downward to the alien force that rolled and twisted inside her abdomen like a winter storm. There was a stirring up above in the loft where Ainsley slept with her little sister, Maire. A tiny, pale face appeared over the edge. Maire gave her a quick smile and ducked back before their mother could direct her glare upward.

"I expect you have a reason for this worry," her mother said as Ainsley rinsed her bowl in the sink.

"I don't," Ainsley replied quietly but firmly.

"Your father is the Ceannaire of the Society. You are his eldest daughter, and you stay out all times of night. You've been matched and will be a married woman before spring, and you behave as though you were a common amadán." Her mother was turning the berries to dust with the force of her thick, muscled arm. Her voice was level, but Ainsley could hear the fire beneath the calm.

"You've been seeing that gra'nna buachaill." Her mother stopped the destruction of the berries for a moment and locked her eyes on Ainsley.

"No," Ainsley replied, her voice small. "He left from Cork Harbour for England months ago, you know that."

"Finnan Rourke is the son of Grady Rourke," her mother stated and emptied the berry dust into a shallow bowl before refilling the mortar with a fresh batch of victims. "Grady Rourke ran off on a merchant ship with an English whore and let his family starve, Finnan included. His son grew to be no better."

"Well, he's gone now, left some time ago and not coming back," Ainsley spat as she spun around to stare out the tiny window into the darkness.

That night, as Ainsley lay on the straw cot next to Maire, she laid her hands on her still unnoticeable belly. It was a secret between herself and the fae—and would be for as long as it could be kept. Next to her, Maire shivered and Ainsley pulled her close, wrapping the end of her blanket over the little girl. Maybe the fae would bring her a moon-shaped boat, and the three of them—Ainsley, Maire, and the baby—could sail from Cork Harbour into the Celtic Sea. Maybe the Old Moon from the fairy stories would pull them up to the stars and they'd spend their nights looking down on the rolling Cork hillsides, far from the rot of the Society. As Ainsley let the last claw of consciousness slip into a dreamless sleep, she let herself feel the hum of the night sky and the power of the darkness that lay beyond. Her fingertips trembled with the intensity of it all, and as sleep overtook her entirely, Ainsley Robertson felt the stars themselves flowing through her veins.

2

CEIT, 1996

"I HAVE NO ONE ELSE TO TURN TO," THE OLD WOMAN in a rough wool dress whimpered. "My husband is dead. I ask you, Matrarc, for your generosity, your sympathy, your pity."

Ceit Robertson considered the pathetic creature before her. Máthair Bedelia had never simpered or cowed like this with Ceit's great-grandmother Mór Ainsley, the previous Matrarc. It spoke of many things, but as Ceit looked into the old woman's face, locking her pale eyes on Bedelia's unfocused and vapid gaze, she knew her to be false.

Ceit sighed. "What is it you want me to do for you?" she asked in a steady tone, already knowing the answer. Beside her, her brother Alan shifted, leaning forward just slightly.

"They stole from me. They took my Aedan's things, they took my memories, all the things I hold dear," Bedelia whispered theatrically.

"This is a very sad thing you tell me," Ceit replied evenly. "And I would like to help, but you have not said what it is you need from me."

"You can call the old ones, the Rabharta, the Siabhra. You can call them to devour these thieves, these monsters." Bedelia looked up cautiously. "I was just a girl when we came to this country with your great-grandmother. Mór Ainsley would—"

"Don't speak to me of my great-grandmother." Ceit cut her off sharply, and the old woman recoiled as though slapped. "I cannot do what you ask. I will not call the old gods and fae to settle your dispute—this is unreasonable. I can help you with a bit of money to replace some of what is lost, and that is all." Ceit nodded to Alan, who stood to take the old woman's arm and lead her out of the room. She started to object, but when Ceit tilted her head and sharpened her gaze, the old woman fell mute.

"Thank you, Matrarc. Thank you," Bedelia murmured, nodding her head sporadically.

Alan returned and closed the door behind him.

"How much are we giving her?" he asked cautiously.

Ceit sighed and took a sip of the now cold tea that sat beside her. "She's upset that the hospital threw out his clothes, and she says they lost his watch. Give her twenty dollars for the watch, and make sure her pantries are full. Take the car and go to the market for her." Ceit leaned back as Alan nodded. "She wasn't here because the hospital staff lost his socks and undershirt. She's trying to see how far I'll go. I do not care to be tested. Give her the twenty dollars and tell her the matter is closed."

Alan nodded and turned to the door.

"And Alan," Ceit called out as her brother turned, "go back and enjoy your party. I will take no more visitors until after we eat. It's your graduation day—you should be proud."

Alan gave her a half smile. "Thank you, Matrarc."

3

AINSLEY, 1924

THE SHEEP NEEDED TO BE RUN FROM THE PADDOCK TO the river, and the old milk cow needed to be tended to before Ainsley set to Cork proper to fetch the shopping. She could hardly keep her mind focused as she hurried the ragged creatures down the path to the River Lee. Her father once had a flock greater than even the farmers who claimed province in upper Cork. *But not any longer,* she thought bitterly as they ambled to the water's edge. She'd have to drive them back or they'd fall in headfirst and drown their fool selves. She could feel the pull of the city. The barkeep at the Standard House had promised to keep any letters that might arrive from Finnan, and while she doubted that any had, it was a welcome respite from the suspicion that had descended around her.

The trouble had started as soon as she had climbed down from the loft, her back aching from the lashing her father had given her when he'd arrived home the previous night. She'd woken to his heavy footsteps and the softly urgent murmurings of her mother.

He had reached up and with one hand pulled her off the loft to the floor below. Ainsley cried out with pain and covered her face as her father brought the elm switch down on her back over and over. Her mother had watched the beating from the corner, her mouth trembling, knowing enough not to intervene. Later, she'd leave a jar of salve on the edge of the loft and never speak a word of it. His face red with anger and his breath heavy, her father had finally relented and thrown the switch to the side. He'd never spoken, but Ainsley knew her crime had been far beyond staying out too late. Her father knew about Finnan, and it had been an embarrassment. She pushed back the thought of what he'd do if he knew her condition. Ainsley had crawled back up the ladder and curled into a ball. Maire wrapped her arms around her, and the little girl whispered the old folk song they sang in the Society—the only comfort she could give.

> *I sing of the fae and the wood and the vine,*
> *And the night that lasts forever.*
> *The ghosts of your loves and the ghosts that are mine,*
> *Will linger there forever.*

But instead of calming, it set fire to Ainsley's anger. She had lain next to her sweet sister, her body shaking with pain and fury. When she closed her eyes, she imagined a wall of fire engulfing her father, a tiger tearing his limbs from his body, the Fomoire of the children's stories crushing him in their great hands. The rage she felt numbed the pain from the bloody lash marks that striped her back and shoulders.

When morning came, Maire still snored softly under a pile of blankets. No one was awake but Ainsley, and a good thing for it. The cast-iron coire, the soup pot, which stood to Ainsley's knees and was heavy enough to need two sets of hands to lift to the fire, lay in severed shards and pieces as though it had been made of fine bone china. The contents, last night's mutton stew, were congealing on the wood floor. It was as though the soup pot had been sliced to bits by a blade of unfathomable strength. Ainsley had frozen in place, her heart beating out of her chest as she surveyed the damage. It was beyond imagining, and nearly as disastrous. The ancient cauldron had been passed down from more generations than Ainsley cared to count, and no one ever gleamed a day when it would be no more. It was the source of so many things in their house, and it was, beyond the bizarre nature of it, an irreplaceable loss.

Ainsley had had only a few precious minutes to let these thoughts settle, however, before her mother had ambled into the great room and taken stock of the damage. Her howls of rage were as much grief and fear as they were anger. She had smacked Ainsley over the back of her head with the broom handle, even though she had to have known this was beyond any mortal person's doing. Her father had been roused and, still fuming from the night before, had stopped in the doorway, eerily quiet. He'd taken the broom from his wife's hands before she cracked Ainsley's skull clean open and, with one gesture of his weatherworn hands, settled the woman back to silence.

"It's not the girl, you fool," he had muttered. "The Fomoire have visited this hearth. We will need to set things right."

Ainsley had been set to cleaning up the impossibly heavy shards of cast iron and scrubbing the crusted stew off the floorboards. Her father, as Ceannaire of the Society, had been off discussing with the elders the presence of the Fomoire and what steps they would take to rid themselves of the spirits. Once the house was clean and her mother ready to be rid of her daughter for a time, Ainsley was finally free to tend the sheep and then escape to town.

The Fomoire were a child's story, and Ainsley swallowed her disgust in the absolute belief the elders placed in it. A race of giants with the strength of the old gods who brought destruction to those who offended them. The lore was that when the fae and forest spirits were finally appeased, the veil would lift and the Society would finally see the next world. The elders laid wild cherry and broomweed out on the river's edge to appease the spirits, and her father would try to lift the veil between this world and the next. He had never succeeded in doing so.

Ainsley was unmarried as yet and considered a child, thus she had never been privy to the ceremony. That hadn't stopped her from creeping out of the house on the nights of the full moon to watch her father standing on the banks of the River Lee—where his sheep now lazily grazed—his arms lifted to the sky and the water angry and disrupted behind him. The elders would chant in the old language and raise their arms to the night sky in echo of their leader. This would go on for hours, and eventually Ainsley would grow tired of it and creep back to her bed, her hands and feet chilled and her head numb from watching what appeared to be a useless, if benign, set of theatrics.

Ainsley rounded up the stragglers and started the trek back up the path to the paddock, the sheep stumbling in front of her. She wondered if the elders would consider her less of a child and welcome her to the ceremonies if they knew her condition. No matter though, she had no desire to be a part of the idiocy. As she pushed the last creature into the pen and latched the gate, she set to the kitchen to gather her things for town. Maire entered with a pail of milk and set it on the table.

"What will we do without the coire?" the little girl asked, her voice small and unsure.

Ainsley kissed the tip of her nose. "I'm sure Da will demand a replacement from the Fomoire, and it will be bigger and better than ever. I bet he'll even have the old gods install the electric lights like the grand houses in Cork."

Maire giggled, but worry crossed her face. "You shouldn't joke. If father heard…"

"But he didn't." Ainsley smoothed the little girl's hair. "And I think the old gods and all the creatures of the woods have a greater sense of humor than we give them credit for."

Ainsley gave her one last kiss before she set out for town. She had taken an extra pence from her mother's purse, enough for a pint in the bar before setting back. She could talk to the barkeep and listen to his stories of America, where he'd spent a year or so before coming back to the damp and cold of Ireland. He talked of streets filled with motorcars and rails that took people from place to place. He talked about a city called Los Angeles, where they made the picture shows that they showed in the movie house in Dublin. Ainsley would sip a dark porter and imagine a different life, one where her entire village didn't cower before their unholy tyrant, one bordered by the water of the Pacific rather than the bank of the River Lee.

4

ALAN, 1996

ALAN DUCKED OUT THE BACK OF THE HOUSE ON
Sinder Avenue as Máthair Shona burst through the front door
with a steaming casserole dish. The elders had arrived some time
ago. The buffet table was being slowly assembled. So far it held four
varieties of pie and two Crock-Pots of various soups. The table was
filled with several inedible casseroles and at least five gelatin molds.
Máthair Ellaine made one particularly egregious lime gelatin with
bits of carrot embedded in its frame that was meant to be topped
with mayonnaise.

The heat of the morning had been trapped under a layer of Los
Angeles smog and clouds, and now the air felt sticky and unclean.
Alan slipped to the side of the house and dug under the loose baseboard for the six-pack of beer he knew was stashed there. He had a
half-full gallon bag of pot stashed back there, too, and the temptation to dip into his wares was heavy. Not worth it though. He had
a delivery due to the boardwalk later tonight, and they'd notice if
he was light. The whole of the Society would soon be filling their

plates with their terrible food, leaving envelopes with a few dollars stuffed in the folds in the box at the door and patting Alan on the cheek, telling him how he'd grown or how proud they were.

Their real purpose, though, was ill-concealed. Ceit would sit in the old Barcalounger in her office, a cup of untouched tea on the low table next to her. The elders would wait, and one by one they would file in to ask for what it was they needed—permission to travel from the cul-de-sac to see a relative or friend, help getting the money back they lost when a shady plumber never showed back up to fix their bathtub. Some might ask for more nefarious help. Alan knew that Máthair Bedelia was not the only one who was holding a grudge and felt the only solution was to unleash the old spirits.

Mór Ainsley had held audience in this way on the rare occasions that she opened her house and welcomed in the members of the Society. It was an old tradition that had carried over from Cork and one that she'd continued to honor after coming to this country. Now it was Ceit's turn. Though she was only approaching twenty-one, Ceit already wielded more power than the previous Matrarc. Alan and the rest of the Society knew it was because she was far more than just the leader of their community. She was an ancient incarnation of a vastly more powerful deity. She was the Bandia Marbh, the goddess of the dead and ruler of the Night Forest that separated the living plane from the deceased. There was little she could not do.

Alan took a swig of the cheap beer. He'd lifted it from a friend's fridge, sliding the beer into his backpack when he'd been left alone in the room. Now that school was over, Alan wondered how he would ever justify to Ceit or the rest of the mostly ancient lot his leaving the cul-de-sac for more than cursory errands. The party today was intended to be a graduation celebration. Eighteen years old, graduated from high school, and officially a grown man in the eyes of the Society, he had been named Dara, or guardian of the Matrarc. He would handle the business that the Matrarc assigned to him. He had accepted the posting with reverence, but a nagging voice deep in his head whispered that he was nothing more than a glorified butler. Alan also knew that the elders expected that he would marry and move into the garden house behind Máthair Shona's tiny bungalow. Eventually, her house would be given to him and his wife when she passed, which gauging by the sour tint to her skin and her ever-slowing shuffle, might be sooner rather than later.

They even had a match for him selected. Ceit had wearily approved the business, and told him later that he wasn't obligated to follow the old rules. Alan had nodded and felt secretly grateful and simultaneously apprehensive at the missive. What was he to do if he didn't follow the old ways? There was very little money for him to go to college. Ceit controlled the scant funds that were shared among the cul-de-sac, and Alan knew that they barely afforded basic expenses. Now that he was eighteen, the checks sent from the state for his care would stop, and he would need to provide the lost income. School was not an easy option.

So why not marry Meg, the girl they had matched him with? She was pretty enough, quiet, and only seventeen, so the ceremony would be delayed another year in any case. He remembered her from his early days in the Society, before the world fell apart. Before his mother fell sick, before he had been sent to live with Aoife and then his father, and then and then. Before the world stopped making sense, he had known Meg as a little girl who did not go to the public school with him and Ceit but instead stayed home and took lessons from her mother. She was shy and his grandmother said a bit simple, but Alan had long ago decided that simple was preferable to the vat of trouble that came with extraordinary.

Extraordinary was sitting in an old Barcalounger in her office, preparing herself for the string of visits that would continue well into the night. It had been only Ceit and Alan in the house since they had returned home nearly a decade ago now. The official word was, of course, that they lived with their grandmother, but that ruse had been dropped as soon as Ceit turned eighteen. She had been his legal guardian for three years now, a bit of legal trickery courtesy of her friend at the Child Protective Services office.

Alan shoved the empty bottle back behind the baseboard and folded a stick of gum into his mouth. He could hear the rustle already building in the house. Ceit would be expecting him to be present in his new role as Dara, the gatekeeper, her most trusted advisor.

With a deep sigh, Alan turned and walked back around the corner of the house to stand in the doorway and watch the activity. It was the beginning and the end of what his life would become.

5

CEIT, 1996

CEIT LEANED AGAINST THE DOORFRAME, WATCHING Alan move through the room. In her hands was a plate assembled for her by Máthair Shona containing a spoonful of every dish on the table. The gelatin with mayonnaise was her favorite. It was a strange combination, and in an odd way it reminded her of her old life at MacLaren Hall. Institutional food, that's what gelatin was, cheaply bought and cheaply made, much like her life here. She mashed the food down into a paste, overcooked egg noodles and seeded grapes colliding. She was restless. After she ate, the elders would start lining up before her office door again. Her office, which had once been her childhood bedroom, was furnished with nothing more than the old Barcalounger and a secondhand desk and chair, which Alan had found on the curb waiting to be thrown out with the rest of the trash.

Eight years had passed since she'd left MacLaren Hall and returned to this house. It had changed little from the time she had lived here with her mother and father as a child. It had taken a bit, but Ceit had eventually moved into her parents' room. The memory of the horror that had happened there so many years ago still lingered, but the taint faded with each passing moon. Ceit had taken over guardianship of Alan three years ago, when she had turned eighteen. The elders had thrown her a graduation party much like this. Karen McAlister had even come. Karen had moved back to the SVU after she'd made the transfer of guardianship of Alan from Shona Robertson to Ceit Robertson as her last official duty in the Child Protective Services office. Since then, she checked in occasionally. It was not her job any longer, but Ceit was glad nonetheless. Few people knew what had really happened eight years ago in the Utah mountains, and while Karen had not been present, she had been the one who picked up Ceit and Alan, nearly comatose with shock, from Salt Lake after that terrible day.

The temptation to return with Chooli to Chinle had been great, but Ceit had known it was too late to go back. She had to step into a role and prepare for the ways she would lead not just these people but others in time. Noni and her ranch at the bottom of Canyon de Chelly had taught Ceit to harness her power, the true nature of her birthright, and exactly how insignificant this cul-de-sac with its old superstitions really was. Still though, the return to Venice Beach had been inevitable. Alan had needed to go home; he had needed something that resembled the life he had lost at age seven.

So here she was. Their father lay in a semivegetative state in the same care home where their mother had died years ago. Ceit hadn't seen him since he broke into MacLaren Hall and tried to gut her with a butcher knife. The curse that kept him staring at the ceiling was a protective measure. Ceit knew the Rabharta took many forms and that his brain was rotten with malice. Neither she, Alan, nor anyone in the Society would be safe if his binding was released.

Alan still visited him at least once a month. She suspected he took the Metro bus to Inglewood to sit by the old man's bedside more often than he admitted, but it was not worth the fight. She also knew Alan blamed her for their father's condition. Never mind the circumstances that had brought it about or the conditions Alan had been trapped in when he lived with his father in San Diego. Never mind all that, Ceit knew for her brother, Boyd Healy Robertson was the last thread to the life he remembered as a child—the last time he had felt safe.

"Are you done, love?" Máthair Shona held out her hands to take Ceit's barely touched plate of food. Ceit nodded.

"Will you find Alan?" Ceit asked. "I will take a few more visitors before nightfall."

Máthair Shona nodded and started to turn away.

"And Shona," Ceit said, stopping the old woman in her tracks. "Prepare the black salt and the bread. We will leave an offering for the Asrai tonight at the stones—the moon is full."

Máthair Shona nodded and continued to the kitchen. Ceit had long ago decided that while the old ways reeked of superstition, she had to walk a very thin line when it came to respecting the lore that her great-grandmother had carried over from the old country. Those who had come to Sinder Avenue and raised families here relied on the fae stories and the offerings of black salt and rosemary to feel safe. The Asrai did not care either way, but Ceit knew they appreciated the attention. A vain sort of fae they were, and dangerous in their pride—as likely to rip skin from bone as they were to give safe passage through the Night Forest. Ceit often appealed to their better senses and left small gifts during their monthly visits to the stones, where she would lift the veil between this world and the next.

But that was later. Now, Ceit would hold audience as Mór Ainsley had once done. She would listen to the requests and problems of her people and, as their Matrarc, try to help them. Most would be small favors: money to fix a broken sink, help with a neighbor or maybe a teacher at the local school. Bedelia's foul request still rang in her ears though. To call the Siabhra was bad enough, but to imply that the Sluagh were to be used for every petty grievance spoke of a rank disrespect for the dark spirits that lurked on the perimeter of their reality. The old woman would need to be watched. She was not capable of calling a dog to a supper bowl on her own, but her intent was likely to set the Rabharta to tapping on the windowpanes, looking for a way to come inside.

6

AINSLEY, 1924

"AND OH, YOU SHOULD SEE IT, LOVE—THE GIRLS IN their dresses clear up to their knees. I once saw a motorcar driving down Beverly Boulevard with a man and woman dancing on the top! Dancing!" The barkeep, a rough man named Bryan O'Malley who spit when he talked and smelled of stale beer, leaned in close, making Ainsley wince. "And you can have a drink only if you knock on the inner door of the hall, and then they ask you the password. It's all very top secret."

Ainsley laughed. "Now I know you're lyin'. I've seen the pictures, the magazines over at the post, the grand parties—there's champagne every which way!"

Bryan leaned back and chuckled. "Well, the rules are different for the rich, but isn't that always the way?" He made a show of cleaning a pint glass and glanced up. "Any word from Finn?"

Ainsley shook her head. "If there was, you'd be the first to know. He's gone like he said he was going to be. You'd tell me if any letters arrived?"

Bryan nodded. "'Course. I keep thinking he'll show back up, he might at that."

Ainsley finished the last swallow of her pint and closed her eyes, enjoying the pleasantly tingly feeling it had given her. "Tell ye what, hold yer breath till does then."

Bryan chuckled and pushed the pence Ainsley had placed on the counter back to her.

"Keep it," he said. "Yer ma will have yer head if she finds it missing. Besides, the boss man is out today. He'll never miss a pint."

"It's appreciated," Ainsley said, pocketing the pence. "I don't know when I'll be back in town. They send me out for shopping only once a month as is now, and with the winter coming, I doubt I'll get a reprieve."

"I'll hold any letters that arrive, or maybe I'll just send him to your door in person when he shows back up." Bryan smiled kindly, and Ainsley nodded in goodbye.

Back on the streets of Cork, Ainsley set out to the market to buy the few things the Society could not make themselves. It was true what she had told Bryan—she was asked to go only every month or so, and as winter approached, she knew the requests would be fewer and far between. The Society largely relied on themselves in their little alcove outside of Cork proper. The small gardens that flanked each cottage grew enough food to be canned for the winter, and the potato field that stretched a quarter mile did the rest. Goats, sheep, cows, and the occasional partridge made up the rest of the meals.

Bryan was one of the few people that Ainsley met with who treated her as a normal girl. The rest—the apothecary, the spice merchant—they all knew where she came from and muttered little incantations to protect themselves from the dark spirits they imagined her hauling behind her. Hogwash it was, and it angered

Ainsley more than she was allowed to show. Her wool dress and shawl waved like a flag that she was not of the city. Even in Cork, the new fashions were peeking their heads, but they were nothing like Bryan's wild stories of America. Finn had always said the nuns of the Bessborough Convent would break a thousand knuckles if a knee showed itself in the streets of Cork.

She had met Finnan at the fish market, where she had been sent to buy the dried cod the fishmonger made with rock salt especially for winter stews. Finnan had stood behind her all the while she made her purchase and then scared her half to death as she turned around. He was the son of the laundress, and Ainsley had seen him pulling his mother's cart to the edge of the River Lee, not too far from the Society.

"You live over the hill, with the..." He paused and grinned.

"With the what exactly?" Ainsley muttered and pushed past him, her hands trembling. The looks and whispers were bad enough, but to say it aloud was quite another thing.

"Yer not Catholics," he called after her.

Ainsley stopped and spun on her heels. "And I expect you'll be wanting to discuss it right here in the street, is that it?" she shot back, the fishmonger staring at the scene along with his disapproving wife, who Ainsley thought resembled the backside of an ocean flounder.

Finn grinned, and his dark eyes caught a flash of the noonday sun, making them glow with a hint of the dawn. He stepped to her, and when the space between them was no more than an inch, he took off his cap, showing a messy lot of dark hair, the same hue as his eyes.

"I only mean that a Catholic girl wouldn't be likely to join me for a pint, but as you aren't a Catholic, I thought you might allow me the pleasure—unless you need to be gettin' back to yer devil worship or fairy magick or whatever it is you do over that hill." He grinned again and glanced over his shoulder to the fishmonger and his flounder of a wife. "I don't think they like me much."

Ainsley felt the heat rise to her cheeks. "We don't worship the devil," she said softly.

"Didn't think you did. But ask Sister Mary Clara over there, it's all the old birds have to keep them occupied, worrying about yer lot." Finn paused. "So how about that pint, Ainsley Robertson, daughter of Rory Robertson."

Ainsley let a small smile curve her lips and followed Finn to the Standard House, where they sat at the back table and drank bitter ale. He told her about his mother and little brothers and sisters. Finn carefully left his father, Grady Rourke, out of the conversation, but Ainsley knew anyway. Cork was small, and the gossip found its way even to the hills. Grady Rourke had left his wife and children last winter. They'd nearly starved before the Bessborough nuns had stepped in with the St. Vincent de Paul castaway blankets, still reeking of the consumption, and the dole for the grocery. By the time Ainsley met him, Finn was working at the Standard House, back in the kitchen, and helped his mother with the laundry she took in. He was saving money to go to England, he told her. He would work for the factories they had blooming like wildflowers there. "Since the war, there are more jobs than men to fill them," Finn said with his dark eyes dancing in the dim light.

It had been only a few short weeks later that Finn had let her into the small boarding room in the basement of the Standard House. There he kissed the back of her neck and whispered in her ears that they would go to England together, marry, leave the damp and rot of Ireland, the prying eyes of the nuns and the sky that held only rain and cold. It would be grand he told her, and she believed him.

Now he was gone, and Ainsley strode to the spice merchant and ordered the rock salt and crushed pepper that was imported from places Ainsley could not even dream of going. She felt nauseous from the pint, and she suspected it was the stir of imagining in her belly that caused it. Finn had been gone months when Ainsley had found herself retching in the outhouse, her monthly long since gone. She had known in that moment what her mind had been denying, and the unsettled terror she carried in her fingertips had never left her. She knew what happened to unmarried girls who were with child. She knew. And Catholic or not, it would not matter a bit that her family lived outside this city and its rules. It would not matter—she would be sent to the homes if her father didn't kill her first.

Ainsley paid the spice merchant and tucked the jars of salt and pepper in her basket, heading to the fishmonger where all this had begun. Maybe Bryan was right. Maybe Finn would reappear and take her back to London with him. Maybe they'd rent a flat, and Finn would work in the factories while Ainsley read books to their child, wearing clothes what weren't made of damp Irish wool. But fairy stories were a fickle lot. Ainsley knew this to be true as much as she knew her hope to be as tenuous as the fae who offered healing potions in exchange for black salt and bread. Her errands done, Ainsley headed out of the city and back to the Society. They didn't worship the devil as Finn once implied, but Ainsley couldn't help but wonder if the devil was perhaps a surer bet than the absent and unfeeling God that resided over Cork.

7

ALAN, 1996

THE BOYS STOOD CLUSTERED IN THE TINY LIVING
room of the house on Sinder Avenue. Utterly unaware of their
surroundings, their wispy forms overlapped, fading in and out.
Their mouths moved—soundless words, breathless efforts. Alan
regarded them with a begrudging acceptance. The eldest of the lot
looked to be in his early teens, the youngest perhaps five or six.
One little boy, who looked to be about ten, rubbed his neck and
locked his dark eyes on Alan's. The others seemed to be lost, as
was expected. They had all passed recently, in the last month, and
it was this one child who had led them here. Alan doubted the boy
even knew why.

He wore too big pajamas that had once been sky blue, long
sleeves and long pants. Mud and dirt stained his ankles and wrists.
The skin on his neck held the angry red indent of a rope, or perhaps
a strong pair of hands; Alan was certain he did not want to know
which. His golden hair was mussed as though he had been awoken
from sleep only to be thrown into death. His face was fragile but

strong. He looked as though he would cry later, but something had forced this spiorad brónach to lead the others to Alan. Beneath his pale, already graying skin, he was angry.

There was a layer of protection that lay over the house; most spirits could not break through the invisible layer of air and light. Ceit had cast it around the tiny bungalow in the cul-de-sac after they had arrived home eight years ago. Ceit did not discuss her methods, and Alan knew better than to ask. He did know, however, that a spirit powerful enough to break through the skein that Ceit had cast over their house was not to be reckoned with. The spirits of the dead often sought out his sister. She ruled the Night Forest that the dead must pass through before their souls were free from this world. But they never came here. She would lead the old ones to the stones on Venice Beach, where Great-Grandmother Ainsley had held audience so many years ago.

But something had gone wrong, and here they all were. This boy had a power to him. He had pushed not only himself but all the souls that followed him through the skein of air and night. He stared at Alan, locking his midnight gaze on Alan's pale eyes, and did not look away. He lifted his thin child's arms, and Alan felt electricity in the air. With one hand, the little boy pulled the night air through the open window, wrapping it around the myriad smoky figures, and instantly they all froze. The little boy in the sky-blue pajamas maintained his preternatural lock on Alan's eyes.

"You're looking for the Bandia Marbh?" Alan whispered, making sure to keep his voice neutral. Alan's breath was shallow, his fingertips numb. He was scared of few things in this life, but the intensity of the little boy's gaze made his skin crawl.

The boy struggled to make a sound, the next world already stealing the last bits of his fading humanity. His voice scratched and retched.

"You," he croaked.

"I'm not the one you need," Alan said softly, dropping to perch on his knees. The child approached until he was inches from his face. He smelled faintly of burn and ash; his death had been rough, as had it been for all the boys that stood momentarily still before him.

"You," the child mouthed, sound barely passing his stiffening lips.

Alan shook his head, his heart thudding. "I will get Ceit, the Matrarc of this place. She will guide you through the Night Forest."

The little boy shook his head again and turned to stare out the window at the full moon. As he gazed at the night sky, the figures that stood frozen behind him faded until they were nothing more than wisps of scentless smoke. The little boy pointed at the sky, tracing the moon with his tiny finger. As he completed the circle, he, too, became translucent, and then his image disappeared entirely.

8

ALAN, 1996

ALAN SHIVERED IN THE NIGHT AIR, THE OCEAN SPRAY riding the cool breeze and leaving a damp smatter on his exposed cheeks and chin. He kept the hood of his sweatshirt tight over his head. The cops paid little attention down here, but drawing attention to oneself was never a good idea. The Sidewalk Café had closed a few hours ago, although he suspected there was still movement back in the kitchen. Only an occasional lone dog walker interrupted his anonymity. Alan was early. His contact was due to be here at 2:00 a.m. Normally Alan would wait until the last minute to sneak out of the house on Sinder Avenue. But tonight, Ceit and the elders were at the stones on Venice Beach, a ways from where he was now, far from what the tourists cared to see. She would not care if he came or went; perhaps she never did. No matter, Alan chose not to make an issue of it and kept his comings and goings discreet.

Tonight was different though. Alan had heard the stir of movement in the living room, not so much the sort of noise that a person would make. No, it was as though the very air had been disturbed. His ears had started ringing and his chest had become tight, making it difficult to draw a breath. He had felt this before, when he'd had to accompany Ceit and the elders to the stones when he was just a child, when his mother had fallen ill. Tonight seemingly had nothing to do with Ceit. The boys who appeared in the living room hadn't come for her.

"You" the little boy had mouthed and pointed at Alan. A breeze swept up from the water, rustling the thick plastic awning of the Sidewalk Café and making Alan pull his hood even tighter over his ears. None of the men in the Society had ever held any power. In fact, Alan had never heard of any of the men even seeing the things that the women were privy to. It was the way it had always been. His father had cursed the lot. Alan remembered Boyd's rants from his time in San Diego. His father, drunk on all manner of cheap liquor, stormed around the house, cursing Ceit, cursing Great-Grandmother Ainsley. Cursing the old women who had raised him. Boyd Robertson was half-crazy even then and full-on by the time he'd left Alan in the house in San Diego and driven himself to MacLaren Hall on that terrible night so many years ago. That was what Alan had told himself for years now, and he was almost sure he believed it.

He'd tell Ceit in the morning. She would know what to do. He wouldn't have to include the bit where he left to sell a handful of dime bags to a drunk LMU student at 2:00 a.m.

His side business had started at Venice High, when he'd sold a bit of pot here and there. Alan wasn't interested in it much himself—made him paranoid, made him remember things he'd done a good job of forgetting—which made him a perfect broker. He upcharged the skater kids and cheerleaders and walked to the collapsing bungalow off Venice Pier, where his supplier grew pot in his greenhouse and dried it in a toaster oven. All in all, Alan had been able to save up enough money that by the time he graduated he could buy a plane ticket to the East Coast if he wanted. Once there, though, that was the problem. So he stayed. *Might as well go through with the match,* he thought bitterly. His intended, Meg, had shown up to his graduation party earlier. Shy and quiet, she hadn't even made eye contact with him and had whispered answers to all his questions.

It made him a bit queasy—but so did all the potential roads of this future. He heard a rustle in the alley next to the café. A tall figure wearing a hoodie equal to Alan's crossed the space and nodded surreptitiously. Alan feigned shaking the kid's hand and passed him half a dozen baggies of Venice Beach's finest weed. In exchange, the kid passed him a thin roll of twenty-dollar bills. The whole thing took less than a minute, and Alan was headed back down the boardwalk to Sinder Avenue, disappearing into the night as though he had never been.

9

CEIT, 1996

CEIT LAY AWAKE STARING AT THE CEILING AS SHE heard Alan's not-so-stealthy reentry into the little house. She heard a scuffle of feet and a low curse. Ceit wondered silently if he was drunk. Not that it mattered, but it was troubling nonetheless. She had seen the soulless pit in their father's eyes all those years ago when he stormed MacLaren Hall, had seen what door the drink had opened. Not that her father's curse could be blamed on liquor entirely—the damnable Satanists and their idiot parlor tricks had done that. Ceit still sometimes thought of Annbeth, her only friend for a very long and lonely time. Flawed as she was, she had never been disloyal. Sometimes Ceit imagined what it would have been like to have Annbeth here, at her side, doing the work she was priming Alan to take on. Annbeth was raised to serve a higher power; she respected the hierarchy. Alan tried, but even as guarded as he kept his mind, she could feel the pulsing resentment just below the surface.

She'd told him long ago he wasn't bound to stay. The elders had arranged his match, and Ceit had agreed only on the condition that it was up to Alan and the poor, slow girl they'd found for him. She'd told Alan he could leave, for college or just another town. But he had not expressed any sign of leaving and had even stepped into the role of Dara, managing Ceit's affairs in the same way Mór Ainsley had had people who took care of the daily minutia of being the Matrarc.

Alan shuffled down the hall, and Ceit heard a door click shut. He was in for the night, whatever business he was running on the side closed for the time being. Ceit breathed deeply and closed her eyes, not sleeping but allowing herself to lift the veil and sink into the edges of the Night Forest. The creatures who roamed this land were frightened of her and hid deep in the dark woods as her consciousness manifested in the low-set meadow on the edge of the darkness. She liked it here; it was a place of calm in a world that was anything but. The old women and the few younger families who looked to her for guidance were relentless. Their way of life was coming to an end. Ceit knew this truth and knew the enclosed little universe in which they had lived for so long could not maintain itself much longer.

She pulled a flower from the thick grass. It wasn't quite a dandelion—nothing here was quite what it was in the waking world. Where the fluff should have clung to a velvety base, waiting to sail into the air, sat tiny pointed spikes. If she shook them loose, they would find their target with preternatural accuracy, burrowing just under the skin, creating havoc on all the tiny nerve endings. Not enough to kill, but enough to drive you mad. The g'nights used the pointed shafts to make their microscopic arrows. A few of them buzzed around her now, the only creatures of the Night Forest who held no fear of her. Ceit admired their foolish courage, and often came to this place where she could hear them zipping past.

The cul-de-sac on Sinder Avenue was coming to an end, and soon the time of the Society would be past. It wasn't anything Ceit wished upon the poor, sad elders who had never known another life. The oldest of the lot had followed her great-grandmother over from Cork several lifetimes ago and then raised their families under Mór Ainsley's watch. Most did not have a working memory of Ainsley Robertson as she had been before she became Matrarc, and most saw her as more fable than human. But Ainsley had been entirely practical for all her mystery, and even back when Ceit was a mere ten years old, when she was already an ancient, Ainsley had known the time would come when the cul-de-sac would be no more.

The business card that held the name of a real estate agent had been long outdated, but the office still existed. And they had record of the deal that Ainsley Robertson had begun talks on back in 1985 and before. The new manager had talked excitedly to Ceit about the plans they had for the land—a new Beverly Hills, he said, art houses and restaurants and fresh, revitalized neighborhoods. The crime, the gangs that worked the boardwalk, would be flushed out, and families and young couples would flood in. The offer was sound. As Matrarc, Ceit held the deeds to the houses on Sinder Avenue. The mortgages were long since paid, having been bought for pennies back in the 1920s when Ainsley and her Society had arrived. It was all profit. A new life for Ceit, for all of them. No more arranged matches and wool dresses. No more secrets, no more whispers from the surrounding neighbors or the clandestine photographers who still monitored the cul-de-sac for God knows what. No more. Ceit had a grander purpose than to man this sinking ship, and the time was coming when the Society would need to end.

Ceit blew the tiny pointed spikes in the direction of the Night Forest, delighting silently as they impaled a low-hanging oak leaf.

With a heavy and somewhat regretful mental push, she shoved herself back into the waking world and opened her eyes to the ceiling of her bungalow on Sinder Avenue. She would free Alan from this life, but he would need to prove he could be trusted not to sink into the darkness of Venice Beach. Finally, she closed her eyes and let sleep overtake her. Halfway between this world and the next, the Night Forest far below, she floated among the clouds until the morning sun broke her reverie.

10

AINSLEY, 1924

AINSLEY WATCHED AS HER FATHER LED THE ELDERS down the path to the River Lee. She was supposed to be watching Maire, but the little girl was already setting to sleep in the loft over the stone fireplace. The last shards of the cast-iron coire were cleaned and in a great pile outside their cottage. The entire village had come by to cluck their tongues and lay a hand on the destruction. A mourning descended, the same as if it had been one of their own human folk. No one could wrap their mind around what evil could do this and what was to remedy it. So the grown ones had set down the path, carrying their props. Ainsley knew one bag contained sea salt, the result of the labors of their annual trip past the southern wall to the Atlantic coast. In another bag was a bundle of dried rosemary, and another was full of sage. A poor, sad nanny goat was being led by a rope at the end of the pack. Ainsley was filled with anger over the goat. She was old and past birthing and her milk had dried up, but she was a sweet thing, and here were all the old ones leading her off to their futile rituals. A woman named

Leanin carried a length of red yarn, spun from the first shave of the spring lambs.

With a last glance inside the cottage to make sure Maire was truly settled, Ainsley ducked around the side of the building and off to the woods. She knew the way to the River Lee without taking the worn path. She would sit just inside the ancient fairy wood and watch as they chanted and moaned, begging the Fomoire to forgive them their trespasses. It hadn't been the war gods who had shattered the soup pot though; Ainsley trusted this as much as she did the Cork fog that settled over the dimming landscape. The Fomoire were a children's story, a way to scare a pack of rowdy boys from running the forest. It was foolish to pretend they were either capable or interested in such things as a human hearth, a cottage, a soup pot. Ainsley wasn't sure what had transpired at the hearth while they slept that night, but it wasn't a fairy story. The ritual and call of the elders would fall on deaf ears, or at most amuse the fae that lurked at the wood's edge.

The priest was coming tomorrow. Father Gerity was as ancient as the Society itself. He had been making his monthly pilgrimage to the little village outside of Cork proper since before Ainsley had been alive. A pale, vapid man, his eyes were a watery vacantness that perhaps had once been blue but now held little color. He stuttered when he talked, and his breath smelled of rotting meat. He would sit with her father at the table and take a cuppa, eat the biscuits her mother would make in anticipation of his arrival. He would ramble about the blessings of the Lord, and her father would patiently allow him to pray and bless the hearth with his tiny vial of holy water. Her father would assure him that all of the village went with God, and even though they might not be Catholics, they were one with the Lord. A lie. The Lord capital L had never had a place in the Society. But Father Gerity would smile with his trembling lips and shake her father's hand, allow whatever younger priestling had accompanied him to help him into the carriage that would carry him back to town. The illusion of conformity would be complete for another month.

Of course, this visit would be on the heels of the darkest of the Society's magick. Ainsley shivered and pulled her shawl tight as she crept into the shelter of the woods and settled down among the soft ferns and blue-petaled flowers that lined the forest floor. She was close enough to the circle of elders to hear and see, but the darkness of the forest kept her hidden. Ainsley could hear the buzz of night bugs in her ears. The presence of the fae was close, but they abhorred the sort of darkness that her father was planning. They would not stay to watch. That was what her father had never understood. Nature did not require the blood of its brethren. The athame that would slit the throat of the poor, sad nanny goat was an abomination to all but the most hideous of the forest folk. The Fomoire themselves, wherever they ruled, did not partake in such ritual. They had no need. Nature relied on itself and followed the circle laid out by the cycle of birth and renewal.

Ainsley balled her fists as the red yarn was drawn in a circle around the nanny goat. Her father raised the athame over his head, speaking in the ancient Gaelic that they used only in ritual. Boughs of rosemary lined the riverbed.

"Glacadh lenár íobairt!" her father wailed to the night sky. The elders mumbled their chants and swayed back and forth.

"Scaoil ár bhfulaingt!"

A rumble of thunder rolled across the sky. The elders took it for a sign and increased the volume of their chants.

"Maithiúnas dár n-imeachtaí!" Her father's voice filled the air, making Ainsley shiver.

Inside the circle of yarn, the nanny goat bleated and jerked back and forth, desperately looking for help. The faces of the elders were tilted to the stars, and they screamed their words to the night.

"Ainmnithe mar ainm duit!" The words roared their way upward, and the crowd rocked in a frenzy as Rory Robertson stepped into the circle, the sharpened athame aimed for the frightened creature's exposed throat. His face was set, and his lips silently recited the incantation.

"Déanfar iad ar an talamh mar atá sé ar neamh."

Surrounding him, the elders fell to their knees, giving Ainsley a clearer view of the nanny goat shaking with fear inside the red yard circle.

"Déanfar do thu."

The chanting fell from a roar to a low rumble. The air seemed to tighten and contract as her father closed his eyes and reached for the back of the goat's neck to hold her steady. A terrified bleat accented the current of the chant as the nanny goat struggled to pull away. In the woods, Ainsley clawed at the forest floor. Tears were streaming down her cheeks. The horror and pain of the old nanny goat flooded her every pore. The image of the elders flooded her vision from the goat's perspective, the smell of her father's skin as he leaned in with the athame, holding it to the tender flesh at the softest spot of the goat's neck.

As of their own accord, Ainsley's hands flew over her head, the dark earth of the forest floor clinging to her fingers. She felt a wave of anger and sadness wash from her toes up through her body and stream out from the tips of her fingers. The ancient words moved her lips without will of her own.

"Déan an olc seo as an áit seo!"

Her eyes were squeezed shut, and the wind spun madly around her face, deafening her. No more was she aware of the elders at the river or the night or the ever-present fog or anything of this realm. The words surrounded her and wrapped her in their pulse. The fae from the edges of the night crept to her side and joined in the chant, their slight, soft presence the only sensation Ainsley felt outside of the beating rhythm of the ancient language.

"Déan an olc seo as an áit seo!"

Suddenly Ainsley was slammed to her back with such force the wind was knocked from her chest. She lay gasping for air, unable to move. Over her stood the old nanny goat, its breathing ragged and a slight bloody nick on its otherwise pristine neck. It regarded her for a moment more, the thick black eyes locked on hers. Ainsley nodded in acknowledgment, and the creature let loose a low-toned bleat before bounding off to the darkness of the forest.

Suddenly the world snapped back into focus. Ainsley sat up, still struggling for breath. The fae had flown as quickly as they had arrived, and she was all alone. On the banks of the River Lee the elders were screaming and running in a panic. Her father knelt at the center of the red yarn circle, the athame still in his hand. Ainsley realized she was still hidden in the darkness of the woods. Whatever had transpired, the elders were not looking in her direction. They wailed and moaned, their panic palpable. Only her father was still. Slowly, he turned his head and looked directly at Ainsley. She knew she was far enough back in the brush that he could not have seen her face, but still he locked his eyes on hers, his face stone and his mouth no longer chanting the ancient sacrifice. Her heart beating louder than the cries of the Society on the bank of the River Lee, Ainsley silently drew farther back into the woods. Still her father stared.

Had she cried the words that had flooded her body aloud? Had she revealed herself? Ainsley had no idea what had transpired during the minutes her body and words were not her own before the fleeing goat had collided with her form. The others did not look her direction. They seemed to be utterly baffled. But Ainsley knew it didn't matter if the ancient woods and the fae magick had hidden her face from the Society and their murderous ritual; her father had felt her presence. He knew she had done something to break the spell, to release the goat, to ruin their sacrifice.

Feeling razors in her lungs, Ainsley fled through the woods back to the cottage. Her dress and shawl were soaked with the night dew. She pulled them off and her nightdress on as she curled under the thick blanket next to Maire. He hadn't seen her face; he could prove nothing. Still the words pulsed in her ears as she pinched her eyes shut: "É a sheachadadh ó olc."

11

AINSLEY, 1924

AINSLEY AWOKE TO THE MURMURINGS OF THE LIFE down below at the hearth. Her father's voice, low and guarded, and her mother's nervous tapping on the wooden floor created an almost musical beat. The sun was just coming up. They had likely not slept, and Ainsley had stolen only a couple of hours at most. The creature inside her caused her bowels to twist, and she gasped her discomfort as not to alert her parents below. Quietly, she crept to the edge of the loft, and staying just out of sight, she tilted her ear to her father's low words.

"I saw the face staring out the woods at me clear as day. It was the Bean Sídhe, the banshee of the fae folk, staring back at me. The goat reared up as though it were one of the Fuath itself and I saw it, I saw the banshee's eyes in the woods. We're cursed. The Fomoire who tore the soup pot to shreds are coming for blood, we're cursed."

Ainsley blinked several times and shook her head in the hidden darkness of the loft. The Bean Sídhe? He hadn't seen her face after all; he had no idea she'd been in the woods. She let out a silent sigh of relief. She'd been ready to have the skin removed from her back when her father and the rest of the village returned, convinced he'd seen her form as she ran back through the forest. But no, his imagination had overtaken him. The banshee—that's what he thought he saw. Ainsley almost let a giggle escape. That notion was even madder than the Fomoire. Her mother's voice drifted upward, full of worry.

"You let loose of the creature's neck is all. No banshees, no nothing. It got away from you, that's all. I saw it happen. The time wasn't right—we need to wait until the new moon and go again. That old goat was an unworthy sacrifice, dried up and useless as she was."

Her father sighed heavily. "Truth to that. But hard to spare the young ones, just starting to give milk, and the nursing mothers are an even worse loss."

"That's why we do it," her mother retorted, still tapping the table with what sounded like her brass thimble. "We prove our worthiness. We give what we cannot bear to not have."

Maire stirred in her sleep, the slight sound making Ainsley's parents look upward. Ainsley pulled back to her still warm blankets. The old nanny goat was spared, hopefully deep in the wood where she'd never be brought back to the village. But it would never stop. Which one of the blameless lot would they drag along the path on the new moon? She pulled Maire closer and closed her eyes. No one would be expecting her awake for a bit longer. She would pretend that all was as it had been months ago, when her belly was empty and she could pretend to run off to the village for a bit of this or that to meet Finn for a pint—or perhaps a walk among the market stalls on Cornmarket Street while he whispered in her ear of the wonders of London. She'd close her eyes and pretend the world was as it had been.

The next time Ainsley opened her eyes, she was alone and the hustle of activity below made her jump to attention. As she peered over the edge of the loft, she saw Maire, dressed and brushed, putting water to boil in the teakettle and her mother beating the very life out of a mound of dough on the table.

"'Bout time you raised yerself!" her mother called up irritably.

"I told her you weren't feeling well," Maire responded pointedly.

"It's true, I'm not," Ainsley replied and realized it was a truth. Her head pounded slightly, and her throat was raw. Her stomach was in knots. "I caught a bit of the draft is all..."

"Well, uncatch it and get down here. The good Father is due before too long, and I still need to get the biscuits on to bake. Can't have a good Catholic girl still in her nightdress when the priest arrives." Mother's voice dripped with sarcasm.

Ainsley pulled on a wool dress, stockings, boots, and shawl before descending the ladder. She paused to drink the tin of boiled river water her sister handed her. Her head felt as though an iron had been pressed to her skin.

"The sheep need to be taken out the barn, and there's milking to be done." Her mother threw the words over her shoulder. Ainsley nodded silently, feeling her body swimming beneath her.

"I can do that," Maire spoke up and pulled a chair out for Ainsley. "She'll catch the grippe out there. Best to leave her be— stay inside today and out of the damp."

Her mother grunted. "Long as it gets done. But don't take this as an excuse to sit on your arse. Your father's in a fine mood today, and he'll beat you raw if he catches you sitting about." Mother glanced at Ainsley and stopped her manic kneading of the dough. "You do look a bit pallid." She paused, considering her next words. "The silver needs polishing. You can sit and do that and still be useful. But have a bit of yesterday's bread first, and a cuppa lavender tea—that'll chase the rot out of your lungs."

Ainsley nodded, and Maire placed the small chunk of yesterday's dark rye bread on a small plate before her. The little girl was already pouring water over the lavender and chamomile leaves, the smell filling the room. The sprite in Ainsley's belly twisted and rolled at the first sip. "Thank you," she whispered to her sister.

"I felt your head when I woke. No use to the lot of us sick. Sit here and polish—I'll take care of the rest." Maire grinned as she sat the silver basket down next to Ainsley, then disappeared out the door.

"You haven't been out, have you?" her mother asked, eyeing her suspiciously. "Running 'round all hours will get you the grippe quick as anything."

Ainsley shook her head miserably and forced herself to swallow the bread. As she reached for a slightly tarnished spoon from the basket, her belly contracted, and she cried out in pain. Her mother jumped in alarm.

"Good lord, girl, what's got into ye?" She knelt before her daughter and looked in her eyes. "Ye eat somethin' rotten? Did yesterday's milk turn?"

Ainsley shook her head as the cramp passed. It was replaced with a stabbing pain that jutted directly up her under regions like a knife. Again, she gasped in surprise. "I maybe ate the last bit of the cheese. It tasted a big gamy." A lie—it had been delicious—but it was a lie her mother would believe.

Ainsley's mother nodded sagely. "Knew it, I can spot a bad stomach. Go lie back down, take the tea. I'll finish this up. We have time before that damnable priest arrives. Go on into our room. Your father's out to the pastures this morning, not to be back for a bit. Go on."

Ainsley nodded and, cupping her tea, crossed into the small room were her mother and father slept. As she suspected, the bed had not been disturbed the night before. Likely none of the elders had slept since the ritual went awry. But what exactly had happened? Was it as her mother had said, the goat simply got away? What of the fae folk that lit on her shoulders and whispered in her ear. *It's the fever,* a voice inside her head repeated calmly. *You imagined the whole thing, and you gave yourself the sickness being out in the cold. The goat reared back and got away, and you did nothing other than getting yourself all riled up and passing out in the forest. Now look at you, sick in ways your mother doesn't even know.*

Ainsley closed her eyes and pulled her mother's thick wool blanket over her shoulders. As she drifted off to sleep, she lulled herself with the rhythmic beat of her mother and the biscuit dough on the rough wooden table outside the door.

It was Father Gerity's rattly voice that next awakened her. Her head felt a bit lighter, and she took a sip of the now cold tea to sooth her raw throat. She would need to cross through the great room to get to the outhouse, which she desperately needed, and she'd have to say something to the priest, a task she avoided whenever possible. Normally, she'd have found some grand reason to be away from the house today, taking the sheep to the far pasture or maybe tending to the goats on the other side of the village. But thanks to the damp and her fool idea last night, she was here, and the pressure on her bladder was enough to make tears rise to her eyes. Never had the urge to use the privy been so intense as it had since her belly had been invaded by this little sprite.

With a sigh, she tidied her hair in her mother's small dressing mirror. She looked pale and run-down. Maybe the priest would think her sick and avoid talking to her altogether. Then she could spend the rest of the visit in the barn with the old milk cow. Ainsley stood and straightened herself. *Just cross the room and be polite,* she told herself. *No need for anything else.*

"It's a grand day for a visit, Father Gerity," her father boomed on the other side of the door.

Ainsley winced. What if he did remember her face from the woods once he saw her today?

"The Lord's business is always grand, Rory, especially on such a fall day as this," Father Gerity murmured in his shaky tone.

Ainsley took a final breath and opened the door of the bedroom, nodding to her mother as she stepped into the warmth of the hearth.

"Ah, there you are, daughter." Her father's tone was unnatural, overly jovial, a show for their guest. "Your mother said you were unwell."

Ainsley nodded. "A bit. Rest helped, I'm much better. I'll see to the sheep, Mum, help Maire."

Her mother nodded, and Ainsley crossed to the door. "Hello, Father Gerity, good to see you again."

The old priest nodded, unseeing, and then turned his eyes to Ainsley. "Young lady, yesterday you were but a child, and now I see a young lady in front of me. Miraculous."

Ainsley cast a look at her mother who gave her a slight shake of her head. The old priest was half-senile. Who was to say the meaning in his remarks?

"A young woman. Not well I hear?" he said. "Soon you'll have a family of your own and your own sick young ones to tend. P'rhaps sooner than anyone might suspect." Father Gerity pointed his stare at Ainsley, and the pulse in her bladder seemed to increase a tick. She had no idea what he was after, if anything at all, but her heart had started beating as it had in the woods last night.

"I suppose so, Father," she said politely. "If you'll excuse me." She nodded at her parents, who looked just as confused as she.

Outside the door, she rushed to the privy and pulled the door shut. He couldn't possibly know. Nobody knew, certainly no one in town who would know the priest. He was talking nonsense, old man nonsense was all. Her parents both knew he was daft, her father performing this bit of theatrics to keep the church in Cork proper from suspecting they were anything other than what they were. The old priest would take his carriage back to Cork and tell whoever cared to know that the village by the woods was a good Christian group, not Catholics but the capital L Lord abounded among them.

As Ainsley crossed to the barn and warm safety of the hay and animal smells, she shook off her worry. Her father and mother had far more to worry about being uncovered than she. The Society worshipped the old ways, the many gods and goddesses of the forest and hills. Those in Cork proper would call it witchery, but it was far older than that. Older than the capital L Lord or the Catholics put together. No, whatever meaning the priest might have had with his odd talk of her as a young woman was less a threat than some night wanderer from Cork proper spotting the lot of the village at the River Lee in the dead of night, terrifying a goat and chanting the old words. Ainsley was safe, at least until her belly swelled more than it already had. Only the slightest bump existed presently, not enough for anyone to notice under all the cloth and cold weather skirts. She was safe for now, and now would have to suffice.

12

ALAN, 1996

CEIT'S PALE EYES BORED INTO ALAN FROM ACROSS the old desk.

"Santa Monica College is a bus ride away. We can afford the registration." She spoke evenly, but there was a distinct edge to her voice.

Alan sighed and leaned back into the uncomfortable wooden chair.

"What's the point exactly? I can apprentice with Uncle Benjamin, join the electricians' union. Meg turns eighteen in the fall and will graduate a semester early. We'll be married then."

Alan heard the falseness of his words even as they left his mouth. He had no desire to join the electricians' union any more than he had interest in marrying Meg in November. More than anything, he wanted Ceit's expressionless face to react to something, anything. Instead all he garnered was a subtle sigh.

"It's your choice," she said. "But, Alan, this place is but a speck in the world. The match means nothing to me. You are under no obligations to fill it. Benjamin Robertson left the Society a decade ago and spends his days drinking malt wine. I'm told he hasn't worked in months. If you truly want to apprentice, I will find you a more suitable mentor. However, I feel your talents will be wasted here."

Alan shrugged, his gut burning in shame. He knew she was right about it all. His uncle had served a few months on an obstruction of justice charge many years ago when their mother passed, and he had never been right since. He'd worked off and on, enough to keep his union membership, but Ceit spoke the truth. He lived in the valley now, having left before Ceit and Alan had returned to this place.

And Meg. He had begun to suspect she wasn't nearly as slow as the elders whispered. She was quiet—that was true—but Alan had seen her ducking out the back fence of her parents' bungalow last week, disappearing down the alley. It had been after sunset. Alan had been on his way to make a delivery to Venice Pier. He hadn't let her know he'd seen, but the idea that she had a secret intrigued him. It also made him wonder if she would be happy to get married in November of her senior year of high school to a boy who her parents had matched her to based on an ancient bit of idiocrasy.

"You have a couple of months to decide, Alan," Ceit said firmly. "Listen to me at this." She leaned forward, and Alan felt the hairs rise on his arms as they did whenever Ceit focused her energy. "This is a dying place. There will not be a Matrarc after I am gone. The Society has outgrown its welcome. We have no stake to this place any longer. You need to prepare for what is next."

Alan nodded, his voice choked with a thousand emotions. "Yes, Matrarc," he whispered.

Ceit's brow twitched slightly. "I am not your Matrarc. I am your sister, and the only family you should trust. Máthair Shona is as much a fool as the others."

"What about Dad?" Alan managed to push out the words.

"Our father was lost long before that night at MacLaren Hall. Make no mistake, Alan. His mind is gone, and he will never recover. Even if he did, he is of no use to you. Our father never saw beyond this cul-de-sac. He could have taken our mother away from here, started a life anywhere else, and instead he stayed. He accepted his match, moved into this house that would never truly be his, and made it so you and I never had a choice in our stars."

Ceit's face remained still, but the blood in her words rose to a boil. Alan found himself holding his breath. The desktop was vibrating slightly, Ceit's anger and frustration manifesting. A little jar of pencils tipped over and spilled across the table.

"Do what you will," Ceit hissed. "But do not accept the life the old ones want to give you so readily. They wish to hold you here. I wish to set you free."

"Then send me away. I'm eighteen now—you can kick me out anytime." Alan felt the heat rising to his cheeks as he spat out the words.

Ceit leaned back. The vibrations rocking the table abruptly stopped, and her expressionless face twisted into a half smile.

"That would be no different than matching you to a girl and pushing you to apprentice with Uncle Benjamin. I will not force you to do anything, Alan. I can only hope that you can see farther than the end of the cul-de-sac. Go now." She nodded to the door, and Alan knew he was dismissed.

On shaky legs he exited the office, closing the door behind him. He wondered how much his sister really knew about his activities outside the cul-de-sac. He wondered if she knew about the sack of weed he kept under the house or the little bags of pills that he sold to the UCLA frat houses on the side. He wondered if she knew that the ghostly little boys had visited him in his dreams every night since their appearance in the living room. They called his name, said he was the only one who could guide them through the Night Forest. He wondered if Ceit knew what Máthair Shona had whispered to him one night when she'd found him sitting on the steps, looking up at the stars. "It hasn't always been a Matrarc," she had whispered. "Men held the power in the Society long ago, back in the old country." Alan had ignored her at the time. What use was it to know this? Ceit was the Matrarc now just as Mór Ainsley had been before her. What did it matter what had happened back in Cork?

But now Alan wondered at the old woman's words. There was a simple truth to be faced. His mother's death, his father's dissolution, everything that happened in between and since all had a common cause. Despite Ceit's words, he would never be free of this place while she was Matrarc. No decision he made would ever truly be his; it had never been. He remembered well how Ceit's invisible presence had ruled his father. How before that, Cousin Aoife had quaked with fear at the idea of displeasing Ceit, child as she was even then. He remembered the smell of the stinking rags that had been stuffed into his mouth and tied around his eyes that afternoon when he'd been pulled off the sidewalk outside his elementary school. He remembered the coldness of the caves, the feel of the lava rock walls, the black glare in the eyes of the Maga as she spoke of Ceit and how she would be there soon. Ceit, Ceit, Ceit—it had always been about her and would continue to be.

Alan stopped by his room to grab the bag of little blue pills before he headed out to the boardwalk. He had a delivery to make and then planned on dipping into his own stash. Buying a forty ouncer from the boardwalk hole-in-the-wall that didn't bother with IDs, popping a couple of the little blue pills, and laying on the beach until the tide rolled up over his exposed skin. Ceit was right about one thing: there was no life to be lived in the cul-de-sac. But she had missed the point. While she ruled this place, there was no life anywhere.

13

CEIT, 1996

"MATRARC?" THE VOICE WAS HESITANT AND TIMID. A small knock followed.

"You may enter," Ceit replied, somewhat wearily. She had spent the last hour or so since she'd talked to Alan taking care of the finances of the Society. As Matrarc, she held the deeds to the houses and paid all the expenses from a common account. She could have arranged for one of the elders to take on the task—Mór Ainsley had done as much—but Ceit did not trust the way Ainsley Robertson had. Alan was the only one she could see taking over this task of managing the business of the Society, and she knew she must do everything to make sure he left this place. His insistence on staying, marrying that girl, turning into another version of their father made her skin crawl. The more she pushed him in one direction, any direction, the more he would dig in his heels. Ceit had known this truth about Alan since he was a child—he would go his own way even if that direction was wrought with disaster. In that, he was a carbon copy of their father.

Máthair Shona stepped inside the office, a small smile on her lips.

"What can I do for you?" Ceit asked curtly, in no mood to listen to Shona's ramblings.

"Matrarc, we are having a slight disputation among some of the members. We need your counsel." Her eyes flew around the room; her inability to make eye contact had always driven Ceit to madness.

"Spit it out, Grandmother. What is it you need my help with?" Ceit responded irritably. The old ones were constantly coming to her with petty grievances about the price of groceries or whether the butcher had slighted their cut at the meat counter. Ceit wondered if Ainsley had listened to such nonsense or if she just locked the door behind them when she had them leave.

"Matrarc... it's Bedelia. She is upset about the loss of her husband's things. She wants your help and is afraid to ask." Shona said the words quickly and quietly.

"Bedelia came to me already, and her request was unreasonable." Ceit motioned for her grandmother to sit down. "She asked me to call the Sluagh on the hospital staff for throwing out Aedan's clothes. It's an unreasonable request. I gave her money to replace his watch, if it truly did go missing—I have my doubts. I have instructed Alan to make sure her pantry is filled and to keep mind of her house. That is all the help I can offer her." Ceit kept an even tone, but she felt the irritation in her voice and the familiar vibrations of her frustration starting to manifest.

Ceit probed and saw that Shona's mind was heavily guarded. Her thoughts were not just foggy but blocked, as though Shona had intentionally built a wall around her mind. Ceit looked at her for a long moment, intrigued. What could the silly old bat possibly be thinking about that would require such measures?

"With all due respect, Matrarc, Bedelia claims that they took

Aedan's good jacket, which she hoped to pass on to her son. She also says the watch came from Cork, from her great-grandfather, who she claims was godfather to my grandfather, Rory Robertson. Irreplaceable is what she says." Shona twitched nervously.

"Bedelia sees our family name as a card to be played whenever she is in need," Ceit said. "Always has. Tell her to search her drawers for the watch, or ask her son."

Ceit steadied her hands to keep the table from shaking again. Alan took no notice when these things manifested, but Shona was likely to break into hysterics. Bedelia and Aedan's son was squarely in his fifties, married to the woman he'd been matched to back in Ainsley's years as Matrarc. Conor had always been a scoundrel. Ceit doubted that watch had ever made it to the hospital at all; it was far more likely that he'd taken the damnable watch as Aedan lay sick, hocking it to support his gambling habit.

His wife was no better. Conor's match had rejected him outright back in the day. As was the way in the Society, the woman had had the final word on whether the match was to happen. Without her approval and blessing, the entire affair was called off. Ceit had only heard about the ordeal; the entire mess had happened before she was born. According to the stories though, Bedelia had visited the then young woman and told her ruin would come to her house if she didn't marry her son. The marriage happened, and Mór Ainsley never spoke a kind word about Bedelia or Aedan again.

Ceit had no idea the truth, but she had never cared for Bedelia and her constant reminders that she had known Ainsley back in Cork and knew what her great-grandmother would do. The old woman had a twisted core, her husband had been no better, and they had given birth to a dishonest and untrustworthy son. Now he and his forever sad-looking wife lived in the back house behind Bedelia's bungalow.

"She crosses a line in coming to me and asking for an ancient evil to be unleashed on the basis of a lost watch and an unsubstantiated claim of theft," Ceit said, losing her grip on her anger. A shudder passed through the table. Shona jumped to her feet, and Ceit could see her lips moving in silent chanting prayer.

"Of course, Matrarc, of course," Shona muttered.

"What exactly is this disputation you came to me about?" Ceit asked directly. The old woman was withholding something; this had naught to do with a lost watch.

Shona hummed nervously. "Some of the elders disagree with your ruling, Matrarc. The watch, it is just a watch, but it is one of the last things we had left from the old country. With Ainsley gone so long, some of the older among us feel a bit like the old ways are starting to be forgotten…"

"Things," Ceit muttered. "You said it, Grandmother. It is a thing, and I would check Conor's pockets and the local pawnshop before I cast eyes on the hospital staff. I will buy her another winter coat to give to Conor, although I will add we live in a place such as hardly needs a winter coat set for the Irish damp."

Ceit stood from her chair, her slight figure filling the room with her growing anger. Máthair Shona shrank back as the desktop rattled and the chair legs started thumping against the hardwood floor.

"Mór Ainsley died at the hands of the monster you wish me to summon for this petty grievance. She died mired in the old ways you claim are absent. Do not speak to me of the old ways. I was not chosen to be your Matrarc—I was born to it. It mattered not whether I wanted the role. Without me, you are impotent, powerless, a hoard of old women and their children. Once the younger among you move away, and I pray they do, your time will die out. I am the only reason the Society maintains."

Ceit leaned across the desk, placing her palms squarely on the rough wood, stopping the vibrations abruptly.

"All those years you banished me from this cul-de-sac. All those years, Grandmother. Do you remember the state you all were in? I came back to delinquent bills, debts you all had run up, your houses falling down around you. Do you remember? At thirteen, I had to clean up your mess because you and all the old ones were incapable of caring for yourselves."

Ceit sat back down. The earthquake rattling of the tables and chairs stopped entirely, and she felt her breathing begin to even out.

"And that was just the common inconveniences. The fae, the Asrai, all the old magick had abandoned you as well. You cannot lift the veil. You cannot summon the night. The Night Forest answers to my call. The Sluagh will not be summoned to settle this bit of vengeance. I will not hear this nonsense again. Tell Bedelia and the others to be mindful of their place."

Ceit nodded toward the door, and Máthair Shona shuffled out, her hands shaking. Ceit stared at the closed door and then crossed to turn the key in the lock. She would take no more visitors today.

Lying flat on the wood floor, she lifted the veil between this world and next. Ceit found herself in the clearing next to the entrance to the Night Forest. The g'nights buzzed past her ears, and the silky grass settled beneath her weight. A rustle from the thick underbrush made Ceit turn her attention to stare into the darkness. From the depths stepped Amon, her demon. He was dressed in an immaculately tailored pin-striped suit, a crisp white shirt underneath a matching vest, polished leather shoes, and a fedora that hid his colorless eyes. His translucent skin glowed with moonlight.

"Hello, my liege. Visiting your subjects?" he purred.

Ceit smiled. "Perhaps. Observing more so."

"You'd do well to keep a close eye on those that you think to trust." Amon walked one foot in front the other, as though he were on a runway catwalk, down the ancient carved stones that lined the path through the Night Forest.

"The old ones are harmless. They think they are more powerful than they are. They can't summon the rain in the midst of a storm," Ceit muttered.

"You'd do well not to underestimate them." Amon stopped in front of her. "Come, I want to show you something."

He held out a hand. Ceit ignored it and stood on her own.

"Follow." Amon turned and walked away from the path of the Night Forest, farther down the hill and into the brush. "Here," he said, pointing to a small mud puddle that collected in a little alcove.

"What exactly are you showing me, Amon?" Ceit asked impatiently. Time worked differently here, and she knew better than to dally; hours could pass in the waking world during the minutes she stood in the field staring at mud with Amon.

"Look deeper," Amon instructed.

Ceit fell to her knees, staring into the mud, and saw little tadpole-like creatures swimming to and fro and the light from the eternal night reflected in the shadows that danced across the dark surface.

"Well, it's mud," she stated flatly.

"You're not seeing, my queen. *Look.*" Amon's voice was a whisper that wrapped around her like a breeze.

Suddenly in front of her, she saw a troupe of little boys. They were all pale and worn as though their bodies had long ago dissolved back into the earth. Their empty eyes stared out. The littlest among them stood in the front.

"They are looking for passage through the Night Forest. Why have they not appeared to me?" Ceit demanded.

"Look closer. What do you see?"

Ceit gazed closer at the image, her eyes straining to see what Amon was stressing. The edges of the little boys were unclear, as though an eraser had smudged the images. Souls appeared to Ceit often, lost in the waking world, seeking passage through the Night Forest. She would light the ancient stones that led from the clearing, give them a blessing that would protect them from the nightmare creatures within. The journey was the work of the soul, but the Bandia Marbh ruled the terrain. But these little boys were different. The edges of their forms were not just smudged, they were inconsistent. As Ceit watched, little details about the boys changed; a pair of empty death eyes turned brown and then green, a maimed leg grew straight.

"They're… they're not real," Ceit murmured in shock. She had never seen such a manifestation. These boys were an illusion— not souls, not spirits, but the imagining of someone's mind made visible. They were more akin to the nightmare creatures that were born of the fears and pain of mankind than the beings of the spirit world. But even then, the nightmare creatures were a mutation of sorts, the fears of man evolved into their own force. The little boys reflected in the muddy water were something else. The sheer force of will that kept them visible was almost unbearable.

"They are an illusion," Amon said quietly. "One of those harmless old bats who couldn't summon the rain, as you put it, has summoned this. You can see the difference—you know these images not to be souls—but would everyone? What purpose would one have to summon this image?"

"It's a parlor trick is all," Ceit said suddenly, standing straight.

"Agreed, and not a particularly good one. But why? Why go to the effort? It's exhausting just to look at it." Amon sighed.

Ceit nodded. "Whoever created this is using every last bit of whatever it is they have."

"Who do you trust?" Amon asked, staring into Ceit's eyes.

"You. The g'nights. And no other," Ceit responded, meeting his gaze.

"Good. Although the g'nights are far more reliable than I." Amon's brow furrowed slightly. "You feel bound to the old women and your brother, too, perhaps. But you are the Bandia Marbh, more things in heaven and earth than are dreamed of in their limited philosophy."

Ceit gave the demon a slight smirk. "You know Hamlet destroyed the lives of everyone he touched."

"All the more reason to cut your ties to that world and let them destroy themselves." Amon tipped his hat and turned to the perimeter of the Night Forest. He stepped back into the darkness and disappeared.

Ceit took one last look at the muddy water, which showed no images now, just the shadows of the unearthly trees that loomed overhead. With a deep sigh, she lifted the veil and shoved herself back into the waking world. Hours had passed, the room was dark, and the moon shone through the window. Someone, somewhere on Sinder Avenue, was dreaming of the troupe of little lost boys, someone who did not know the deathly images were no more substantial than the glare of the moon.

14

AINSLEY, 1924

"YOU'RE NOT HAVING A PINT THEN TODAY?" BRYAN leaned against the bar and studied Ainsley playfully. She sipped the tea she had ordered instead.

"My stomach is rebellin' me." Ainsley glanced around to see if anyone was listening. The pub was largely empty. The sight of a woman, single as she was, sitting by herself at the bar was scandalous enough, not that Ainsley cared much; the town already talked themselves to a frenzy over their notions of what the Society was or wasn't. But still, it wouldn't do to give them more to gossip on about.

"Bryan, Finn's mother, do you think she has a way of contacting him? Do you?" Ainsley's voice sounded far more desperate than she intended. She'd practiced on the way here. Luckily the salt had all been used in the elder's useless ritual, so she'd been sent to Cork proper with a small list, salt at the top. After what the priest had said the day before, Ainsley knew she needed help of some sort. Whether the old man's words were ramble or whether he suspected, Ainsley knew it was only a matter of time before the truth about her condition was painfully obvious.

Bryan shook his head. "Can't say for sure, but I doubt it." He poured himself a pint and took a swig. "They weren't on good terms when he set off. Ye knew that didn't ye?"

Ainsley shook her head. "I didn't. I knew he helped her with her business, but he didn't speak much of her." Finn had moved from his family's cottage to the boarding room at the Standard House before she'd met him, but she knew he'd helped his mother with the laundry she took in when he could, lugging the cart to the river and back again. "I didn't see him on that last day before he boarded the ship." Her voice broke a bit, and Bryan looked at her pityingly.

Ainsley had meant to see him off. Finn had left on a Tuesday morning from Cork Harbour, bound to England. Ainsley had planned on leaving early from the village, setting off to be there on the dock when he was set to board. But the goats had gotten loose in the night and the village was in a frenzy, so Ainsley couldn't sneak away. No errand in town could be invented. She'd sat by the edge of the River Lee that evening as the sun went down, her heart already pulled in a thousand directions.

The last time she'd seen him, they'd sat on the edge of the dock, the far end away from the arriving ships and prying eyes. "I'll write you every week," Finn whispered softly in her ear. "I'll send 'em to the pub. Bryan will take care of ye while I'm gone. I'll send for you as soon as I have a proper flat. The factories, they have housing for their workers. I'll tell 'em we're gettin' married, and we will as soon as you arrive."

Ainsley leaned in, feeling his soft lips on hers, the sprite in her belly, unknown to her at that point, a silent witness. "And no priest will marry us," Finn whispered into the nape of her neck, his breath hot against her skin. "No robes and crucifixes—no, we'll go to the court proper, we'll make our own religion."

"Bring me soon," she whispered.

But no letters arrived. She was not sent for, there was no flat in England, no court proper, no religion, and no God as far as Ainsley could see. And Bryan was the last living soul who knew what Finn had meant to her, and might understand why she needed him so desperately now.

"Look, Ainsley." Bryan paused, considering his words. "Look, love, I hate to say it, but I fear he threw you over, both of us. He promised me things too—he'd write, send money for me to follow him there. They need barkeeps in English pubs too, he said. We're both abandoned."

Ainsley shoved the tea back at Bryan, spilling most in the process, swallowing a sob. "I'm going to see his mother. He didn't throw me over—he couldn't do that to me. He loved me."

She stood abruptly and lost her balance momentarily, grabbing the bar and barely holding steady. Bryan ducked around the end and caught her right as her grip on the polished brass rail slipped. "Easy there, love" was the last thing Ainsley heard before darkness hit.

When she awoke, Ainsley stared around at a small boarding room so similar to the one Finn had occupied. A racing in her heart threatened to knock her unconscious again. He was back, he had never left, it had all been a long, odd dream. But reality set in a moment later. An unfamiliar shaving brush and toiletries lined the small sink. A barkeep's jacket hung on the back of the door. This was Bryan's room. Finn was gone, not to come back, and had left her behind. A knock at the door interrupted her misery.

Bryan's face peered around the frame. "You okay there? I brought you some water."

He entered and closed the door behind him quickly, setting a glass of water down on the small table next to the bed. Ainsley suddenly felt extremely uncomfortable and exposed. What was she doing lying on this strange man's bed? Was she as bad as the loose women in the south ports the old ones whispered about, one man to the next?

"I'm fine. I have to go, I have to get back…"

She started to rise, but Bryan laid a hand on her arm.

"Wait, for my sake, wait a few." He looked back at the door. "No one saw you fall, good to be an empty day, and I managed to make it back here without any attention. But they're unloading a big order a hall over—no way you can slip out the way you came in without being seen. You might not care, but I have a reputation to upkeep."

Despite herself, Ainsley let a giggle loose. Bryan grinned back and nodded to the water. She took a drink.

"You want to tell me what's going on while we have a minute to talk?" he asked.

"Don't you work?" Ainsley asked, half-joking. If she spoke further it would be nearly impossible not to tell him. He was the closest thing to Finn; it was almost like telling Finn himself.

"Taking my break. I have thirty minutes to hear your woes, so talk fast." He grinned again.

"I'm expecting," Ainsley whispered.

"I figured that," Bryan responded.

Ainsley felt as though a hand had slapped her face, her body growing hot and cold simultaneously. "But how, why? I'm not showin', at least not so anyone can see. I'm not, no one can know, no one can…"

Bryan put his arm on her shoulder. "Calm yerself. I didn't suspect it till today when you ordered a tea and nearly fainted at the bar. I have five sisters, all older, all of which have a brood of children each. I know an expectant woman."

"You can't tell anyone! You can't. I need to tell Finn. He's going to marry me, we are going to live in a flat in England, we're—"

Ainsley lost her words to sobs that ripped through her entire body. All the grief at Finn's leaving, all the fear of the gentle swelling of her belly, all the knowing of what would happen when anyone found out, it all erupted. Bryan folded her in his arms and stroked her hair as she sobbed.

"No fear, love. I have no one to tell. Nor would I," he whispered. "Don't go tellin' Miss Grady though. Finnan's mother has a streak of the hellfire and brimstone in her that would set the priests to shame. Most the reason that Finn moved into these shitehole rooms was to get away from her." Bryan pulled Ainsley away and looked into her eyes. "Look, love, I don't know what you'll do, but I'll help no matter. How far along are ye?"

Ainsley shook her head. "I don't rightly know. My monthly's been gone some four, maybe five months now."

Bryan nodded, thinking. "It won't be much longer before you can't hide it. We need to do whatever we're going to do in the next month or so."

"What will we do?" Ainsley whispered in a shaking voice.

"You'll set some water to your face, get rid of those red eyes. Go on with your shopping, come see me next week. I have some savings. We need to see about getting you out of this country— you know what will happen if the church finds out."

Ainsley nodded. The mother and baby home loomed on the top of the hill on the far side of Cork proper. She'd heard the stories: it was a work home, an orphanage for babies who had living mothers, a purgatory.

Ainsley snuck past the workers and out the back door just as she'd done when she'd been in these quarters with Finn. As she went on about her errands, she dared to feel a shred of hope. Bryan would help, she would sail her own passage to England, and she would find Finn on her own. They'd have their flat and marry in a proper court. They would forge new gods from the ashes of their past.

15

AINSLEY, 1924

AFTER THE SUN SET THAT NIGHT AND MAIRE DRIFTED to hard sleep next to her, Ainsley crept down the ladder, pulling her boots on and her shawl around her shoulders before slipping out the cottage door. She'd had a dream, at least the beginnings of one—the sort that creep in as you drift to sleep and make you wonder what is real and what is not. In it, she'd seen a clearing in the old woods, a patch of green in the gnarled and ancient tree trunks. In the center stood the old nanny goat. It stared at her with its sideways eyes, and she kneeled to meet its gaze. Around her, the forest started whispering, the very leaves and branches murmuring words too ancient for Ainsley to understand. The nanny goat did not blink or break its gaze in any way, and the gold surrounding the eyes' black centers had glowed like fire.

Ainsley had bolted awake and known right away she needed to go to the woods. Maire had taken a lifetime to get to sleep, and her father had stomped out of the downstairs bedroom twice to look out the window and stare into the pasture. Ainsley had begun to think she was trapped. But then Maire's breathing leveled out, her father's snores could be heard from behind the wooden door, and she dared to sneak out the door to the night beyond. It was getting colder. If her calculations were correct, her baby would be born come spring, when the first flowers were finding the new season. But there were months to go before then, and something waiting for her in the woods.

Now Ainsley stole along the side of the house until she reached the protection of the worn path that led to the River Lee. No one who might be looking out their windows would see her beneath the heavy trees and overgrown field grass. The woods were silent, the moon barely a sliver in the sky. It should have been wicked dark, but the trees seemed to glow as though the moon was full. With a deep breath, she stepped beyond the perimeter and into the dark protection of the trees. The sharp end bits tore at the exposed skin on her hands and neck and she wrapped her shawl around her head, shivering. The wind whipped through the night, and Ainsley felt as though her very bones had turned to ice. Still she walked, drawn by an invisible cord that connected to her very core. Ainsley knew she should worry that she might not find her way out, but it didn't matter. She knew with a foggy certainty that the way there and back would be made clear.

The clearing wasn't quite so neatly tamed as it had been in her dream, just a small patch of reprieve from the thick overgrown elm and oak trees. The field grass and bristly undergrowth made for a stern bed as Ainsley sat on the dew-sodden ground. There was no nanny goat with glowing golden eyes, no whispers from the trees. Suddenly Ainsley felt exceedingly foolish. A silly girl, sitting alone in the woods, waiting for God knew what to come and eat her for its dinner. At best she'd catch another chill and die of the lung rot;

at worst the wild boars would drive their sharpened tusks right into her gut, killing her and the sprite. She was about to stand and turn to leave, shaking her head at her idiocy. She could hear her mother. "Imagine," she would bark, "following a dream of a lost goat to the woods in the dead of night."

Just as Ainsley stood, however, a rustle from across the tiny clearing stopped her. The leaves shook and the soft sound of movement through the underbrush made the tiny hairs on the back of Ainsley's head stand at attention. A boar—it was a boar and it would charge through the black at any minute. *With my luck,* Ainsley thought, *I've stumbled across a momma and her piglets and will be gored to death for the crime of interfering with their evening as sure as anything. I'm a damn fool.* As her breath caught in her throat, she laid a hand over her belly.

The leaves parted. What stepped into the clearing was neither boar nor nanny goat. It stood about three feet high, and its very limbs seemed to be made of thin wooden branches. It paused as it entered the clearing, and Ainsley saw what appeared to be a small-ish, rather spindly tree. As it moved toward her again, she saw a pair of moonlight-silver eyes lodged in a small, oval head perched on top of the unlikely body. Ainsley opened her mouth to scream or cry, she did not know which. Instead, all that emitted from her was a soft sigh. She was not afraid of this small creature. She suddenly realized what it was that stood in front of her. The old ones had long spoken of the hidden folk, the first people hidden from the sight of man—unless, of course, they chose to be seen. In the stories, the hidden folk were the sons and daughters of the ones who came even before the fae. The Catholics in town who dared to tell such stories said they were the bastard children of Eve cast out of paradise by God himself. Her people talked of the old Druidic stories, of the forest creatures who ruled this land before man and woman came to muck it all up. The hidden folk were the first to touch the soil, the first to smell the night air, the first to welcome the fae and the water creatures that dove between the waking world and what lay beyond the veil.

The small creature stepped hesitantly closer and reached out a tiny hand that was the same color as the juniper scrubs along the riverbank. Ainsley sat again and with a shaking hand reached out. The creature extended a rough, dry touch to her palm and then sat itself. Ainsley blinked several times. It had to be a dream, as the nanny goat had been. She was asleep in her bed and would jolt awake at any minute.

"Not a dream," the creature whispered. No lips moved, and the sound wrapped around Ainsley like a soft breeze.

Ainsley stared at the tiny creature, and its moonlight eyes locked on hers.

"See." The word sounded as though it was whispered through a warm breath behind Ainsley's ear. "See."

As she stared into the creature's eyes, shadows turned to shapes and shapes to a scene—a great black horse and a cloud of smoke, black as night, that wrapped around the small cottages of the Society. Ainsley shook her head. A tall figure, its face obscured, raised its hands, and Ainsley could see pale skin that matched the creature's colorless eyes. Ainsley realized her entire body was shaking, and the images disappeared as suddenly as they had begun.

"See," the creature whispered as it stood with effortless grace and walked back into the thicket.

Ainsley let out a half cry, half moan as all the air she hadn't dared to breathe escaped her lungs in a rush. She stood awkwardly and turned back the way she'd come. As she'd suspected during her trip to this place, the path out of the woods was laid clear. Not knowing how, she stepped with surety of direction even though there were no markers to line her path. Later as she lay in bed, Maire still sleeping heavily as though Ainsley had never left and her father still snoring below, she reached a hand out to the darkness, feeling for the rough touch of the hidden folk.

16

ALAN, 1996

MÁTHAIR SHONA'S EYES WERE GLASSY AND UNFO-
cused. She stared blindly ahead at the television screen where
some sort of laugh track was accompanying a family in a kitchen.
Alan eyed the nearly empty bottle of red wine that was propped
up next to her. He sighed and surveyed the scene for a moment
before he pulled the bottle away. Only a slight reflex emitted from
his grandmother; she was far too drunk to really react. Alan placed
the bottle on the table and went back to turn off the television. He
came next door to check on her more often than he admitted to
Ceit. Ceit's mind was to leave the old woman to her own devices.
Alan had seen what that brought, especially in the last few years.
Anymore, Máthair Shona was liable to be lost down a bottle of
liquor as soon as she thought the rest of the cul-de-sac had gone
to bed.

"Okay, that's it. Show's over. Time to go to bed, Grandma,"
Alan said with an edge to his voice.

She looked up at him and smiled.

"Such a good boy," she murmured. "Such a good boy. You know, my grandfather was head of our village back when we were in Cork, you knew that though…"

"Head of the village, was he?" Alan said, pulling Máthair Shona to her feet, then pulling her down the hallway to her bedroom. "I thought the Matrarc was always the head." Alan knew better than to egg her on, but in her current state, she was more likely to spill whatever she had been hinting at about her grandfather in Cork.

Máthair Shona stopped in her tracks. "No," she said firmly. The glaze that had filmed over her eyes was gone, and her aged face was filled with intent. "No, love, it hasn't always been that way. My mother was the first. She became a Matrarc when Grandfather died. And what a death it was."

"You're not making sense, Grandma. Let's go to bed. You drank too much again. I know the stories. You left Cork when you were a baby—you couldn't have remembered all this." Alan tried to pull her along.

"No," Máthair Shona nearly shouted, and in his surprise, Alan let go of the old woman's arm. She swayed for balance and then focused her gaze directly on him. "No. My grandfather was eaten alive by a demon. It was summoned, and woe betide those who stood in its path."

Alan shook his head. "What are you saying?"

Máthair Shona took Alan by the shoulders and leaned in until her fetid breath was inches from his face. "I'm saying that my mother took her place in the Society in a most foul manner, and then she passed her line on to your darling sister." The old woman leaned into Alan's ear, her fingernails digging into his shoulders and making him wince with the pressure. "But that's not the only way it has to be. What was taken by force can be taken back again."

With that, the bleary-eyed glaze reappeared over her face, and

Máthair Shona slumped against Alan drunkenly. He barely caught her, the weight of the old woman making him grimace.

As he pulled her down the hallway, she began to sing in off tones and broken melody.

I sing of the fae and the wood and the vine,
And the night that lasts forever.
The ghosts of your loves and the ghosts that are mine . . .

The old woman cackled at the song, and Alan held in his temper. As soon as the sun set, she was drunk more than sober, and he was tired of the job he had given himself.

After Alan had pulled a wool blanket over his grandmother's shoulders and closed her bedroom door, he walked back out to the kitchen and poured the rest of the wine into a clay mug. His great-great-grandfather was but a whispered name among the oldest of the Society. Scant few were so old as to have actually met the man. The oldest among them all, such as Bedelia, had been no older than his great-grandmother Ainsley when they'd come over from Cork. His grandmother had been just an infant, from what he gleaned from the stories. Shona was least qualified of them all to talk on the subject. He could still remember as a little boy, Cousin Aoife's whispered stories about the fights between Ainsley and Shona, how the two of them would yell and scream. Still, crazy as his grandmother was, there was some truth to her words concerning the history of power in their family. Alan found himself musing as to what it would be like to have an ounce of the power that had been given to Ceit. He sipped the cheap wine and let his mind imagine what it would be to call the Sluagh, the sound of flesh ripping from bones, the sound of the veil between this world and next ripping asunder for all times.

17

CEIT, 1996

"AND YOU HOLD THE DEEDS TO ALL THE HOUSES?" The neatly suited man regarded Ceit suspiciously.

She nodded, barely containing her impatience with his skepticism. The deeds had been signed over to her on her eighteenth birthday, and she held power over them as her great-grandmother Ainsley had done. It had always been the job of the Matrarc, but it was pointless to explain this to the wisp of a man who sat in front of her. Sinder Avenue lay on the periphery of a new revitalization project they were working on for Venice Beach, and the cul-de-sac was prime real estate. Its worn and crumbling houses were begging to be torn down. The proximity to the beach, the construction that dotted the areas to the east and west—all these things made the voice on the other end of the phone very attentive when Ceit had said she wanted to speak with someone about the logistics of selling.

"And you have tenants?" the suited man asked, checking something off on a list in the interminable stack of papers he held before him.

"Yes. I have tenants, and the sales would not be immediate. My tenants have lifetime rights to their property," Ceit said firmly.

The man looked up from his papers and regarded her curiously. "That's an unusual lease to say the least."

"It is an unusual situation," Ceit shot back, an edge to her voice. It was not the fault of this man that she felt uneasy about this entire query. It was a betrayal of her role as caretaker. Mór Ainsley had watched over the people of the Society, managing the houses and back houses, making sure everyone was taken care of. She had moved the younger families into the bungalows as the older ones passed on. There weren't many younger families any longer. Meg was the youngest of the children, and she would be done with high school soon enough. Ceit knew that Alan's match to her was a sad attempt on the part of the old ones to start a new generation in the cul-de-sac. It wouldn't work; the Society was dying, and only a handful of old women remembered Mór Ainsley as she had been back in Cork. Bedelia was the oldest of the lot, and she was looking more and more like she was halfway out death's door.

"You know what we are, I presume," Ceit said bluntly. They had been dancing around the topic since the man arrived.

"Yes. We know that this is a, um, community as it is," the man stuttered.

"*Community* is a word for it," Ceit said dryly. "I am in charge in this community, and I hold the deeds to the houses that my people live in. I have no interest in carrying this community through another generation, and I suspect as my great-grandmother had your agency's card in her desk, neither did she."

"Well, that's straightforward," the man said, straightening his tie and sitting back to meet Ceit's gaze. "If I may ask, what do you plan to do with the money—and it will be significant—that you will garner from the sales?"

"That is not your concern," Ceit snapped. "What I need are facts."

"Okay then," the man said. "Let's talk numbers."

With that, he began the process of laying out the approximate values and potential plans for the area. Ceit listened intently. It would have been more difficult for Mór Ainsley to have put this plan in action. When Ceit was a child, there were several younger families in the cul-de-sac. There were other children. Now no young families remained, and the houses could be sold as soon as the occupants died—or were convinced to leave this toxic little cave and move out into the world. Ceit was sure of one thing— Alan couldn't be allowed to marry the girl the old ones had matched to him, even if he wanted it. It would breathe life into a creature that should be laid to its final rest. No, Amon had been right. It was time to close this chapter and release her responsibility to these sad creatures. It was time to take her role as Bandia Marbh. It was time to rise.

18

AINSLEY, 1924

MUM STARED AT AINSLEY FROM ACROSS THE COTTAGE. For her part, Ainsley kept to the task she had given herself, skinning the last of the fall apples for canning. The rough kitchen knife bit into the smooth skin, and she created one long ribbon. The skin would be boiled down in a separate pot; it could be made into a tart jam on its own. The apples were already starting to go soft and brown, and Ainsley's fingers were sticky with juice.

"There's something the matter with ye," her mother declared as she stomped across to the hearth where the kettle was starting to sing.

"I'm fine, Mum, tired is all." Ainsley focused on her apple. The rind broke and fell into the bucket at her feet.

"No, there's something. I heard tell you were in the town last week." Her mum poured a draught of the steaming water into the bowl of flour and yeast and plunged a hand into the mixture to mix the dough.

"I was," Ainsley said softly. "I went for spices."

"I don't recall sending ye," Mum said curtly. "Wouldn't have known you had gone 'cept the butcher's daughter, Anna or whatever she's named, said she saw ye stepping out the back of the Standard House."

"She talks too much, that one," Ainsley muttered. The girl, Annie, was a wretched little thing with a face like a side of her da's rib roast. She liked to make devil horns over her ears whenever Ainsley passed and had on more than one occasion poked her dirty fingers into the packages of mutton and kidneys on the rare event Ainsley had been sent on a mission to buy supplies from the butcher's shop. Ainsley had made it a rule never to eat the meat that came back from town for that reason, and luckily it was a rare errand to be sent on.

"So why would she see you coming out the back of the Standard?" Mum asked again, landing a fist into the firming dough. She sprayed the mass with rough salt and pounded it again, punishing it for the news a bitter little girl had gossiped into her ear.

"She didn't. She's a fool. The spice merchant is out along Newmarket Street, and I was taking a shortcut is all, cutting through the alley behind the Standard. She's a bored child, and I swear it's her filthy little fingers that gave everyone the bellyache last time we had to take the mutton chops from that damnable butcher's shop."

Mum stopped her abuse of the biscuit dough for a moment and considered Ainsley's words. "You might be right 'bout that mutton—foul stuff comes from town in general. Just make sure you aren't anywhere where people could talk. They have quite enough to talk about as is."

Ainsley took a long look at her mother. A fresh bruise peaked over the edge of the neckline of her dress. Ainsley took note that she kept her sleeves down even though they'd be best rolled out of the way for the work she was doing. A surge of anger rushed through her; she knew how those bruises had come to be. Next to her an empty cup tipped over on its own accord and rolled to the floor. Her mum looked up, surprised, and Ainsley let a long, uninterrupted string of apple peel drop into the bucket and tried to steady her hands.

Her mother's tone told her that the matter was dropped for now, but the idea that the little witch had not only been spying but had had the audacity to spread what she saw was unnerving. Bryan had told Ainsley to return to the tavern in a week's time; she had a few days left to pass before she'd have to invent an errand that would take her to Cork. She had to figure her way out of this place, a way back to Finnan and a place where her baby could live soft and safe.

19

AINSLEY, 1924

"AND WHAT IN THE HELL COULD IT BE ABOUT THEN?" Her father's voice rang out into the bitter morning. Her mother made a noncommittal grunt and continued on whatever task she'd set herself on. Ainsley ducked out the front of the cottage with a basket in hand to collect the morning eggs and paused, just out of sight of the door, but still within hearing.

"The damnable priest shows his face once a month on our hill, that's our arrangement, and now he's back before I had a chance to curse his fool name properly. What have you heard from town?" Her father's voice was agitated but not angry, not yet. Ainsley shivered in the biting wind and crept closer to the house and the slightly open window.

"I told ye, I don't know," her mother answered impatiently. "I do know that his arrival means I have to push aside all my work and make it hospitable around here, which is hard to do with your blustering and carrying on. Will ye get and do your work so I can do mine?" Her voice was even but there was an edge. She hadn't mentioned that fool girl Annie's report on Ainsley again since they'd spoken on it. Ainsley wondered if she and her mother were thinking the same thing, that the little girl and maybe her ham hock of a mother were spreading stories in Cork, stories the old priest was likely to believe.

Ainsley scuttled off to the barn and the henhouse. Maire was already inside milking the nanny goats. Later she would help their mother make the salty cheese with a hint of field lavender that made Ainsley's stomach growl just to think on it.

"Heard old Father Gerity's comin' back today," Maire called out, not looking up from her pail.

"He is. A messenger from the church came in this morning. And wouldn't you know it, the old horse even sent along what he wanted Mum to bake for him?" Ainsley laughed despite herself. Maire looked up from her milking and grinned.

"You're serious, you are?" She coughed back a guffaw. "He loves his biscuits and English tea."

Ainsley set to reaching around the oblivious hens, pulling small brown eggs out to put in the basket. They'd take the extras around to the other cottages soon enough. No one in the Society kept all their pull for themselves; it was shared among the group. The old ones who couldn't bake or light their hearth properly were taken care of by the young. It was part of Ainsley's job to make sure they had a fair share of the morning's pull of eggs and milk. Maire would do this when Ainsley was gone. For a moment, Ainsley stopped, her senses overwhelmed. She wanted Finn to come home. She wanted them to marry and move into a cottage of their own on the hill, safe from her father's temper. A home where her sister and mother could come and live in peace. They'd have their own barn with a milk cow and a hutch full of chickens. The baby would grow up as she could have, had she and the rest of the Society not been under the thumb of their Ceannaire. She'd forge her own forest rituals, learn her own ways to honor the fae and the wood folk. Ainsley could see it all as it could be. Her old life with the bits of beauty here and there, and a new one, forged of her own making.

It wasn't to be, she knew that. Wherever Finnan was, he wasn't likely coming back. It was her only hope to make it to Cork tomorrow and meet Bryan as they'd planned. She couldn't go out the back of the Standard again though. That little sneak Annie had proven herself to be a proper rat. No, she'd go in the front as though she were there for a pint, and they'd make a plan. She'd catch the next ship to England, she'd find Finn, and they'd forge their new life together in a new place.

"You dreamin' of his lovely blue eyes aren't ye?" Her little sister broke her reverie. "That black collar really sets off the pox in his skin. I can see ye, I can, riding off in his priest wagon... aah love." She giggled madly and turned back to her goat.

Ainsley turned and glared. "You're funny, you are. But thanks for the gooseflesh on my arm you've given me."

Out of the corner of her eye she caught a movement near the back of the barn, and she spun around. A single spindly finger reached over the edge of a hay bale; it was the same color of the juniper scrubs that the sprite from the forest had been. But surely that had been a dream? Ainsley felt her head growing dim. She could hear her sister's voice at a great distance, still making perverse jokes about the old priest. But it was as though Ainsley had been thrown down a deep and terrible well, and all—the noise of her sister's voice, the soft mewling of the various animals, the wind that tore through the loose planks of wood—sounded as though it was a thousand miles away, as though it were a memory. As she watched, the single, preternaturally thin finger tapped the hay bale three times, and then it slid back out of sight. In her ear a voice meant only for her hissed softly.

"The old one means you harm."

Ainsley dropped the basket, the contents shattering against each other. She could hear Maire's distressed voice nearer now and knew it must be right in her ear, but it still sounded as though a great fog had descended around her. The creature was right there; she could go pull it out of the hay and show her sister, her father, the rest of them. She could show them it was real, and that their blood and chants weren't necessary, show them that the little folk were around whether or not you tried to charm them into appearing. Her stomach rolled and the skin grew rock hard, stretched to breaking. A sharp, searing pain flooded her belly as though a blade had been thrust into her womb. Ainsley grabbed her stomach and lurched forward. She would show them all that the creature behind the hay needed no blood, needed no fealty. It existed within and without their world.

It was her father's voice that broke the spell ultimately. "Ainsley, for wood and stone, wake up, girl!" He roared the words, and Ainsley suddenly felt as though the world was spinning. She turned to see her sister, out of breath from running to the cottage, and her parents all staring at her from the barn's entrance, the sun casting them as little more than shadows.

"The hidden folk—the first folk—I've seen them, once in the woods and again here by the hay," Ainsley whispered.

Her father strode across the space and held her firm with both hands on her shoulders. "You've got a bite of the fever again, you have."

Ainsley shook her head vehemently. "I don't. I saw them, like sticks and leaves come to life they were. It's right there, Da, look!"

Her father looked back at her mother and sister, who were

casting skeptical glances around the space. "Perhaps you did see them," he said. "Perhaps the demon who destroyed the coire is lurking closer than I imagined." He leaned in close, his gaze steady and his voice a low threat. "You know the veil can't lift for one who is still a child, don't you? And you are still a child, are you not? There's whispers, daughter... vile, evil whispers. If you bring shame to this house, I will skin your back before sundown." He stepped back and regarded her coldly.

"The veil does not lift for you either, does it?" she said as he started to turn away. Her hands were shaking but her voice firm.

He spun around, facing her again. Ainsley's mother pulled Maire close and hid her eyes, anticipating what was to come. With one precise movement, the palm of his great hand landed against Ainsley's jaw, knocking her to the ground. She lay stunned, her ears ringing.

"Watch your mouth, girl," her father said simply and strode out of the barn.

Maire started to run to her, but her mother caught the little girl and directed her back to the house. Taking a step into the barn, she said in a soft voice, "We'll take care of the priest, who should be here within the hour, and then we'll tend to this. You'll need to clean yer mess." She pointed at the egg basket, rich golden yolk leaking out the bottom. Ainsley just nodded silently, tears forming in the corners of her eyes. For the first time, Ainsley had seen her father regard her with fear—and he was like to destroy what he could not understand.

As she scrubbed the sopping eggshells out of the basket, Ainsley glanced over her shoulder to the hay. What was the little creature trying to tell her? And why was the old priest arriving on this day? The hairs on the back of her neck rose one by one, and she knew with certainty that if she were found near the cottage while the priest was set to visit, it would be the last time she'd see the little stone hearth with the loft overhead. She had to leave for town immediately. She had to find Bryan, and she had to leave this place.

20

AINSLEY, 1924

AS AINSLEY EXITED THE BARN, HER HANDS STILL shaking ever so slightly, she heard the clack of the horses coming up the hill. It was too late—the old man was early, and her mother would set to a fit. Nothing was prepared yet; Ainsley doubted the water had even boiled. She froze in place. Even though she had no reason to believe it, she could hear a nagging whisper in her ear telling her to run from this place, from that man in his robes and collar. "Flee," it whispered, soft as a breeze.

Ainsley returned to the cottage and spent a frantic few minutes laying out the tea service. Just as the carriage drew up to the door, her mother pushed Ainsley and Maire out.

"Go, get back to yer work in the barn—this is no concern of yers!" she barked.

Maire obediently ran back to the goats, but Ainsley ducked behind the cottage. She heard the priest enter and the door close behind him. Only then did she creep to the side of the house, next to where they would be sitting at the table. A loose stone made a small gap in the structure, and she and Maire had often listened to her father conduct meetings and Society business through the secret listening hole. If they looked out the window, they would see her curled up against the outside wall, but there was no reason for anyone to seek her out. Inside, the clatter and ting of teacups and spoons filled the room. Ainsley waited patiently, holding her breath.

"It's a pleasure to host you twice in the same month, Father," her father said jovially. "To what do we owe the honor?"

Ainsley grimaced at the sound of his voice, her jaw aching.

"I am afraid, my friend, I have some disturbing news, and I suspect you may already be somewhat aware. It's a delicate matter—I wonder if Mrs. Robertson should perhaps step outside?"

There was a rustle at the table and another great clang of china and spoons. Ainsley didn't jump away in time to avoid her mother, who had ducked around the back and had headed to the same listening hole that Ainsley crowded. She glared, but calling Ainsley out would draw attention to her as well. Instead, she crawled next to Ainsley and leaned in. The two women looked at each other and pressed their ears as close to the gap as they could.

"Rory, there's talk in town of your eldest, Ainsley."

"Father Gerity, all due respect, I think I know what you might have come here to say. There was talk some time ago of her and the Rourke boy, and I can tell you, it's ended now. Ainsley is set to be married in the spring to a match she and her mother have chosen. A good, strong boy who fears the Lord as much as you do."

"Rory, it's more than that." The priest's voice was cracked and uneven. "She was spotted by a member of our diocese in the tavern at the Standard House. It seems there's talk and... well, there is no good way to say it. Rory, I fear she's hiding an act of shame. I fear she is carrying an ill-gotten child."

There was a silence, and then her father replied in a voice so calm it made Ainsley's blood run cold.

"Father, if this is true, I will break the neck of the young man who compromised her purity. We will deal with this in our way, in our time."

"I do not doubt this, Rory… I know you to be a godly man. There are places where her shame can go to the good of our blessed Lord…"

The priest kept talking, but Ainsley pulled away from the wall. Her hands were numb and her body had turned to ice. How did the old bastard know? Bryan had said no one had seen her faint that day in the pub, and what did that prove anyhow? Someone must have heard her as she talked to Bryan? But how? Unless… Bryan was not to be trusted. She pushed the thought from her mind. She saw his face and heard his voice in her head. He was on her side, he had to be. Bryan was the only one who understood her situation truly. He was the only one who could help. Annie—it had to be the little butcher's brat. She had told everyone about seeing Ainsley that day in the back of the Standard. She had made up a story, and lucky for the little git, she'd been right.

Ainsley fell back and struggled to her feet. If her father or the priest looked out the window now, they would see her standing in the late autumn chill, her face pallid and expressionless. Ainsley looked down at her mother, who was staring at her with anguish that overwhelmed anger. She mouthed Ainsley's name and reached for her. Ainsley shook her head. She needed to leave, and now. The old priest had told her father—God knows what he was suggesting—that she needed to leave. She needed to find Bryan, and she needed to be on a ship before dawn. She cast her mother one last look, a silent apology full of everything she wished she could vocalize, then she ran.

She took no care to hide her trail. If anyone looked out their window now, they'd see her running like a banshee across the field. Ainsley couldn't care about that now. The only thing she was left with was a grim certainty that the old priest would cause her harm. As she fled toward the old woods, she stumbled on overgrown roots and nearly fell, but she righted herself and, with scarce a glance behind her, ran on. The slope of the hill propelled her forward. From far back she heard the scuffle and clang of the horses' bridles as they kicked impatiently at the dust. They couldn't see her now if they looked out beyond the barn. She was on the downturn of the hill, nearly to the shelter of the ancient trees. Her belly clenched and tightened again, a shooting pain running across her taut skin. Ainsley doubled over, still stumbling forward. She had to make it to the forest; the same voice that warned her of Father Gerity's intentions was guiding her to the woods. Only inside the safety of the trees could she rest.

As Ainsley stepped foot into the woods, the roots of the oak and elder trees twining their way underfoot, she felt the panic dissipate. Time worked differently here—it ran slower, it hid things from those who did not know to look. Ainsley walked deeper and deeper, not entirely sure what it was she was seeking but knowing the whisper that had led her here would tell her when to stop. She did not feel the cold even though the morning air had more of winter than autumn in it. Her stomach relaxed, and the sprite inside gave a mighty kick, reminding her of its presence. Numbly, Ainsley rubbed the slight bump as she walked. Past the low ferns and the mossy trunks of massive trees whose canopies blocked the sun and created a night out of the day, Ainsley placed one foot in front of the other and walked on. She knew she should turn and leave this place, run for Cork, go to Bryan, tell him the trouble and how she needed to leave tonight.

Perhaps her father was right—perhaps she'd seen a demon, the same one who had torn a cast-iron cauldron to bits as they slept. She very nearly stopped her feet from marching, but the voice hissed in her ear. Ainsley winced at the sound and kept walking. She could never return home; she knew that now. The reality of it all sunk in as she walked deeper and deeper into the old woods. The priest would be sitting up at the house now, drinking his tea and wiping the crumbs off his withered lips. That is if her father had not already raged out the door, looking for her. Ainsley cringed at the thought of it.

She kept walking, and then suddenly with a jolt, Ainsley was pulled backward by both shoulders, stopping her from going any farther. Directly in front of her was a grand old tree, its trunk as big around as three men with their arms outstretched. The dark green of its leaves seemed a tone entirely of its own. Ainsley knelt without being asked to do so. Her legs were aching, and she could feel her heart beating fast.

"Hello," she said aloud, her voice firm. Ainsley did not know what could possibly answer her here, but the sound of the greeting made her hands tremble a bit less. There was no response, and Ainsley closed her eyes cautiously, letting the exhaustion she was suddenly overcome with wash over her in waves. The sound of the forest—the bright chirps of invisible birds, the hum of insects that flew past her ears—seemed to pulse and throb, the pressure in her ears magnifying the tones one minute and dampening them another. Ainsley covered her ears with her hands, trying to make the pulsing stop.

"Hello," a woman's melodic voice answered.

Ainsley's eyes shot open, and she looked around her wildly.

"Who are you? Where are you?" she asked as calmly as she could manage, the last "you" coming out in a shrill squeak.

"You were right to come to us. They mean you harm, even though they may not know it yet." The voice came from the far side of the giant tree. Ainsley strained her neck to try to see around the curve of the trunk.

"Your father calls to us, he leads your people in search of us, but they are confused. They offer us blood when we want for only grain and salt. They offer us prayers when we ask only for fealty."

As Ainsley watched, wide-eyed, a child-size figure stepped from around the ancient tree. It wore a long white tunic of a fabric far too thin for the chill air, but it did not seem to feel the cold. Its face was angular and oddly proportioned, the eyes too large. Its hands gave way to fingers that were impossibly long and thin, like the hidden folk. Its skin was as dark as the bark of an aged rowan tree, and its exaggerated eyes shone gold. It stretched its thin lips into a grin, and Ainsley jumped when she saw two rows of sharpened teeth. Its feet were bare, the toes more akin to claws.

"What, what are you?" Ainsley whispered.

"My people have many names," the creature answered. "And there are many more who are unlike us here in these woods. You are here at our invitation, but it would not be safe without our escort. Your father and his followers would do well to remember that."

Suddenly the bush behind the creature rustled, causing Ainsley to start, but it was only the old nanny goat, who ran up to the creature's side and looked up at it plaintively. The creature's lips stretched into another smile, and the irregular hand reached down to stroke the goat's snout.

"You have our attention," the creature said, coming closer as the nanny goat followed. "You asked us once for a draught of poison to solve a problem that needed a fix. Is that what you still seek?" It nodded to Ainsley's belly.

Ainsley shook her head. "No... I mean, I don't know. I can't have this baby here, but I cannot, I cannot..." Her voice trailed off. The oddness of the creature looked less startling the more she stared, as though it were an ordinary thing that she'd always seen.

"It's not a judgment, the remedy we provide." The creature gracefully sat across from Ainsley. "It's not a punishment to go to the world beyond. One could see it as a mercy."

Ainsley considered the words. The creature inspired no fear in her, just as the hidden folk had not. "Why did you bring me here?"

"To warn you," the creature said softly. "Your trust is too easily given. You feel as though you are alone, and that frightens you when it should not."

"My love, the young man who... I need to get to him and away from here. If they find out my condition, I can't say what will happen." Ainsley felt tears escaping from the corners of her eyes.

The creature regarded her curiously. "Escape perhaps, but be wary of following. You were not meant to follow any man or woman. You are the leader of these people."

Ainsley coughed in surprise. "No, I'm not. I'm not, I... I..."

The creature gracefully rose and waved a hand slowly through the air, which seemed to tremor at its touch.

"You will see. But beware those who offer help too readily. Find us again if troubles chase you. You have the ability to speak to the old world, and it has been watching you for some time now."

With that, the creature stepped backward into the wood and disappeared as though it had never been. Ainsley let out the breath she had been holding in her chest. She knew what she must do: find her way to Cork and Bryan. Follow or run, it wasn't a choice. The old priest was wise to the condition she was in, and she knew her fate.

21

CEIT, 1996

UNDER THE MOON OF THE SUMMER SOLSTICE, CEIT held a meeting of the elders at the stones. The air held a slight chill, not odd for the season, but there was an energy that accompanied it, as though lightning hid behind the marine layer. As she lifted the veil between the worlds, the air crackled with electricity. The old women of the Society passed uneasily into this space that lay in neither reality, a holding spot of sorts where the energy of the new world and the old intermingled. Ceit gestured for the elders to sit and waited patiently while they situated themselves on the sand. The night ocean stretched out, the waves gently creeping farther and farther onto the shore. This was not the same water that flowed with the tide on Venice Beach; this ocean lay in the in-between, and its waves were full of lost words and intentions. The creeping eternity of the horizon line went on until the end of things to come, its depths black as night and unfathomable. Under the surface, the ancient creatures of the old world hunted. The Asrai, with their scales and claws, leaped from the night-black waters, scanning the beach. They would leave Ceit and the elders be, but only because Ceit held the keys to the Night Forest. Without her present, the Asrai would tear the flesh from the bones of the old ones, or anyone who dared to enter this space without their blessing.

Far out at sea, the surface of the water rippled and a shape dove in a perfect arc from the depths, just catching the moonlight before slipping back under the surface. Ceit could feel a collective shudder emanate from the elders, and she smiled. They who had sought to destroy her now relied on her for protection. She could feel their apprehension as she scanned the circle and locked eyes with all who did not turn away.

The Asrai were not the only ones they had to fear. The old ones muttered about the Carman and her sons, Dub, Dother, and Dain. They left offerings on the beach in the waking world for the kelpies and their kin. Ceit allowed them their foolishness but knew their wards to be useless—not because the ancient evils did not exist, but because an ancient hag such as the Carman had no reason to take notice of the Society and their impotent magick. The Asrai themselves would never touch a human while in the waking realm; they were simply not worth the bother. It was only when the veil had been lifted and the elders entered this space that the Asrai and the rest of the ancient evils had even a glimmer of their existence.

The Sluagh that had attacked Ceit's mother had had to be summoned. On its own, it would never have dredged itself from its comfortably icy depths, bringing along with it the scavenger Rabharta. Someone had summoned it and opened a door through which it entered Ceit's house and found her mother so many years ago. The Maga had sworn it was not her, and Ceit had no choice but to believe that was the truth. It had been someone who under-stood the old world and had held a bit of the power of the Matrarc.

Ceit had often mused that it could have been Mór Ainsley herself, except she had no reason to set such things in motion as caused her own death. Ceit rested with the knowledge that the answer would come soon enough.

Ceit closed the circle with a wave of her hand and perched on her knees, her back straight, facing away from the black night ocean.

"Coinnigh mé ciorcal cumhachta, ag mo thoil agus ag mo fhocal. I conjure the Circle of Power, a boundary between the worlds, mar sin bíonn sé."

The chant was largely for show, but it created the energy among the elders that Ceit needed to calm the ocean winds and bring the weight of the night sky to the center of the circle. They met in this place every full moon and every solstice, as they had done with Mór Ainsley years ago. When Ceit left, they would wait until her return to meet again; only the Matrarc could lift the veil and summon the night sky. A tiny flame burst to life in the very center of the circle. It fed on nothing and belonged to nothing but this in-between world. It danced on top of the sand, illuminating the faces of the elders, who stared in awe and reverence.

"On this gealach lán we call upon the world beyond to bring us beannachtaí for the time to come."

Ceit intoned the words, feeling a deep rumble in her voice. She stood and lifted her arms to the sky. The stars seemed to reach back, each bright stone catching the light of the full moon and echoing in response to Ceit's chant. Around her, the old women chanted their own summoning for blessings for the time ahead, each praying to the night in her own way. Ceit watched their faces. She felt a twinge for the lack of regret she had for plotting the end of their world. They would be locked from this place without her, and would fall even deeper into their superstitions. They left little dishes of salt and bread on their windowsills to appease the púca, convinced that every stray cat that entered the cul-de-sac was evidence of the shape-shifter. Ceit was surprise they didn't have a shrine to Bríg in every front yard. Ceit swallowed a smile thinking of how the FBI would love that. They still, on occasion, took photos of the cul-de-sac, and Ceit was sure there was still a file on the Society that lay largely dormant, waiting for another incident to bring it to the fore.

With a deep breath, she closed her eyes and focused on the energy that was lifting up to the star-filled sky. She could see the tiny particles, like bits of ash and burned paper, floating up from the mouths of the elders and into the in-between.

"On this gealach lán we call upon the world beyond to bring us beannachtaí for the time to come," Ceit intoned, feeling a heat in her core. Something else was here at the stones with them. She knew nothing would hurt the elders as long as she was present, and no creature of this night world would dare to lash out at the Bandia Marbh. It was something new to this place. Ceit could feel its uncertainty, its fear. The old women kept chanting, oblivious to the shift in the wind and the fact that the night ocean had ceased to ebb and flow. It lay dormant, still as a lake. Ceit turned to face the water and gazed out into the eternity into which it stretched.

A figure approached from the horizon line. It walked gingerly, as though it expected to sink into the layered depths of the ocean at any moment. It looked to Ceit's eyes as a spirit, but the vision was too tremulous, too cloudy. In an instant, she knew what it was she was seeing—the false image that Amon had shown her. It was here, which meant whatever force had created the illusion in the first place had the power to cross into both worlds. Ceit stared in fascination. It was little more than a mirage, entirely false yet convincing nevertheless. If she had not been shown the true nature of the creature, it would have given her cause to question what manner of spirit was approaching. As was, the shadow, a spell creature, walked across the water toward her. A little boy in ragged pajamas, his eyes large and dark. Ceit glanced at the old women in the circle. They were all captivated, their lips moving in silent chant. They believed this creature to be a true spirit if their expressions of awe were to be believed. The figure stepped foot onto the beach and stared up at Ceit, his eyes entirely black and unseeing.

"What are you little one?" Ceit knelt down to look the boy in his eyes. "What magick created this illusion?"

Behind her, Bedelia gasped and choked on words that sputtered out her mouth.

"Illusion, my Matrarc? Do you not see the spirit here as we do?" Her voice was a bit too indignant, and Ceit was immediately overcome with suspicion.

"Silence," she commanded, and the rustle of whisper and prayer ceased. Ceit spun to observe the old women, their fear betraying them. "I do not know who summoned this illusion, but yes, it is an illusion, a photograph, a thing that someone imagined into being. This is no true spirit."

She spun to the little boy who stood before her. He was already growing wispier, the strength of the magick that conjured him waning. The boy opened his mouth and with considerable effort forced the words out. "You are not the one I seek," the little boy stammered, choking like a machine with a loose connection.

"I imagine you are programmed to respond as such," Ceit said gently. "And I doubt very much you are even capable of saying, but who is the one you seek?"

The boy shook his head.

"I figured as much." Ceit sighed and turned back to the old women. "It takes a great deal of energy and intention to conjure such a thing. Whoever thought it would fool me will greatly regret her error."

"Go now. You do not exist," Ceit whispered to the boy, who was already becoming as insubstantial as the ocean spray.

The boy twitched as though the words were so foreign to him that his body had trouble computing them, then he disappeared entirely.

Later that night, as Ceit lay in her bed and stared at the ceiling, listening to the winds whip around the trees outside her window, she played the little boy's words over in her head. It was extraordinary really, the conjuring of a magician's foil, an illusion that in the right age would have made an ordinary man look mythic. It was easily spotted, but she could not help but feel a cold tingle on the edge of her spine. Who had done this thing? And for what purpose? Who was it meant for? Ceit closed her eyes, shutting the visions out. As she slept, the last of the spring winds whined and wailed into summer, a farewell song to the passing of a season.

22

ALAN, 1996

ALAN HEARD CEIT REENTER THE HOUSE WELL AFTER midnight. He knew that if the solstice gathering had gone this late, something had gone sideways. He did not dare ask. It was not the business of men. He had lain awake for a time longer, then gently crept down the hall and out the front door. There was no particular destination in mind, rather he just wanted away. Sometimes he played a game in his head, imagining where he would go and what he would do. In one version, he took the money he'd already made off the UCLA frat kids and the Loyola potheads and left California altogether. He'd heard word you could buy passage on steamer ships like in the old days, do menial work for passage to the next port. Alan stared up at the stars as he imagined where he might end up—far down the coast of South America, north to Alaska? Maybe he'd cross the ocean entirely, build a new life wherever he got off next.

The frustratingly irrational part was he knew Ceit would support it. He could leave tonight and silently be doing her bidding. She wanted him to leave this place, to stop his match to Meg, to run. He knew she would even give him money, and he had the money from the support checks sent for his care from the state all those years. Shona had managed to blow through quite a bit of it, but Ceit had stopped that as soon as she gained guardianship. Now he knew it was sitting in an account, waiting for him to take it. Ceit would like that.

What would it prove to stay and spite her? To marry Meg and sire a dozen new Society members? What would it serve? He'd followed Meg the other night as she snuck down the alley and out the cul-de-sac. She caught a bus headed downtown, and Alan watched it pull away, his head swimming with curiosity. She wasn't slow, and he wasn't entirely sure she wanted this match. For her part, Meg didn't offer an opinion. Her parents had told her what to do, and she did it. Ceit couldn't hear the girl's name without rolling her eyes. She had not encouraged nor enforced any of the matches that had been attempted during the last eight years. If Alan married Meg, it would be the first match to be completed since Mór Ainsley's passing.

He'd had the dream again the other night—the troupe of little boys, led by a figure in stained and ruined pajamas, red welt marks around his neck, his eyes black as night. The little boy looked up at him and mouthed a single word.

"You."

Alan had awoken shaking. His first instinct had been to tell his sister, to find out what manner of spirit was following him. In the Society, the men did not carry the spiritual power. They were not the ones who could lift the veil or be invited into the night world. But though his grandmother's drunken rambling had been nonsense overall, he couldn't help but carry a seed of wonder from it. What if his great-great-grandfather had run these people? What if he had been a man who, according to Shona, could lift the veil and see the spirits?

Now, with a great sigh, Alan turned his head again to the night sky that was starting to give way to dawn. He wondered what the first light looked like over the Alaska shoreline before he resigned his imaginings and trudged back to the house on Sinder Avenue.

23

AINSLEY, 1924

AINSLEY STOOD OUTSIDE THE PUB ENTRANCE WET and shivering. The rains had kicked up minutes after she fled down the road that led to Cork. She had carried on, walking as fast as her rapidly contracting belly would allow. She knew it was not time for the baby yet. She had assisted in births among the Society before, and she knew these early pains were not uncommon, probably the result of the stress and fear that had driven her here. A couple of young men veered around her and turned back to look at her curiously. Ainsley was shaking with fear and adrenaline. With a deep breath, she entered the pub and immediately caught Bryan's eye. He gestured for her to come to the side of the bar, away from the booths and the young men drinking an afternoon pint.

"Go around back," he whispered. "My door's unlocked. Do you remember how to get to my room?"

Ainsley nodded.

"Try not to be seen as you enter. Wait there and don't make a sound."

Ainsley nodded a thank you, aware that the young men in the booth across the way were watching her curiously. She forced herself to walk slowly and calmly until she was around the side of the building. Then, risking the little rat from the butcher's shop seeing, she ducked inside the back door of the Standard. She knew the staff would be largely busy with the afternoon tea time, but still, she grabbed an apron from a metal rack as she entered and tied it around her. She didn't look like an employee after a first glance, but most didn't offer that much attention. As was, she didn't see a soul except for the shapes of figures hustling back and forth at the end of the hallway that led to the kitchen. She pushed on the door to Bryan's room and breathed a sigh of relief when the knob gave way. He had no valuables to steal, and like Finn before him, he didn't bother to lock the door. Finn always told her it was more likely he'd lose the key before anyone would enter his cubby of a room and steal his toothbrush and bar of soap.

She pulled the apron off her and sat on Bryan's stiff cot. Her muscles ached and her belly throbbed. She didn't dare lay back with her wet clothes and ruin the thin sheets, but her eyelids betrayed her and she woke to the rattle of the doorknob. Quickly she sat up as Bryan stepped inside and closed the door behind him. His face was contorted in worry.

"What are ye doin', girl?" He sat next to her. His tone was soft, but there was a controlled panic behind it. "Were ye seen entering?"

Ainsley shook her head. "I don't think so anyhow."

Bryan's face relaxed some. "Well, that's a bit of luck." He looked at her and shook his head. "You look a mess."

Ainsley started to reply, but the words were replaced with choking sobs. Bryan wrapped an arm around her and spoke directly into her ear, like Finn used to do.

"Come on, girl, you're a'right. What made you run here?"

"You've got to get me on a boat," Ainsley whispered frantically. "I can't tell you how, but the old priest, Father Gerity, he knows. They'll lock me up, they will. He came to see my father. Someone told him, but you're the only one who knew."

Bryan looked at her with incredulity. "Ye don't think I said something, do ye? Finn was a brother to me, and yer a sister now. I didn't say a word."

Ainsley examined his face for a moment; his eyes were full of shock. "I don't. I do think that little rat of a butcher's daughter created a story for herself to tell around, and it happened to be true this time." Ainsley paused. "Can you get me on a ship to England? I can travel in the hold with the animals, I can work in the galley— whatever needs to be done!"

"Sh… girl, sh. Yer talkin' mad. I'm not puttin' a pregnant woman in the hold with the sheep and cows and settin' her to work peelin' potatoes."

"But you've got to get me out. The old priest, he told my father. He'll kill me!" Ainsley could feel the baby roll and contort in sympathy.

"I couldn't even if I wanted teh." Bryan sighed. "I don't have the money even for the trip you're discussin'. I need a bit more time. We get paid at the end of the week, and then I might be able to wrestle up a third-class ticket on one of the steamers. But I don't have anything to give ye to start off with."

Ainsley felt a lump stick to the core of her throat. "No need to, I'll manage. I'll go to the dole office the minute I land, tell 'em my husband is there. They'll help me."

"Ye weren't properly married, unless I missed something." Bryan sighed. "Won't they ask for the papers?"

"I'll tell 'em they washed overboard off the ship. I'll show 'em my belly." Ainsley could hear her voice racing as fast as her circling thoughts. "I don't need much time. I know I'll find him once I get there, I just know it."

"Well, ye can't stay here, and I'm guessing going home will be a bit sticky?" Bryan asked, his voice firm.

Ainsley shook her head. "I can't. I just can't. My father…"

Bryan looked hard at her for a minute. "Is yer father like to be lookin' for ye yet? Would he think you'd come to Cork? To the Standard House?"

Ainsley paused. She didn't know. She only knew that every muscle in her body told her to run, and the creature in the woods had told her the priest meant her harm. She hadn't given much thought to what it would mean for her father and the men from the Society to follow her.

"I can't say. They'll be lookin' soon enough if not already. It'll be a matter of time before they come here. Annie." She spat out the name. "Annie, the little witch, told them she saw me sneakin' out the back door the other day." The corner of her eye twitched as she spoke. "I have to leave this place. They'll send me away, they will. They'll lock me up in the convent, you know they will!"

Bryan considered her words and slowly nodded. "I know a place you can stay for a few days. You absolutely can't leave and go into town, and you can't let anyone know yer there. I'll bring you food and drink at the end of the day. It'll be the leavings from the kitchen, but you'll do right enough for a few nights."

Ainsley nodded.

"One of the fellas here, he has a little hunting cabin on the other side of town. Let's us stay in it at times. It's a real piece of shite, ought to have been knocked over years ago. But with the weather turnin' the way it is, no one will be there. You'll freeze more likely, but there's a hearth and it's far enough out that no one will pay any mind to the smoke from the chimney." Bryan paused and looked at Ainsley closely. "Yer ready to say goodbye just like that to yer mother? Your sister? Finn told me how dear she is to ye. You leave like this, disappear this way, they'll assume the worst."

Ainsley felt her heart beat against the cage of her chest. "I'll write them the minute I reach England. And after I find Finn, after the baby is born and we're properly married, I can come back. It's not goodbye, not just like that."

"A'right," Bryan said with resignation. "I've still got a bit of work, but I'll be back in an hour or so and we'll get you out the way you came in, and settled in the cabin." He paused. "If yer absolutely sure."

Ainsley nodded. The little sprite deep in her belly kicked in solidarity. She wasn't entirely sure, but she knew that this was the only way she'd be allowed to keep her child and find Finn. She shuddered at the whispered stories of unmarried mothers and the convent prisons. She knew even her own family would not shield her from such a fate. Her father had never shown anything other than rigidity when it came to the matter of morals, and in his eyes, she had betrayed the most sacred promise of all. She knew he would be slow to accept her back even with a husband and a child proper, but without, she would be banished into the hands of the church. So she nodded and rallied the courage she knew she would need.

24

AINSLEY, 1924

BRYAN HADN'T BEEN EXAGGERATING—THE CABIN was a piece of shite. There were gaps in the planks that made up the walls, and the nearly winter wind whipped in and out. Ainsley huddled by the hearth, a thick wool blanket pulled tight around her shoulders. Bryan had left a crate with some leftovers from the Standard House kitchen, bits and pieces meant to be tossed out—a morsel of cheese that was ripe to turn, some stale bread, a few meat pies that had been too long in the oven but were fine nonetheless, a jug of water and another of milk. It wasn't much but it would do until Friday came and Bryan could book her passage. She hated how dependent she was on his help. It wasn't her natural way to not be able to manage for herself. If it wasn't for the baby, she'd never have even thought to ask. There was no choice here. She would pay him back for his kindness when she reunited with Finn, and she'd never let herself become so helpless again.

Ainsley stared into the flames of the hearth. Bryan had assured her that the cabin was far enough outside of Cork that no one would notice the smoke from the chimney. That assurance only served to grow another anxiety of being abandoned out here in the woods with no way to find her way back. And then the opposite fear snuck in, that of someone traipsing out here unawares and discovering her. She knew it would take only one person to see her out here, hiding, before the word would get back to her father. He'd skin the flesh from her back in his anger. She'd been gone two nights now, and Ainsley knew her mother and sister were likely frantic. Her heart ached for it, but there was no choice.

Ainsley shifted uncomfortably and wrapped the blanket tighter. The sun had gone down some time before, and there was no reason to believe that Bryan would be coming out to the cabin that night. The food would last her till the end of the week no problem, and he had promised to come when he had something solid in the way of a plan. It nagged at her that it was unnatural he should be so helpful. He and Finn and been mates, that was sure, but Ainsley wondered why he was so invested in aiding her. She'd half expected him to turn her away when she'd run to his room at the Standard. *He'd have been right to do so*, she thought glumly. There was a voice in the back of her head that kept scratching away at the worry. It told her to ask more questions, to not trust anything so blindly. She tampered it down again and again. She had no choice in this. She had to leave Ireland, she had to run, and Bryan was the only one to help.

A snuffling and shuffling of the earth outside broke her reverie. A low, guttural voice barely more than a whisper seeped in through the cracks in the wall.

"Ainsley Robertson," it said simply, no command or expectation connoting the words.

Ainsley felt ice creep down her spine, and her throat went so dry she couldn't eke out a cry. The shuffling scratch at the forest floor traveled the perimeter of the cabin until it found its way to the rickety front door that locked only with a weak chain that latched from the inside. With stiffening limbs and a frozen certainty, Ainsley stood, and putting one cautious foot in front of the other, she slowly crossed to the door. The certainty that she had to open the door and greet whatever creature waited there was the same as that which had told her to run from her family's cottage, the same that told her danger lurked for her in town. It was a deep, unknowable thing, a seeing that came from behind her eyes.

Her breath was rapid and shallow. The skin of her belly tightened and relaxed in rhythm. The door squealed in complaint as it swung open, revealing a thick blackness that smelled of things long dead. Ainsley sucked in her breath and steadied herself against the frame of the door. In the solid darkness, a shape took form. A great black horse, tall as she'd ever seen, towered over her, staring down at her with midnight eyes. The blackness seemed to swirl and shift, giving it form and shape. The mane was ink, and the form seemed to blend into the eternal night that followed it.

The old ones in the Society had spoken of the púca, the night fairy who shape-shifted into the form of a great black horse. They spoke of the destruction it brought, how it could trample a man to death before he even knew what had been set upon him. They spoke of how it would appear as a swarm of potato bugs that would devour the entire harvest in the blink of an hour, or a sharp-toothed gnome who would dart from the shadows, screaming obscenities and setting the little ones to cry all night. It was a story meant to keep the men in the fields and the windows latched at night. Yet, here it was. Ainsley knew after this past year that as Master Shakespeare had written, there were more things in heaven and earth than she could ever have dreamed of.

Ainsley stood her ground even though she felt sure the walls themselves would be knocked down for the way her body was shaking. The creature regarded her with its vacuous eyes, its form appearing as a mist of coal dust, settling and shifting constantly. It was said the púca would lure you out with the call of your name and then strike with its impossibly heavy hooves, killing its chosen prey instantly. What it wanted from Ainsley, she could not tell. What was her life worth to this creature? What reason would it have to kill her here? She felt an odd lightness overcome her body, the myriad problems of her mortal life seeing their end. In the next world, whatever that might be, she could start anew.

Steadying herself for the blow, Ainsley stood tall, breathed in deeply, and opened her eyes, meeting the púca's gaze. Then, as Ainsley watched in utter amazement, the creature did not rise to its full height to trample her where she stood. Instead it knelt with improbable grace on one knobby leg. Its great black head lowered, and it cast its eyes to the dirt floor of the cabin. Ainsley gasped in shock and felt the trembling that had nearly overtaken her return.

"What... what are you?" she whispered.

The creature looked up, meeting her gaze. "My liege," it said in a rough whisper.

Ainsley stared in shock.

"I'm not... not..." she whispered.

The creature nodded, rose to its full height, and in a swirl of darkness, disappeared entirely.

25

CEIT, 1996

"MATRARC?" THE LOW VOICE FROM THE OTHER SIDE of the door carried an air of urgency that made Ceit look up from the accounting she was working through, trying to figure the costs of the repairs that had been requested in the last month.

"Enter," she said firmly.

Máthair Shona stood timidly in the doorway.

"Where is Alan?" Ceit asked irritably. He should have been here to filter this visit, find out her problem, and then bring it to her when she was ready for the old woman's nonsense.

"I don't know, Matrarc. He is not here right now. Please, Matrarc, it's urgent," Máthair Shona said softly.

Ceit nodded, prompting her to continue, though not trying to hide her irritation.

"It's Bedelia, she's taken ill. I think she ought to go to the hospital, but Conor refuses to call. Says she's better off in bed. Will you come see?"

Ceit nodded wearily and stood. "I will come and see, but if the woman is ill, she should go to the hospital."

As she led Máthair Shona out of the house and across the way to Bedelia's bungalow, she took a deep breath to calm her growing annoyance. Conor had insisted on keeping his wife home last winter when her flu had turned to pneumonia, claimed the spirits were attacking her and he could release them himself. Eventually, the poor woman nearly died in her bed before Ceit had called an end to the nonsense and phoned the emergency line. He was doing the same thing to his mother now, although in all fairness the woman was well into her nineties and it was a bit exasperating that she was still alive at all.

Ceit was struck back by the smell of unwashed flesh and rot as she entered the front door.

"What in whose name is going on in here?" she muttered. Conor stood by the door, his pasty face dour.

"My apologies, Matrarc," he said carefully. "My mother has let the housekeeping fall by the wayside recently."

"You're her son are you not?" Ceit snapped. "Leave me to Bedelia, and you get to cleaning up whatever is making that ungodly stench."

Conor nodded and scuttled off to the little kitchenette. This bungalow was even smaller than Ceit's—just one bedroom and a small loft that was built into the attic. From where she stood, Ceit could see the sink overflowing with dishes and dirtied pots and pans still on the stove. *Conor hasn't been inside here in an age, even though the backyard cottage isn't more than a dozen feet from the back door*, she thought angrily. Bedelia had been sickly at the solstice gathering and had needed help walking to the stones at Venice Beach. Sick as she'd been though, Ceit had still not been able to read the old woman's thoughts. She kept her mind heavily guarded, her thoughts confused and swirling, but hidden nonetheless.

But now all those barriers were down. Ceit could hear Bedelia's thoughts and fears swirling in the house like a cyclone. They were largely nonsensical, the product of fever, but she could see bits and pieces that shone clearly. A bright summer day, Conor as a little boy with light hair and a sunburn across his cheeks. Aedan on his bed in the hospital, unconscious and attached to a ventilator. She also saw Shona and the other elders. As Ceit tried to make sense of it, she stopped before entering the old woman's bedroom.

"Matrarc?" Máthair Shona asked cautiously. "Is everything okay?"

Ceit looked into her grandmother's eyes; the weepy blue color had always made her think the irises themselves were melting clear from the sockets.

"You all met with Bedelia recently," she said curiously. "Why?"

Máthair Shona froze, and her face paled by a shade. "Matrarc, I…"

Ceit waved her hand. "Never mind. Anything you tell me will be a lie. I will find out soon enough."

Moving around her, Ceit entered the bedroom, which stank of incense, stale air, body odor, and sweat-soaked sheets. Bedelia lay in the bed, her breath so shallow that at first Ceit wondered if she lived at all. If it had not been for the unending swirl of thoughts that emanated from her dying mind, Ceit would have known her for dead.

"Bedelia?" Ceit said with a firm tone. "Can you hear me?"

The old woman managed a soft moan, and her head moved back and forth slightly.

Ceit crossed and sat on the edge of the bed and placed her hand on the old woman's forehead, which was as hot as fire. "Máthair Shona, call 911 immediately."

Shona left the room, and Ceit turned to Bedelia. "I am sorry they left you in this state. I do not know what you have tried to conjure or what your intentions are as of late, but you do not deserve what has been left to you."

Bedelia's eyes fluttered open, and she tried to focus on Ceit, her lips moving soundlessly. Ceit waved a hand before the old woman's eyes. "Don't try to speak, I can see your thoughts. Focus on what you want to tell me. Focus on what you need to confess to me now. Help is on the way. You are dying. I think you know that, and I cannot stop death. But they can make you comfortable and take you from this rotting place. Take comfort in that. Now focus."

Bedelia's face calmed and she closed her eyes. As the wail of the siren could be heard on its way to Sinder Avenue, Ceit's head was filled with a tale she could not have imagined since her days in Chinle. A tale of spirits, of trickery and deception that Coyote himself would be proud of.

26

ALAN, 1996

AS ALAN TRUDGED UP THE ALLEY BEHIND THE CUL-DE-sac, he saw Meg sitting on a fallen tree branch that served as a sort of makeshift bench.

"Old Lady Bedelia died," she said simply.

Alan sat next to her, balancing carefully. "Huh," he said. "When?"

"Little over an hour ago. My mom called from the hospital." Meg's quiet voice had an edge of something Alan didn't quite recognize.

"Why was your mom there? Were you all close to Bedelia?" Alan asked.

"Aren't we all close? I mean we're all some sort of fucked-up cousins or whatever in this thing—there's no fresh blood anywhere. You and I, we're probably brother and sister for all I know." Meg grinned, and Alan couldn't help but laugh.

"Trust me, you'd do better not to be related to me," he said gently. "But I suppose you're right. They've been marrying all of us to each other for so long it had to cross paths at some point."

"Are you sad about Bedelia?" Meg asked suddenly. Her look was quizzical, as though she were waiting for him to give just the right answer.

"Not especially," Alan said. "I'm sad I was down at the pier when I was supposed to be here with Ceit. She'll be pissed about that. Figures, the minute I step away, someone has to go and die."

"I'm not sad either," Meg said. "She told me once that I was retarded and there was no point in me continuing school and that I had been hit on the head as a baby."

"Were you?" Alan asked, trying to suppress his grin. "Hit on the head as a baby that is?"

"Not that I know of. I'm not retarded either," Meg said defensively. "Bedelia always smelled like fruit that's turned to rot. Her breath was the worst."

"I'm lucky to never have been that close to her," Alan said, then cocked his head slightly. "Where do you go on the bus, when you head toward downtown?"

Meg's face stiffened, and she tried to swallow her reaction. "You've seen me then?" she said. "Are you going to tell my parents?"

"I can't see why I would," Alan said. "I'm just curious. I suspect both of us are far more interesting than we let on."

Meg grinned. "You can't tell. Seriously—you can't."

"I promise." Alan nodded solemnly.

"I'm taking a course at FIDM. No one knows. I saved up the money from babysitting and odd jobs here and there. My parents don't want me to think about college. They have no money anyhow, but they won't even let me apply. So I'm taking a design course at night. I told them I'm babysitting in Culver City. They think I'm saving for our damn wedding." She smiled, and Alan was taken aback by the way the genuineness of the expression lit up her face.

"Yep, you are officially much more interesting than anyone would suspect," Alan replied.

"Perhaps we both are," Meg said softly, staring off over the tops of the houses where the sun was starting to set. "I don't really want to marry you," she said suddenly, still staring ahead.

"You don't have to," Alan said, joining her eyeline as the sky began to streak with peach and gold. "You shouldn't really."

"You're not insulted?" Meg asked. "The Matrarc won't be angry?"

Alan chuckled. "Ceit? She'll throw us a not-getting-married party. She hates the tradition of matching—that was something the old ones were hustling up. What about your parents?"

"I'll be gone before they can object. You just need to act as though it's all on track. I have one more semester of high school left, and as soon as I'm done in December, I'm leaving." Meg turned her eyes to him.

"Where are you going?" Alan asked softly.

"Anywhere else," Meg replied, and her gaze returned to the sky.

Alan sat in silence beside her until the sun disappeared entirely and twilight kept watch over the coming night. Then, without words, they climbed through the loose fence plank that let them back into the cul-de-sac. Meg gave him a long look as she turned to walk up the steps to her house.

"You could come with me," she said. "We could go anywhere else together."

Alan breathed in the night air; his chest was tight. "I can't leave this place. I'm bound here—all the more reason you should leave."

With a final glance, Meg turned and entered the house. Alan walked slowly to the little bungalow where he knew Ceit would be mired in the business of death. He steeled his mind and tried to forget the peach-and-gold sky setting over the rooftops of the alley.

27

AINSLEY, 1924

AINSLEY WAS OUTSIDE THE CABIN COLLECTING DRY twigs and leaves for kindling when Bryan rode up on an aged mare.

"Everything okay then?" he asked by way of greeting, swinging a burlap bag off the saddle as he looked around the woods anxiously.

Ainsley stood tall, tucking the sticks and leaves into the folds of her skirt. "As well as can be, considering." She emptied her finds into the pail by the front door and turned to face Bryan. "Friday has come and gone, you know. I have no way to tell time out here, but I know more than three nights have passed. What's gone wrong?"

Bryan strode past her, setting the bag on the table. "This will get you through a few more nights, and I brought another blanket from Standard. Winter is settin' in." He looked around and shivered.

"You didn't answer my question. What's goin' on in town? Why haven't I left? What's goin' on with my parents?" Ainsley was cross. She'd eaten the last meat pie on what she had guessed to be Friday morning and had been subsisting on the remains of the stale bread and what she scavenged from the forest. Two days had passed that way before she found a rabbit, with fresh claw marks in its neck, laid out on her doorstep. Without asking, she knew those that lived deep in the woods had provided for her. She'd roasted the creature over the fire, a messy business, and the cabin still smelled of her efforts. It made her ache for the well-settled scents and comforts of the cottage on the hill with her family.

"You've been cooking." Bryan looked around suspiciously. "Has anyone been here? Anyone know?"

Ainsley sat down in the worn wooden chair and stared at Bryan. His face was flushed, his manner distracted. She was suddenly intensely nervous, realizing how little she really knew about the man. How little she knew about Finn himself. She felt a fool for letting herself follow him out here now, but at this point, it was almost too late to go back. How would she explain her absence, not to mention her belly that seemingly overnight had started to bust the waistline of her skirt clean to breaking?

"No," she said simply. "No one has been here. I caught a rabbit. You didn't return the way you said you would, and I was left with next to nothing to eat. What of my father?"

Bryan sat down and started unpacking the burlap bag, removing potatoes, onions, a loaf of dark bread, several tins of salted meat. It was enough food for a couple of weeks, and Ainsley felt a chill growing at the base of her spine.

"Your father is tearing the town apart trying to find you. It's too dangerous to set off just now. All the men at the shipyard would recognize you in a minute. I need to wait for the tanker from Holyhead to arrive, then we'll get you aboard." He spoke rapidly and avoided looking Ainsley in the eyes.

"And when does that happen?" she asked in a measured tone. "From the looks of it, you're settling me in for a stay here."

"Week from tomorrow."

"And do we know for certain that my father won't find this cabin? Is it that well hidden then?" Ainsley asked, almost fearing the answer.

"Yes, no one knows of this place, 'cept me. The lad who owned it caught the train to Dublin last season, and the others who used to come here have all moved on." Bryan paused, surveying the spread of goods on the table.

"Not quite as you told me then," Ainsley said carefully. "You said it was a hunting cabin, and all you at the Standard came up here quite often."

"Look at the state of the place." Bryan rose suddenly, the chair nearly falling back with the force. "Good gust of wind would knock it clean over. No, no one uses this place anymore, no one knows of it."

Ainsley felt her heart pick up the pace. She'd ridden out here with Bryan at night. He'd driven the small cart the Standard used to transport wine barrels from the port. He had instructed her to crouch in the cart, several layers of thick blankets over top her as though she were a sack of potatoes. She felt a fool entire for it now, but she had no idea where she was or how far from town. That night it had seemed they traveled forever, but she had chocked it up to the stress of the moment.

"Bryan," she said in as calm a voice as she could muster. "Maybe I ought to come back with ye. Maybe this is a fool's errand, and I hate the notion that you might come to trouble over it. Take me back to the edge of town. I'm sure my father or someone from the Society will come across me soon enough, and I'll have it out with them. If they send me to the nuns, then have it be, but I can't live with the idea that yer riskin' yer neck this way. Yer too good a friend for me to allow it." She said the last bit in a soft voice and rose to stand behind him.

Bryan spun around and looked down at her, his eyes cold. "No. There's no goin' back now. You'll be a'right here until I can get you set off properly. I'm headin' back—they'll notice the mare gone before me. Stay inside, it's settin' to winter out there."

With that, Bryan moved around her and out the open door, pulling it shut behind him. As Ainsley heard the clop of the mare's hooves grow farther away, she closed her eyes and sent a silent call out to the creatures of the woods. If they were watching her as they had said, they would hear her cry.

28

CEIT, 1996

"THE CAOINE IS A TRADITION YOU CANNOT TAKE from them, Matrarc. Please hear me." Máthair Shona's eyes were glistening as she swayed gently back and forth in Ceit's office.

"The Caoine is a superstitious ritual that violates nearly every health code in California. We cannot do it even if I thought it meaningful, which I don't." Ceit glanced up from the papers she was sorting. The business of Bedelia's death was more painful than her passing. The old woman had died within hours of her arrival at the hospital, but at least they had been able to ease the pain she was in. Ceit still seethed to know how long she'd been lying in her own waste, suffering in the way she was. Bedelia was not honorable, and it was a relief that she had passed, but Ceit knew the old woman had deserved a more graceful exit. She was making her way through the Night Forest now. It would not be a difficult journey; the benefit of old age and long life was the quick transition to the next world.

Máthair Shona continued her rocking and sniffing. Ceit looked up again and felt an unhealthy anger in her spine. The glass vase of street corner carnations tipped over from the force of it, the water dumping right onto her grandmother's shoes. The old woman jumped back in surprise.

"My pardon, Matrarc. I do not mean to offend, but the Caoine is—"

"The last time the Caoine was performed properly," Ceit cut her off, "was not long after I returned, and old Elsbeth passed. I allowed it then only as a concession to you and the others. I do not need to make concessions now. And I will add," Ceit said as she rose to her feet, the glass vase rolling off the desk and landing with a dull thud on the wood floor, "that it has not been performed in as many years. We've lost others from the Society after Elsbeth, and I never approved it then and I will not now."

She sat back as Máthair Shona edged to the door, her hands visibly shaking. "It's just that Bedelia was from the old world, Matrarc. Elsbeth wasn't—she was born here, so were the others. There are so few of us left from the old country. I was just a babe when we left Cork. There are two others who came as children. The rest, well, they didn't know the old ways. Bedelia though, she was a young woman. She knew Mór Ainsley. They were young women together... She knew my grandfather..."

"Stop," Ceit snapped and the sturdy wooden chair in the corner of the room flew back against the wall of its own accord. "Do not now or ever talk to me of Mór Ainsley. You were not the next Matrarc, and neither was my mother. You do not lead these people. I will instruct the funeral home to wrap Bedelia's body in the eslene, and you can wail and carry on all you want tonight, but tomorrow she is going in the ground."

Máthair Shona backed out of the room, her lips murmuring silent pleas. Ceit relaxed back into her chair.

"Alan," she called.

"I'm showing Grandmother out—will be right there," he called back. He appeared in the doorway a moment later, a small suppressed grin on his lips. "Yes?"

"Can you call the funeral home and confirm that the wake is set for tonight? And let them know to prepare for a real shitshow," Ceit muttered as she went back to the deed and house titles to Bedelia's bungalow.

"Will do. Do you need me to take the eslene to them?" he asked quietly.

Ceit sighed. The eslene was a shroud made of woven muslin cloth, a tradition from the old world. The body of the deceased was to be wrapped and buried in it. That part she would allow the old ones. The rest of the Caoine was not happening, not now or ever again. If Shona had her way, Bedelia's body would lie on her kitchen table on display for three days. Then the old women would gather around and wail chants to dissuade the gods of death for another seven. After a full ten days, right when the body was good and ripe in the July sun, they'd allow her to be buried. Ceit had permitted the ceremony only once. Elsbeth had passed not long after she'd returned to Sinder Avenue. Ceit was only thirteen, and as sure as she had been of her right to the seat of Matrarc, she had conceded far more than she ever would now.

Elsbeth had rotted and bloated and grown a colony of death flies that lit on the branches of the magnolia trees on the street for weeks. A delivery man who'd ventured up Sinder Avenue at the time had called it in to the police. It had been Shona who had had to try to explain the bizarre tradition. It had been Karen McAlister, Ceit's long-known patron in Child Protective Services, who had convinced the state to let her stay with her grandmother despite the incident. It had only served to prove to those who still surveilled the Society that they were odd, other. They were strange and frightening. Ceit was done with it. She had told Máthair Shona at the time that she would never again allow the tradition, but Shona had a short memory.

"Take Shona with you, and one of the other old bats. They can dress her body the way they see fit. And see that the others get to the funeral home. It's just off Rose, right?" Ceit looked up, grateful that Alan was grown and capable of taking some of the load now.

"Got it." Alan paused. "And yeah, it's on Rose. They can take the bus. That'll be fun for the Metro system."

Despite herself, Ceit snorted a laugh. "Alan, the timing of this question is off, but have you given any further thought to that damnable match and what you plan on doing with the rest of your life?"

"Big question, Matrarc." He took a step farther into the room and surveyed the mess left by Ceit's anger. "Wow, Grandmother pissed you off good, huh?"

Ceit nodded impatiently. He was hiding far more than he was telling. She'd seen him talking to Meg, and the idea of them marrying and staying in the cul-de-sac heavied her heart. "Yes, she did. What about it? Thoughts?"

Alan shook his head. "I... don't know. I'd like to stay on for a bit at least. Meg is still in school, and there's no rush to confirm the match. I have no other plans, and I rather like running your errands."

Ceit frowned. "You should want for more."

Alan met her gaze. "So should you. The wailing of old women is a sad state of affairs."

Ceit nodded. "Perhaps we are both meant for a bit more, little brother. Now go take care of the wailing or Shona will be back in here."

Alan nodded and left. Ceit looked down at her papers. In

Bedelia's dying thoughts, she had seen exactly why Shona was so cowardly in her presence. She had seen why her grandmother was insisting on the Caoine and trying to revive the old tradition. She knew what was in their hearts, and she was prepared to end it all—the Society, Sinder Avenue, the whole lot of it. But unlike Alan, she could not just up and leave. It would take time to unwind the web her great-grandmother had spun over this place. Mór Ainsley had had the sight, and her power, if not equal to Ceit's, had been comparable. However, Ainsley had been myopic in her vision. She had seen Venice Beach and the cul-de-sac as a means of escape, and once there, had burrowed in so deep the roots ran clear to the bottom of the world. Ceit would pull them up one by one and destroy the hold superstition and fear had on these people. They would hate her for it, but she hardly cared about that now. She sighed as she checked the time. She had to call the lawyer; the papers for the deed of sale of Bedelia's house would be signed by the realtor as soon as they could manage it. Ceit could feel a rumble deep below the earth, the harbinger of the storm to come.

29

AINSLEY, 1924

TWO NIGHTS PASSED FROM THE TIME THAT BRYAN left the cabin until Ainsley heard the knock on the splintering door. Three sharp raps in quick succession. Her first thought was it was Bryan, and he'd taken to acting even more mad than he had during the last visit. The next thought was it must be a passing hiker, a traveler, and a glint of relief had allowed itself to light in her heart. She could go with this person, go to town. Leave this place and figure out how to make amends with her family.

But the notion was a fleeting one. A chill filled the drafty cabin. The fire in the hearth lowered to the darkest of low blue flames, and Ainsley could feel her fingertips growing numb with the cold. Three sharp raps again. Ainsley knew without being told that whatever was on the other side of the door was not of the waking world. It would be like the púca, who had not reappeared but she swore to hearing the low huffing of its breath at night in the forest. No, this was a creature more like her, more human than animal. The raps were strong and fast and came from a height that suggested someone at least a head taller than she.

Again, and this time the striking of the wood carried an air of impatience. Ainsley had summoned the creatures of the woods two nights ago as Bryan departed, and here she was, ignoring their response. She knew her reaction made no sense, knew she had asked for this visitor, although she was unsure what she really needed in order to unwind herself from the situation she'd found herself in. She took a deep breath and crossed to the door. Her hand on the knob, she closed her eyes and unlatched the chain that served as a lock. Without giving herself a chance to think, she turned the knob and stared up at the figure who waited on the other side.

His skin was as pale as she'd ever seen, his eyes colorless and glass-like. His hair was dark and waxed back under a wool travel cap. His suit was a dark-brown wool, the like of which she'd seen only in the American magazines they kept at the grocer. Over it all, he had a long black overcoat of thick wool. He looked a character stepped off a stage. The man smiled.

"Well. Aren't you a sight?" His voice was melodic and deep, a singsong tone that made it sound lyrical.

Ainsley could only stare; her entire body felt numb. A faint smell of burn came from him. It wasn't entirely unpleasant, but its potency made her eyes water a bit.

"I'm coming in," the man declared and stepped past her. "I don't mind the cold in the same way you do, but there's an audience out there and what we have to talk about rather needs a bit of privacy, don't you think?"

Ainsley swallowed hard and regained her voice. "Who are you?" she said as firmly as she could. He didn't look entirely human—his face was too angular, his fingers too long, his eyes, although seemingly devoid of color, held a glint of gold that caught the firelight.

"I have many names, and many places. Here I am best known

as Deamhain Aeir. Across the ocean they have called me the Nain Rouge. Other places I am known in other ways. I am the one who makes sure the last cinders of your fire are out at night. I am the first to wake and the last to sleep. I am the one who hears the approaching hooves of an old mare riding through an ancient woods well before you are aware. I am the one you called."

Ainsley caught her breath, her heart pounding. Her father had told stories of Deamhain Aeir, the air demon that controlled the winds and cold. Her father's story told of an ancient evil that lured farmers off their paths, stole the breath from sleeping children, left the bones of the livestock cleaned and bare in its path.

The man laughed lowly, his pale lips pulling back to reveal perfect white teeth. "Such stories, the real ones, will make your head spin, little one." His accent was crisp and deliberate, practiced and perfected. "You sent out a cry for help the other night, yes?"

Ainsley nodded, a thin covering of gooseflesh spreading across her skin as she realized the Deamhain had heard the thoughts she had not voiced. "I did. But I don't know what I was asking for. I don't know what I need."

"Oh, I don't think that's true. You need safe passage from this place, a way to stop throwing yourself at every single man who shows you a bit of kindness." The man curled his lips and waited for her response.

"I don't... that's not—" Ainsley sputtered.

"You do. And you'll stop soon enough." The man cut her off, not unkindly. "You put your full fool's trust in a young man who left you straight away." He watched her mouth open and close. The words were harsh, but Ainsley knew there was truth to them. "You then allowed another to feed your fear and bundle you up all the way out here." The man's brow furrowed slightly as though he were trying to figure out a riddle. "You have no idea where you are, truth?"

"Aye, it's true," Ainsley whispered.

"Your body would be found cold and dead under a tree sooner than you'd walk your way out, I can tell you that much. There's no path out to this uafásach piece of shite. All you need is for it to be made of candy and you'd have landed yerself in a fine fairy tale. Or maybe you already have. The big bad wolf is on his way back to ye. I can hear his borrowed horse, riding steadily on. Something has broken in his brain and heart and he thinks you his. Are you ready to be his?"

Ainsley shook her head, her voice gone.

"Take a seat, love. In your condition, you shouldn't be so worked up," the man said flatly.

"How do I break from this place—how do I get back to the Society? My family?" Ainsley asked, her voice shaking.

"You can't. Not so simple as all that. You are far more powerful than them, and your father knows it. He's seen evidence of your strength, as have you. You're a threat to him. He's known it since the night you tore the coire to shreds while the moon hung high in the sky." The man smiled again, his pale lips almost disappearing entirely.

Ainsley shot to her feet. "But it wasn't me! The Fomoire are the only demons capable of such a thing, my father said. It couldn't have been me."

The man waved a hand, dismissing her words and indignation. "The Fomoire are more myth than reality. They live on the very edges of your world and couldn't knock a pitcher of milk off the table if it were demanded of them. No, you went to sleep angry that night. You were hurt and bleeding. You went to bed upset at the thing that grows in your womb and the world you live in. You went to sleep with a prodigious fear of the Bessborough nuns and what will come of you when that little monster became impossible to hide. Which is about now, I presume. I can see the outline of the little creature—it grows and kicks, does it not? That night you lay in bed, full of fear and resentment and anger, and you dreamed of ugly things, of what you'd do if all the shackles that contain you in this world were released. Am I wrong?"

Ainsley stepped to the fireplace and sat on the thick blanket on the dirt floor close to the fire. She was unnaturally cold, and her legs would no longer hold her. Everything the Deamhain Aeir had said was true. She had gone to bed with a wild grief in her heart that night, and she had dreamed of a world where she burned the Society to the ground, where her belly no longer grew, where Finnan plunged to the bottom of the sea in penance for his recklessness. She went to bed full of anger and hate. She envisioned herself tearing apart the seams of her world and woke to the same prison she had created for herself. The creature she had summoned was not wrong.

"We have precious few minutes before you, too, will hear the clopping horse of the one who seeks to keep you here. I am here to offer you my services. And if you accept, I am bound to you and yours for eternity. Your line will be powerful, will eventually give way to an awakening the likes of which have not been seen. Eventually, there will be one who is born with manifest power to rule the Night Forest. When such a one is in her full power, the world itself will kneel. But I cannot come into a house that I am not invited into." The man knelt to meet Ainsley's eyes.

"You came in here uninvited," Ainsley whispered, her heart beating in her ears.

"This is not your house, love," the man whispered back. "You need to reclaim your people and your seat at the table, and I can help or I can watch as you fail."

"What if I refuse?" Ainsley asked, her voice as steady as she could keep it.

The man shrugged. "I leave and go on about my business, which is vast. But this d'iarr ceann who is headed your way now will arrive soon. He controls you here, and you are right to be afraid."

"What if I accept your help?" Ainsley's voice dropped a tone deeper, her head feeling as though it would float away. The firelight caught the stillness of the man's eyes, and she could see the reflection of the flames.

"Then you will have made a deal that many would not dare to make. You will have a partner, but I do not work for free. I help you now in the knowledge that one day I will sit at the right hand of the throne, the Bandia Marbh. I help you now, I guide you away from this place, I bring a bloody vengeance on those who have wronged you—and there will be many. But your anam, your biotáille are mine." He leaned in, and Ainsley could smell the soft, sweet scent of burning elm.

"Then I would be no more free than I am now," she replied in a voice so soft it was nearly lost to the crackling of the flames.

The man smiled and let a melodic laugh burst from his throat as he sat back, looking into the fire. "True enough, love. True enough." He leaned, reached into his pocket, and pulled out a cast bronze locket. "You may change your mind, and when you do, use this to call me." The man handed her the bronze locket and chain. The front was carved with a strange double circle pattern, four letters in the place of where the directions on a compass would be: A M O N.

"Amon. That is your name." Ainsley looked up at the colorless eyes, and the demon smiled back.

"One of them. Amon of the Forty Infernal Legions, Amon-Ra, Amon of Judah. I have many names and as many titles as there are stories of darkness. I seek to help you, little one, and I will be watching. Open the locket." He nodded to the small clasp.

Ainsley swung it open to reveal a small mirror.

"Catch the light of the sun or moon, and I will respond. You must invite me into your house, Ainsley Robertson, next Matrarc of the Society." He stood with effortless grace and glanced to the door.

Ainsley struggled to her feet, her belly making her stagger. "I'm not... not, we don't have a Matrarc... we don't..."

"Hush, little one. Your gentleman caller approaches. Be wary of his intentions, and watch his rise to anger—his anam is an ugly one, stained with illness. His mind is clouded. He thinks you his now, and thinking such things can be a dangerous path." Amon turned to the door and put his pale hand on the knob.

"You wish to make me yours," Ainsley said in a surprisingly firm voice.

Amon turned from the door and cocked his head slightly. "No. I do not seek to possess you—I seek to serve. I seek to be your valet, your butler, your lady's maid, your solicitor. I seek to tamper down the cinders of the fire when all have gone to bed and make sure the sun is high before you wake."

Ainsley did not have time to respond before the man tipped his wool travel cap and slipped out the door. As Ainsley collapsed into the chair, the beating of the hooves far off in the forest grew louder.

30

AINSLEY, 1924

THE DOOR TO THE CABIN FLEW OPEN, AND AINSLEY could hear the old mare huffing and shuffling about outside. Bryan appeared in the doorway. The forest was preternaturally bright, although Ainsley had not seen a moon in the sky. He was red faced and wrapped in a wool scarf, hat, and tattered overcoat. He carried a large burlap bag, which he swung down onto the table.

"You should keep the door latched—who knows who would wander in," he muttered, avoiding Ainsley's eyes as he unloaded the scant provisions he had brought: a canister of lamp oil, what appeared to be more stale meat pies from the Standard. Ainsley felt her stomach turn. *If I make it away from this place,* she thought darkly, *I will never eat another meat pie as long as I live.*

"And who would be comin' out this way?" Ainsley asked sharply. "You said yerself that this cabin was lost to the rest of Cork, that no one knew it to be here. Who do you think would have found me out here where you've locked me away?"

Bryan spun around and looked her up and down, his eyes unfocused and glassy.

"You asked for my help, you did," he said softly. "I saved ye. Yer father tears the town apart daily, and I haven't said a thing, not a damn thing. And this is the thanks I get." His voice broke slightly, and Ainsley remembered the demon's warning to not let it rise to anger.

"Yer right, I'm just tired of waiting," she said to appease him. "It can't be so long now, can it? You could just take me back to town and let me be near the docks, and I'll figure out the rest. You don't have to do anything else." She took a step forward, trying to keep her voice soft even as her hands shook.

Bryan shook his head. "Not my best girl, no. I'll not leave you at the dock like that feckin' bastard Finn did. I'll not leave you to that. No, we're to catch the train from this place up to Dublin, we are. I wrote to the Shelbourne and as soon as the Standard can send my references, I'll have a job. I'll get us a little flat in town, with a rocker for the baby, and that will be that…" He trailed off, the speech sounding as though he had practiced it a hundred times to himself, metered and weighed, every word just so. Bryan unwrapped his neck scarf and pulled the hat from his head. His unruly hair was matted and greasy, and Ainsley could see it had been some time since he had washed. He turned and crossed to the door, opened it, and looked out at the night.

"Or we could just stay here. I can till the land and we can grow our vegetables. I'll snare us rabbits… We could just stay here. I could patch these walls." He spun around, his eyes blinking rapidly, his voice thin and desperate sounding. "We could just stay here," he repeated in a near whisper.

Ainsley could feel her heart beating. She reached up and placed a single finger on the place where the locket lay hidden. She had concealed it beneath her dress and shawl when Bryan approached, and the cool metal against her skin was the only thing keeping her from fainting dead away. In her belly, the baby—Finn's baby—kicked and spun. Ainsley had no doubt that the words that Bryan spoke made their way to the womb, and even the sprite knew the danger they were in.

"Oh, Bryan," Ainsley said as calmly as she could. "This is no place for a baby, and the Shelbourne is a fine inn. We could go back to town tonight, and I could tell my father we're setting off and not to worry further."

Bryan snapped out of his reverie, his eyes dark and angry. "No," he said firmly. "You won't tell a soul. You want to leave me, is that it?" He stepped forward, the wind whipping inside through the open door. "You ungrateful cow, you want to leave and run back to yer father?"

Ainsley retreated until her back was against the cold stone of the hearth where the dying fire lay in embers. Bryan stepped in, his face a shifting landscape of red and purple. Ainsley could see a vein in his temple pulsing fit to burst. He reached out one filthy hand and wrapped his fingers around Ainsley's thin neck. She shook with the sudden restriction and pain. She could feel the pressure behind her eyes as she gasped for fleeting scraps of air. Bryan's coal-black eyes bore into hers, and she saw no humanity there, no trace of the man she had known in town—the friend, the confidant, the barkeep that Finn claimed as his best mate. Ainsley was overcome with anger and frustration. The Deamhain Aeir was right; she had thrown herself at every man who had shown her a kindness. Flailing, she reached to her chest where the locket lay hidden beneath her dress. Bryan saw the bronze of the chain around her neck and released her abruptly. Ainsley fell to her knees, her throat raw and her lungs screaming. The baby kicked and beat her insides with all the fury she felt in her head and heart.

"You have had visitors, haven't ye?" Bryan roared. He reached down and, pulling on the chain, wrenched the locket up into the light. He pulled with a strength that should've broken any ordinary chain, but this held tight, strangling Ainsley in an entirely different way.

"Stop!" Ainsley croaked, desperately reaching up to grab the chain or Bryan's hands or anything that would stop the searing pain of the metal slicing into her skin. "Stop!" Blackness clouded her vision, and she knew if she gave into it and passed out she would never see another dawn, and then not even the Deamhain Aeir could save her. Bryan reached for the locket and then fell backward in shock. Ainsley collapsed forward, her arms circling her belly as she once again tried to regain her breath.

She peered up through the static gray spots that obscured her vision and saw an angry red burn on Bryan's palm, the exact shape and size of the locket. He stared at it in fascination and pain. The kaleidoscope of mottled anger that stained his pale skin lessened, and his eyes locked on Ainsley. This time, though, the anger was replaced with another emotion—fear. Through the burn of her lungs and the sharp bite of the cuts the chain had made on her neck, Ainsley allowed a small smile to dance on her lips.

"You'd do well to treat me more kindly," she whispered. On the other side of the cottage, she could hear the huffing breath of the púca. The old mare was whinnying in fear from where she was tied to an oak in the line of the open door. Bryan tried to stand and fell backward, still holding his hand aloft, the perfectly round burn of the locket still smoldering and singeing his flesh even though he had touched it for only a moment. Ainsley took it in her hands and held it aloft. "There are those who know I am here, and I do not think you wish to anger them more than you already have."

"Yer a witch," Bryan muttered, his tongue thick and the words muddy. "Yer a witch, just as Finn always said ye were. Ye prob'ly have yer familiars out in the dark right now, ready to tear me to pieces."

Ainsley heaved herself to her feet despite her spinning head and throbbing neck. It was important that Bryan fear her in this moment; she would sink into her pain and misery later. Now she rose to her full height and pulled her shoulders back, holding the locket out before her.

"I need only call them, Bryan. Shall I do it?" She kept her voice soft and urgent. Bryan scooted on his back end to the door, his face white as a sheet now. Behind him the silhouette of the púca filled the doorway, standing taller than the cabin itself. All Bryan saw as he turned was its massive chest, black as midnight and rippling with otherworldly strength. It brayed softly, asking direction from Ainsley. Ainsley took a step forward even though her legs shook under her skirts and threatened to give out entirely. She had no idea how to command the creatures in these woods, and had even less knowledge as to why they looked to her with respect. Amon had said she was the next Matrarc, but she knew that to be a falsehood. Demons lie, she knew that for a truth. The Society had no Matrarcs; the men held the line and always had. She was nothing, a girl, a whore, a witch as Bryan had aptly called her.

She nodded at the shape of the púca and then at Bryan. "It will allow you passage to leave this place if you do not return, ever," she said in a voice that she hoped spoke of authority. She had no idea if the púca or any of the creatures that lived in the woods would listen. Perhaps Bryan would be torn to shreds before he rode a mile. Ainsley realized she would not be sad were it to happen. But the púca stepped aside, and Bryan scrambled to his feet, his eyes still locked on Ainsley.

"Yer a witch," he repeated. "You'll burn for it."

"Not before I kill you where you stand, Bryan O'Malley. Now

go before I forget my manners and let the púca stamp you to a smear in the dust. And don't speak my name in Cork—I'll hear it." She leaned in on the last bit with what she hoped was enough to scare Bryan to silence.

With a last flurry of feet and hooves, Bryan jumped astride his borrowed mare and tore off into the forest. Ainsley crossed to the door, slamming it shut and latching it to lock. She then strode to the fire and prodded the embers back to flame, adding another bundle of dry sticks until it rose to full height. Only then did she allow herself to collapse to the floor, releasing the terror and pain of the last hour. She sobbed into her hands and shook so she wondered if the splintering walls of her prison would tumble.

She had to leave this place before Bryan could spread the tale of a witch in the woods and those other than her father came looking. She knew him to be right about one thing: she would burn if that were the truth that took hold. Ainsley held the locket with its deceptively cool bronze surface. A bloody vengeance the Deamhain Aeir had said. He would be her butler, her lady's maid, he had said. All she had to promise him was her soul and that of her child and grandchildren and all the line of those to come. That was all—promise Amon of Judah a claim to whatever demonic thing he believed would be born from her line. Perhaps he was right and she did possess the power to tear the coire to shreds with her dark thoughts, but her child need not be sold to that darkness.

Ainsley tucked the locket under her dress again and rubbed at the raw wounds on her neck. She should get rid of the damnable thing, throw it to the woods, let the forest take it back to the demon. But she did not. *Plenty of time for that,* she thought absently. Now she needed to rest for a bit and then flee this place, set off before the sun rose. She would follow the little creek from where she had been drawing her water. Maybe it would lead her to the coast and she could find her own passage away from this place, though the idea of finding Finn was lost to her forever. He was a dead thing to her now. It was only her and the child. The creatures of the forest would provide for her just as they had brought her the rabbit. Ainsley murmured these false comforts to herself as she heated a bit of water to ease her pains. Outside the thin walls of the cabin, the night waited for her to decide her fate.

31

ALAN, 1996

THE CAOINE WAS AS BIG A SHITSHOW AS CEIT HAD said it would be. The funeral home on Rose Avenue had been warned, but they could not possibly have been properly prepared for what had been transpiring for the last four hours. Grandmother Shona led the wails at a siren's pitch, and a half a dozen of the elders crowded around in chorus. Conor, Bedelia's sour-faced son, and his miserable-looking wife sat to the side, watching the old ones as they sat on their knees and emitted incomprehensible notes. The funeral home attendant had nervously looked in several times, and Alan had given her a nod. Alan knew Ceit had told them it would last until they kicked the old ones out entirely, but the attendant was not prepared for the tone and tenor of the theatrics.

On the elevated bit of stage at the front of the room, Bedelia's body was wrapped neatly in the eslene. Shona herself had wrapped the old woman and muttered little blessings and curses the entire time. Alan knew she was fuming over Ceit's refusal to allow the tradition in its entirety. Alan also knew that there were layers amid layers to the animosity that lay between Ceit and all the elders. Bedelia had been little more than a child when she'd come over from Cork with Mór Ainsley so many years ago, and Bedelia's death was the loss of the steadily dwindling Society members who remembered the old country. Máthair Shona saw it as a sign, but Alan took a deep breath to stave off the eye roll he felt inevitable. She had died because her fool son had stopped doing much of anything to help her. Her insulin was found untouched in the fridge after she passed. Conor had sworn up and down he checked on her every day, cooked her meals, cleaned her, made sure she took her daily insulin shots. He was a liar. Alan had been in charge of cleaning out the old woman's house after the initial chaos had settled. It stank of neglect. Ceit knew it as well as anyone. He wondered if she'd known that Bedelia was lying there in her own filth, dying minute by minute. He wondered if she let it happen so she could deny Conor and his terrible wife the right to the house. Alan knew these were thoughts he would be better off banishing entirely; there were no answers, and he would never stand up to the Matrarc, even if she was his own sister.

No one else knew Conor was being denied the house. Alan knew only because he had been charged with watching the door as Ceit met with the realtor. He knew she was arranging to sell off all the houses. He didn't know how or when, but he knew well enough that Conor would never move his scant possessions into that bungalow. He suspected Ceit would evict them entirely before that would happen. But where would they go? The Caoine wail reached a note that made Alan's skin crawl and he winced as he stared at the man and his wife sitting impassively to the side of the madness, watching his mother's body overtaken by the foolish tradition.

Alan remembered his own mother's funeral vividly. He remembered the old ones rushing at Ceit, he remembered his father's ugly words, he remembered the dark-haired woman who had stood with Ceit. He remembered his sister, her frame tiny and significant in the fog-filled morning. Even then, she had looked a queen. He had clung to her until his father pulled him away. His father was as close to breaking as he came while still functioning in the waking world. It wouldn't be too very much longer after that he would leave Alan without a word and drive to El Monte with a butcher knife intended for Ceit. He still couldn't hate him; he'd tried. There were times Alan wondered if his life would be happier, kinder if his father had found his mark. He immediately erased the thought. He knew Ceit could hear his thoughts if he was lazy enough to let his guard down. It amused him that her power in that capacity was so limited when it came to him. It would figure that the queen of all things dark and terrible would be able to do as she pleased, but even the Bandia Marbh had limits.

"A anam a ardu`," Shona keened, her face tilted to the fluorescent lights that lined the cheap paneled ceiling. "A anam a ardu`."

Across the room, Conor shifted uncomfortably and caught Alan's eye. Alan shuddered at what he knew would happen next. Conor rose uncomfortably and motioned to his silent wife to stay put. He crossed the room with a feigned authority. He wore a suit taken from the box of giveaway clothes that was collected every month or so from the secondhand store. It was ill-fitting, and he walked with an awkwardness that belied the confidence he was trying to project. Alan held more sway in the Society at eighteen than this fool did at sixty-five.

"Hello there, son." Conor sat down next to Alan and leaned forward, as though interested in the moans and cries of the Caoine.

"Son?" Alan asked dryly.

"It's just an expression. I didn't mean, I mean, I beg your pardon," Conor stuttered.

Alan nodded. "I'm sorry about your mother."

Conor nodded, not looking back at Alan. "She was a wonderful soul."

Alan swallowed his disgust. This man had all but killed her, and here he was in his cheap suit and false sadness. "What do want?" he asked bluntly. One of the perks of being Ceit's Dara was that he was not required to uphold the social graces the others held so dear.

Conor sat back and shifted uncomfortably. "I... I need to talk to you. I can't talk to the Matrarc—she won't even see me."

"She's busy," Alan responded flatly.

"Yes, I mean, I know she is, but this is a matter of some importance." Conor's pasty face was growing splotchy red. Alan was beginning to enjoy this greatly.

"Out with it." Alan cocked his head and stared the older man in the eyes as he spoke. Conor broke his gaze and fumbled.

"It's just that, and I ask more for my wife than myself... it's just that we need the Matrarc's permission to move into the main house. We've been in the guesthouse for our entire married life, and it's time we take the house—it's only right. We need the clearance from the Matrarc, and she won't even give me a meeting. My wife, she's desperate to know when we can move."

Alan sighed. "I cannot answer this for you. You need to speak with the Matrarc on this matter. Your mother has not been dead even two days and you already want to move into her house. Give it some time, man—you sound downright unsympathetic."

Conor's face flushed scarlet, and Alan saw a flash of anger in his eyes that he could never openly express to the Dara to the Matrarc. Yes, Alan was definitely enjoying this now.

"I can pass on your request to the Matrarc, but I suggest you get ahold of your emotions before I do. You look a bit scattered. Ceit doesn't like scattered."

Alan nodded and stood, stretching his legs. The funeral home assistant was standing at the back of the hall. It was beyond time for this thing to be over. He gave Conor one last look, the man's face devastated and livid at the same time. All that impotent anger, nowhere for it to go. Conor held no power in the Society and was ill-equipped to leave. He'd spent his entire life in the service of the mythology that was spouted from the old women's lips.

Alan crossed to the back of the room to settle the affairs and end the Caoine. They would all do well to look at him with more respect. Dara to the Matrarc was a worthy title, but perhaps he was something more.

32

CEIT, 1996

"AND WHAT OF THE AFTER?" CEIT ASKED, HER VOICE
low enough not to disturb the g'nights that twirled in tiny cyclone
clouds at the end edge of the Night Forest.

"Next, my queen?" Amon replied lazily. He sat next to her,
watching the dance of the tiny creatures. "Next, you leave this
damnable cul-de-sac once and for all and start the business of your
true work."

"You told me my true work was to be the Bandia Marbh, to
rule the Night Forest," Ceit said pointedly, turning her head to
stare at the demon, who was currently wearing artfully shredded
stonewashed jeans, blindingly white Converse sneakers, and a Gin
Blossoms concert T-shirt. "I am doing that."

"Yes, you are, my liege—you are the best part-time goddess of
the dead that ever there was," Amon replied dryly. He reached his
thin, unnaturally pale hand into the night and plucked a g'night
from its spinning frenzy. He pinched the tiny creature between
two fingers while it raged silently, trying to reach its tiny bow, but
it was useless; Amon's fingers rendered the tiny monster impotent.

"I have responsibilities, responsibilities I can soon discard but not immediately. I need to make sure my brother is not trapped. I need to make sure the Society is dissolved entirely before I can depart." Ceit reached out a hand and swatted Amon's wrist, disrupting his hold and allowing the tiny g'night to fly free. "Don't torment them."

Amon smiled, his perfect teeth catching the light of the full moon overhead. "Your brother is more capable than you think. And more dangerous. You'd do well to trust less. The Society will dissolve on its own when you depart, and your brother will do as he pleases." Amon cocked his head, considering his words. "You have looked into the matter of the false visions? The hologram—is that the right word for it?"

Ceit nodded. "Yes. It is coming from the old ones. It's a weak spell overall, but I fear whomever they are tormenting with it cannot see all that and take it for reality."

"You'd do well to trust less," Amon repeated.

"Tell me what you know, Deamhain Aeir."

"I know nothing," Amon responded, "except that you are still far too tied to the concerns of the humans. You are the one who can take back this world, break the barriers of the Night Forest, turn reality back to a time when fae ruled and humans bent the knee to the darkness. Instead, you are signing contracts and approving shopping budgets and allowing some old women who know little more than parlor tricks to undermine you."

"Perhaps you're right," Ceit said calmly. She knew him to be true, but she also knew that Amon wanted too much too fast. She could not leave the Society until her brother was free of it. Until he decided to leave of his own will, she could not risk him being ensnared by the old ones. It wouldn't matter if she sold off all the houses and left the old ones to the streets. If Alan had not severed his ties, he would rebuild and remain as one drowning for all his days.

Before them the ancient forest stirred, and a pair of great bright eyes peered out and darted back. Ceit smiled. The wood elves were curious and reverent. She liked to follow their path deep into the forest, the flat, carved stones that led to the ancient lake. It was there that Ceit would sit when she knew she would not be disturbed for some time. It was there the eyes of the creatures of the Night Forest would surround her, respectfully watching. She could see them gnash their sharply pointed teeth as they kept watch with her through the endless night. She knew they would fight with her and for her. But she was unsure of what they were supposed to be fighting for. A revolution? The times that Amon hungered for, the days when fae and human existed side by side, were the terrible tangles of the darkest fairy tales. They were the stories that lay hidden in the darkest of nightmares. This was the world that she ruled, and Ceit was not sure it should be led into the light. She had seen her fair share of humans who deserved to have their necks ripped out by the wood elves sharp teeth. She had also seen the result of ruling with fear. The sight of the Maga and her false temple in Salt Lake still haunted her. The faces of the families and children who cowered in the corners of that foul place, Annbeth's eyes as she had died in her arms—all these things reminded Ceit that perhaps it was best to keep the veil intact, to keep the line between this world and the human realm strong.

"As you wish, my lord and lady," Amon said in response to her unspoken thoughts, and with mock reverence and rose to his feet, stretching his arms over his head. Ceit shook her head. He was no more human than the g'nights and in no need of such ritual. His corporeal form was for her benefit only. She had seen his true self, and it did not need to stretch and bend as Amon was doing now.

Quietly, Ceit closed her eyes and lifted the veil as she entered back into the waking world. The transition was always a bit painful, a tugging at her chest, a reminder that she was not entirely suited for this reality. She opened her eyes to the darkness of her bedroom on Sinder Avenue. It was late. Alan would have shepherded the old ones back from Bedelia's service by now. The old woman would be fed to the flames by sunup. Ceit moved from the cold floor to her bed and lay down again. As she closed her eyes to the realm of sleep, she wished for a dreamless slumber.

33

AINSLEY, 1924

AINSLEY'S FEET AND FINGERS WERE ENTIRELY NUMB from the chill, but still she walked. On her back, she carried a small satchel with some of the food that Bryan had brought, leaving the damnable meat pies for the rats. She'd been walking for some time now, how many hours she could not say, and still she was seemingly no closer to anything that resembled town. She'd followed the direction that Bryan had set off in. Of course, she reminded herself continually, she had no idea where he might have changed course or if, in the light of day, there was a path she should be following. If Ainsley could make it to the dock, she could try to barter for passage on a ship—a ship anywhere would do. Wherever it took her, it would be away from Cork, away from Bryan and her father and the nuns that lurked at the back of her fears.

Occasionally, she heard the huffing breath of the púca deep in the woods. The sound had ceased to frighten her, and she found it a comfort of sorts now. The Deamhain Aeir had told her she commanded these creatures. What truth to that would be scant, but one thing Ainsley knew was they meant her no harm, at least not on this night. Her mind wandered as she forced her feet to keep marching forward. Perhaps it had all been a dream, the result of too little nutrition and too little sleep. Perhaps it had been the hysteria the old women had spoken of that came with pregnancy. Her own mother had told her how, when she was expecting Maire, she had taken to thinking that the roof would cave in one night as it rained. Instead of anything that might have made sense, her father had found her leaning out on a ladder, shingling tile in hand in the wee hours of the morning. He'd set to pitch a fit, mother had told her. "Where was I?" Ainsley had asked. "Asleep, dead to the world," had been the reply.

If this was a dream, it had been going on for some time. The creatures she'd seen in the woods near the Society, the damn goat—what it all meant, Ainsley hadn't a clue, but she wished to be asleep and dead to the world now, as she had been when her mother hammered in shingles in a torrent of rain. Her mind was foggy, and her arms felt numb. Occasional sharp and biting pains ripped through her stomach. It was far from her time. Ainsley knew the baby had no intention of arriving any time soon, but it was angry and would let its opinion on the matter be felt. Despite it all, she held no resentment toward the sprite. Nothing would be too terribly different without it. She'd be at her family's cottage, sleeping in the loft above the hearth with Maire. She'd hear her father's raging temper below, and she'd cover the bruises he left on her back and arms with wool shawls. She would bear the weight of her mother's sadness and her sister's fear. She would have been married off before too long anyhow. Her father had already been talking matches. The cluicheálaí had met with him the previous spring, early perhaps, but it meant she was setting her sights. At the time, Ainsley had giggled to Finn about it all. He kissed her and told her he'd march up to the cluicheálaí and declare himself the match. It wasn't to be, of course, and Ainsley knew it, but still, she'd smiled and let herself imagine.

Now the image of Maire's face kept flashing before Ainsley's vision, blocking the dark path. The little girl would not see the end of their father's temper. Ainsley had stood between the two of them many times, and now she was gone. Funny how when she had dreamed of a boat and England, Finn and the baby, she had let herself forget this. Funny how she'd wrapped herself up in selfishness and vanity. But whether she'd left with Finn or whether she jumped a ship to the nearest shore at dawn, Maire would still be left to bear the burden.

Beating your wife and daughters was, by no means, a rule in the Society, but it certainly was not a thing the Ceannaire would meddle in. How a man ran his own house was how he ran it; women sat at the periphery, and they didn't raise their voices, they didn't object to their lot. *Perhaps the nuns had it right after all,* Ainsley thought glumly as she stumbled over the root of a massive elm. They lived with their sisters in a place devoid of men, and they worshipped the mother goddess, albeit by a different name and face. They swore themselves a life absent the pain and labor of children and family. *Perhaps I should be more generous,* Ainsley thought dimly.

Ahead a light was becoming more and more apparent; it was dancing between the trees. Ainsley froze with fear. It must be Bryan, back on his old mare to find her. It could be her father, scouring the woods with a whipping rod in hand. Instinctively, Ainsley ducked back into the cover of the forest and crouched low against the trunk of a willow. The light bobbed and ducked, dancing in and out of her line of vision, but it was growing ever closer. Ainsley strained to hear, but there was no sound to accompany it, no voices, no footfalls. Whomever it was walked these woods silently. Behind her, Ainsley heard the huffing breath of the púca and was glad for it. It had defended her once—perhaps it would again. The physical aura of the púca's presence rose up over Ainsley's huddled form, and she felt it broaden its muscular chest.

Slowly she rose and without looking back gestured for the demon horse to follow. The heavy hooves fell right at her heels as Ainsley continued her hike. *Let me meet the bearer of the light,* she thought madly. *Let us meet, and the one who wanders these woods in search of me will never leave intact.*

The light grew closer still, and it became apparent that it was a lantern held high by a metal rod, the sort the lamplighters used. Ainsley's apprehension turned to curiosity quite against her will. What was this trick? A single lamplighter walking the woods at night in search of—what? Her? A rogue streetlight in need of illumination?

The thought made her snort a laugh of the most inappropriate manner, the sound carrying farther than she imagined it could. Behind her, the púca's hot breath warmed her neck as the great demon horse bent its head. The lamp stopped abruptly. Ainsley was filled with an icy dread. She had brought this upon herself, and now she would be uncovered.

"Hello?" a small voice called out.

Ainsley paused. This wasn't her father or Bryan or any man for that matter. The voice belonged to a child.

With great hesitation, she responded, the púca at her back making her spine stand straighter. "Hello."

"I've lost my way," the little voice called out. "Can you help?"

Ainsley paused again. It could be a trick, or it could be a child lost to the woods. Either way, she didn't know the way out, so they were more likely to die of the cold together before she found herself to be any great help. At her back, the púca stamped impatiently. *Let me charge*, she heard it think. The demon's thoughts filled her head effortlessly, and suddenly Ainsley knew that if she gave so much as a nod, the púca would destroy the child belonging to the voice and lamp. Whatever its intentions, it was a child nonetheless, and the idea that the babe would be torn apart by the forest monster it knew only as a nightmare story was too much.

Ainsley turned and shook her head slowly, pushing the púca back into the night. The púca huffed its objection and then turned on its massive hooves and charged off into the dark, away from the world of man. Instantly, Ainsley knew she had lost her protection. However alone she had felt before, she was truly alone now. The great horse had followed her since she'd left the cabin, and now its loss echoed in the night sky. Whatever came her way now, it was hers alone to face.

Ainsley swallowed, her throat aching. "I'm lost as well and no help to ye."

"Yer all alone, too?" the child asked.

"I am," Ainsley replied, the night insects buzzing past her ear in the chill.

"I'm sorry," the voice called helplessly.

All of a sudden, Ainsley felt her arms wrenched behind her, and she was shoved forward. Her feet tangled in the undergrowth as she nearly fell. Overhead, the first streaks of light were beginning to mark the sky. Ainsley felt her stomach drop. She wouldn't have made it to the docks anyhow. Her plan, however flawed, was hopeless. The arms that held her shoved her roughly into a small clearing, and Ainsley could see the distant lights of town a little ways off. She had been so close—if she had made it just beyond the mass of trees, she would have been able to make her way without any help at all.

Her voice was frozen; a scream lay deeply hidden beneath layers of exhaustion and pain. The baby kicked a sharp foot into her side, and she doubled over. The arms released her, and she could hear gruff breathing behind her.

"Who sent ye?" she managed to say. "That coward Bryan O'Malley?"

"Spit on Bryan O'Malley," a deep voice rumbled, and Ainsley felt a stab of fear and relief. Her father stepped into the clearing, his frame blocking the rising sun. "That fool was screamin' high heaven about a witch in the woods. We followed his tracks as far as we could. You were like to die out here, ye stupid git."

Ainsley straightened her back and stared at her father, his face flush with anger and cold, his eyes hard.

"Well, you see me," she said with more surety than she felt. "And you know why I ran."

"I can see the old fool of a priest was telling the truth. That's what I see." He turned to nod at the men standing behind her. "Go get the horses, we'll head back to the village."

The men, who she recognized well enough from the Society, cast her sheepish looks and trudged past to what she could see now was a rough path. A little boy she now recognized threw her an apologetic look and followed.

"What do you propose to do?" Ainsley asked, wishing the púca would feel her desperation, but she knew it was long gone. It was an unruly creature of the night under the best of circumstances, especially when it had been turned away.

"Get you fed and cleaned up and then we'll see," her father said, staring at her burgeoning belly. "Is it Bryan's? He seems to think it is."

Ainsley coughed a laugh that was more anger than amusement. "I would never let that lot touch me. He said he would help me get a ship—that's why I let him take me out to God knows where in the woods. I didn't know him to be mad. It's Finnan's. He said he would marry me. He said he'd send for me and I'd meet him in England, where we'd marry. He said—"

"A great many things, I suppose," her father cut in, his voice surprisingly gentle. "Does he know?"

Ainsley shook her head. "I didn't see the signs till after he left."

Her father shook his head. "C'mon now. I'll take care of Bryan O'Malley. You look half-frozen."

Begrudgingly, Ainsley let him guide her by the shoulder to the horses on the other side of the clearing. As they rode back through the breaking dawn to her mother, sister, and all she had ever known, Ainsley knew with a surety that a fresh hell was just beginning.

34

AINSLEY, 1924

AINSLEY COULD SENSE THE APPROACH OF THE PRIEST'S cart long before the rumble of the wheels was audible. For the last five days, she had been fed endless heaping bowls of stew and plates piled high with boiled potatoes and the last of the summer vegetables. Maire had followed her about making sure her shoulders were covered and the fire was stoked. Her mother had not spoken a word to her, just grunted and avoided eye contact as she plunked more food down before Ainsley. There was a fresh set of bruises lining her mother's cheek, and Ainsley felt the old dread in her gut. Her father had been largely absent, and Ainsley feared what business he was attending to. The rest of the Society went on about their own business, casting long stares at the windows of the cottage as they passed. Ainsley knew her disappearance had thrown the village into turmoil, and she knew full well all those who passed with their carts and baskets, leading their goats to the River Lee or out to pasture, all those whose fates were intertwined in that of the Ceannaire had suffered due to her actions.

This morning, as she sat leaning against the window frame, the frost already gathering on the glass outside, Ainsley felt the rhythmic clatter of the old priest's carriage. The others would not hear its approach for another mile or so, but Ainsley felt it in the back of her neck. She could smell the sour stink of the priest's skin, the smell of old meat and milk gone bad. She could see the clouds forming on the edge of the woods. She ran her fingers over the locket that she kept close to her skin, hidden below the layers of wool that guarded her against the winter wind. Neither her mother nor father had seen it, and it was all for the better. They'd think she'd whored herself to have such fine jewelry. They'd see it as further evidence of her fallen character. Only Maire had seen the locket with AMON etched onto the bronze surface. Ainsley had shown her one night as they lay close in the loft above the hearth. She'd made sure to block the light of the moon as she'd opened it to let Maire see the polished silver reflection inside.

As the cacophony of Father Gerity's carriage drew close enough for those with astute ears to hear its arrival, Ainsley knew that the demon could help her in this moment. She knew what was likely to become of her, knew why the old priest was coming. Ainsley also knew he was not alone. She closed her eyes and saw a black-robed nun and two figures in work clothes. She knew they were coming for her, she knew there was no choice in the matter, and she knew above all that she could not call the demon if any of them were to survive.

"Are you a witch?" Maire had whispered to her one night as the autumn chill turned to winter on the other side of the thin roof planks.

"You're mad—of course I'm not," Ainsley had said softly.

"Da said you're a witch," Maire whispered back, undeterred.

"And he's one to talk, is he? What do you think the priests in

Cork would do to him and the others if they'd ever seen them out by the River Lee trying to lift the veil, chanting their fool heads off, torturing any goat unfortunate enough to go lame or age out of her milk? Da would be the first one to hang from the witching tree in the center of town. He knows it as well as I do—they all do."

"It's different." Maire curled closer, her hand on Ainsley's belly where the baby was kicking. "He was talking to Mum, and he said you are different. He said you are the black magick of the old forest, a fae witch—he said it and spit on the floor."

Ainsley paused at that, remembering the massive chest of the midnight-black púca and the fine-featured creature in the ancient woods as it regarded her with its maple oak eyes.

"A witch I am not," she said. "I possess no magick. But perhaps I am a bit of the forest fae. Maybe I was a changeling, a fae babe left behind by the ancient ones. Maybe yer real sister is running wild in the woods right now, naked as the day she was born and all the more free for it…"

There was a long pause, and then Maire started giggling. "Do ye think they'd let me visit? Like the rich folks on holiday? I could stay the summer naked in the woods, come back here when the chill took the air?"

Ainsley started giggling to join her. "I can't see why not—just tell them yer sister's a fae witch and could they very kindly pour a cuppa?"

"I'll bring biscuits to make sure they know I mean business," Maire gasped out between bouts of laughter. At that their mother had hit the ceiling with her long cane, and they had quieted their giggles and gone to sleep, arms wrapped around the other. That had been a night ago, and Ainsley had lain awake for as long as sleep allowed her, not wanting to forget the feel of her little sister in her arms.

"Father Gerity's on his way up the hill," Ainsley said matter-of-factly as her mother stormed in from the woodpile, her arms laden with freshly cut logs. She did not answer Ainsley but instead grunted a general disapproval and set about ladling the morning's porridge into a bowl and setting it in front of Ainsley. Ainsley wasn't hungry. Her stomach had hardened into a tight drum, the baby pushing all her insides up into her chest. Every bite made her think she was fit to burst. Despite it all, she took the wooden spoon her mother held out to her and started eating the tasteless mush.

"The priest's on the way," Maire announced loudly as she entered, stamping the damp from her boots in the doorway. She cast a worried glance at Ainsley and turned to their mother. "You want I should find Da?" she asked.

"He knows. He'll be along shortly," her mother said curtly, the tone making Ainsley's skin grow cold. "You'll want to eat faster than that." She directed the instructions at Ainsley but looked away, into the fire in the hearth. A new soup pot hung over the flames, nowhere near as grand as the original. This was little larger than the kettle, a poor substitute for an irreplaceable loss.

"Why is the priest coming, Mother?" Ainsley asked pointedly. Maire stood her ground in the doorway, and their mother rocked back and forth before the hearth.

"That damnable Bryan O'Malley ran to the church before yer father could get his hands on him. He's been sleeping in the basement of the rectory. Good thing for you the church folk think him mad, as does much of the city I expect. But they know of the baby—says it's his and he's set to marry ye."

"He's a liar!" Ainsley choked, feeling the desperation closing in. Beneath the layers of her winter dress, the Deamhain Aeir's locket lay cold against her skin. "The baby's not his—I'll never marry that bastard."

"You'll do as yer told." Her mother spun and faced her, her eyes dark and sad. "Ye don't and ye know where they'll send ye. Bryan O'Malley is better than the Bessborough Convent."

"I could stay here. Ye could tell the priest I married in secret in Dublin, and my husband is off at sea or he fell ill and died or anything. I could stay here and have the baby. You could protect me." Ainsley felt the hopelessness of her words.

"Ye stupid girl." Her mother's voice was soft and sad. "Ye don't think I tried? How'd ye think I got this?" She raised her hand to her cheek where the black and blue was turning to yellow and green. "Yer father's done with ye—ye embarrassed him. The old ones whispered that ye outsmarted him after ye ran off. They whispered about that night in the woods with the old goat, and they think they've seen yer face in the trees of the forest. They think a lot of things. The boy who found ye that night yer father brought ye back—little Grady—he swears he saw a great black horse, taller than a tree as he tells it. He says he saw the beast standing behind ye in the dark, swears he saw ye whisper to it. He swears even after his father beat him to pieces for sayin' it."

"Ye think I'm a witch as well?" Ainsley stood, her legs shaking.

"I don't care," her mother said with a rush of venom. "We follow the old ways in the Society. We look to the old gods and the fae of the forest. I don't care if yer a witch or not, but ye have made yer father look foolish and weak, and God help ye for that."

The clatter of Father Gerity's carriage came to a stop outside the cottage door. Ainsley could hear the old priest climbing down and the shuffle of others. Without being told to do so, Ainsley stepped to the entry, gently moving her sister aside, and opened the door as Maire regarded her with tear-filled eyes.

35

AINSLEY, 1924

THE PRIEST WAS ACCOMPANIED BY TWO NUNS IN THEIR black habits. The young man who drove the carriage stayed outside, shuffling nervously next to the horses. Father Gerity nodded a hello at Ainsley's mother and surveyed the room.

"I expect Rory will be along shortly," the priest muttered, his dry lips barely moving.

"Of course, Father," Mum said and pulled a chair out for him to sit. She motioned to the nuns who nodded a hello but remained standing by the door.

"Tea?" Mum asked. "Maire, can you take the kettle from the fire?"

Father Gerity shook his head. "I fear, my dear, we will not have time for such niceties. I thank you though, as do the good sisters."

Ainsley had shrunk back to the hearth, hovering in the doorway to her parents' bedroom. Maire had followed, clinging to her hand.

"Come here, dear." Father Gerity motioned to Ainsley. "We understand there has been quite a bit of trouble of late, and we're here to help with that."

"There's no trouble that needs your help here," Ainsley growled, her voice low and guttural. Her mother spun around and shot her a look full of fire.

"Girl," she said as a way of telling Ainsley to shut her mouth. She turned to the priest. "Yes, you can see the trouble…"

At that Ainsley's father appeared in the doorway, the nuns shuffling to the side as the door blew open and his massive frame blocked the daylight. Outside the horses were snuffling, and Ainsley wished beyond measure that the púca would reappear, charge this place, and tear the priest and his nuns to morsels of bone and flesh.

"Your Grace," Rory Robertson said solemnly. "Thank you for coming. As you can see, the girl has brought disgrace on herself, and now that we have her back from where she was hiding, we need a way to keep her safe from herself and others."

Ainsley felt her body turn to ice. A growing anger was building at the base of her spine, and she reached up to place a single finger where the locket lay hidden beneath many layers of wool. All she had to do was catch the daylight in the mirror. Amon would reappear, if he was telling her a truth. He would reappear and burn this cottage to the ground, and the priest with his watery blue eyes and the marble-faced nuns would be ash. Next to her, Maire squeezed Ainsley's hand as though she could see her dark thoughts, and Ainsley immediately drew her finger away from the hidden locket. She could not, not while the wrath of the Deamhain Aeir might harm her sister, her mother. She suspected that this Amon would not discriminate in his bloody reckoning. She could not, no matter what came of this.

"I will leave this place, as not to further disgrace my family or home. Set me on a ship to England, and you'll never hear from me again." Ainsley spoke the words in a slow meter. Her mother's lips twitched slightly, and she could hear tiny sobs coming from Maire.

"No." Her father's voice was also measured, but she could hear the rage behind the word. The nuns exchanged looks, then stared at Ainsley with blank eyes. "No," her father repeated. "You'll not run off like the whore you are. We offer you a choice—either marry the father of the baby today and we can tell the village the marriage happened months ago or go with the good sisters to the home."

Ainsley sputtered in confusion. "Marry? Finn is here?"

Her father crossed the room in three great strides, the door open and the cold air rushing the space. "No, ye stupid git. Bryan O'Malley claims the child is his, and I'm not to counter him. He cried ye a witch but will shut his mouth with some acreage and a share of the land. I'll sell ye to him, as a penance for yer damnation."

Ainsley violently shook her head. "He's mad! The child isn't his. I'll never marry him."

Her father regarded her for a long moment, his eyes full of dark thunderheads.

"I think I knew ye'd say that." He turned to the priest. "She's ready to leave. Her mother packed her things earlier."

At that, Maire let loose a wail to wake the dead and wrapped herself around Ainsley's extended belly. The little girl's tears were soaking Ainsley's apron. Ainsley felt her body go numb, and she stared at her father as he reached to pull Maire from her side. With one swift motion, Ainsley raised a single hand, and all the anger and despair that had been building in the length of her spine released. Her father flew back against the far wall as though a thousand men had pushed him, even though Ainsley had not placed a finger on his person. He slammed into the wood frame with such force that the cottage shook as though Earth itself had shifted.

The effort leaving her fingers pulled all Ainsley's strength with it, and she collapsed to her knees, Maire clinging to her neck. Her father sat up, his face stunned and fearful. She saw his dark eyes grow entirely black. The rest of the room might have seen Ainsley push him, but he had seen the truth, and so had Maire.

"Damn eegit. Take the girl—now." Her father pulled himself to his feet and stepped out the door, waiting.

The nuns approached Ainsley as her mother pulled Maire away, the little girl still wailing. All the strength that Ainsley had in her body had been expelled in her anger. The nuns easily lifted her and half dragged her out the door to the carriage. Her eyes fluttered closed, and she could feel herself shoved into the back, the nuns taking their positions on either side. A heavy satchel packed by her mother at a time when Ainsley had not noticed was placed before her. Father Gerity took his seat, and the carriage began its descent back down the hill. Ainsley looked back to see her mother and Maire, both standing disconsolately against the cold winter morning sky. Maire's tears were dry now. Her mother wrapped an arm around the girl's shoulders, and the two of them watched the carriage drive away. Her father appeared behind them, a dark and vile force. Even in her weakened state, Ainsley knew she would rise from this hell and bring the fire that Amon promised back upon him.

36

ALAN, 1996

ALAN STARED BLEARILY AT THE ANTISEPTIC WALL OF the examination room. His left eye was already swollen nearly shut, and he could feel loose teeth shifting in his mouth. The nurse had given him a couple of tablets for the pain—aspirin, as though that would touch this. Alan couldn't wait to get home and break into the stash he'd set aside for a USC frat order. They'd have to do without a couple of Percocet. Although in all truth, Alan could scrape the sides of a Tylenol down and mix them in the bag with the rest. Idiots would never know the difference.

It had started off as a routine delivery. Alan had been down across from the Sidewalk Café. It had long since closed for the night, and the only people around were the bums and the occasional night surfer. Alan had been waiting for a guy who'd ordered a tenth of meth, not Alan's usual trade but the markup was killer. Alan preferred to stick to pot and painkillers; the heavy shit was out of his league and not worth the headache. But this was a special deal—for what the guy had said he'd pay, Alan could pay a year's rent outright on the little studio downtown near Pershing Square. It was only a single room and bath, the kitchen a tiny counter with a hot plate and microwave. The bed folded into the wall, and when down it nearly blocked the door, but it was enough. Meg could move out of her parents' house. She could graduate in December like they'd talked about and start full-time classes at the design college downtown. No more bullshit, no more Society.

Meg. She was so much more than anyone in the cul-de-sac gave her credit for. She'd shown Alan her sketch pad; it was full of designs for dresses and suits, all sorts of things. She wanted to design clothes. She wanted to move to New York. She'd never make it if she stayed here. A couple of years at FIDM, a couple of years away from the suffocating madness of their lives on Sinder Avenue, and she'd be out, she'd be free. She had asked Alan to come with her, move into the tiny studio in downtown LA, then, one day, move to New York. He had stayed silent. He could never leave this place, no matter what his sister said, no matter what anyone did. Alan was bound here. He could feel the weight of his mother, the lost and blind gaze of his father. He could feel the tendrils of the Society choking him, and Alan knew that the only way out was in. He'd seen what had happened to his father when he'd tried to leave, seen the way the man had slowly unraveled. His father had started off clean—he'd left the Society a father, a husband, a settled adult. He hadn't even been a drinker in the beginning. Alan was so far gone already that he'd collapse in weeks. He knew the Society was a slow-acting poison; it rotted you from the inside out. His only hope was to try to get Meg out. She'd never been privy to all the weird shit he'd had to see. She'd never listened to the old women and their pleas to the Matrarc. Meg could still escape.

The money from the meth sale was their security, a year's rent, a year where Meg would have no cause to return to Sinder Avenue.

Alan had used his savings to secure the space, security deposit and a few month's rent, but the meth sale would have been the end to their worries. Then he'd only have to work to get Meg food money and keep the lights on, pay for her classes. It was all a wash now though. The money was gone, so was the meth. The guy had come out from the dumpster in the alley behind the café. Alan hadn't seen the plumber's wrench in his left hand until it had hit him across the side of his jaw. After that, Alan had pretty much blacked out; the only memory he retained was of a searing pain and sense of release, the idea that maybe he was dying, and how he'd never again have to see the visions of the dead little boys, their eyes black and gone.

"Mr. Robertson?" a deep voice from behind him said.

Alan turned his head, wincing at the pain in his neck, and saw a uniformed officer. He automatically stifled a muttered *fuck.*

"That's me," he answered wearily.

"Can I ask you some questions?" the officer asked, and Alan nodded. He entered the exam room and stood so Alan could stop turning his stiff neck.

"The nurse said this was a good time. The doc will be in shortly. If you'd rather wait, that's fine," the officer said, his voice impassive.

"Now's as good as any," Alan said resignedly.

"Okay, so we have a rough idea of what happened from the officer on the scene. He said the guy jumped you down on the beach walk. Any idea who this guy was or what he was after?" The officer looked up, studying Alan.

"I told the guy at the scene, no idea. I was walking home. He came out of nowhere," Alan said quietly, hoping his bruises helped to make him sound honest.

"It's a dangerous place at night, as you can see." The officer paused and looked Alan up and down. "Here's the thing, son, the responding officer found a bag of pot on you at the scene, more than allows us to look the other way if you get my meaning. Were you dealing?"

Alan sighed. "No, it was mine. I'm not a dealer."

The officer nodded and jotted something down on the little black pad in his hands. "I see. Thing is, you have a misdemeanor for possession on file already, and you had a pretty healthy stash on you tonight. Were you selling to this guy?"

Alan stared back at the officer with his one good eye. "If I was, don't you think he'd have taken it? What's the point of fucking me up just to leave the goods?"

"True enough, son, true enough. Unless you were selling him something else." The officer stared back at Alan. "You're just a kid—you don't want to get messed up in that crap. We have a whole wall of morgue shots down at the station of guys who started off with pot and started making bigger and bigger deals until someone beat them to death, or shot them, or they overdosed. Consider that."

Alan nodded. "Good talk. What are you going to do about the pot?"

The cop looked annoyed. "I'm writing you a citation for possession, and you will need to appear in court. I suggest you adjust the attitude before you go before the judge."

Alan was about to speak when a voice behind him interrupted.

"Officer, can I help?" Ceit said from the doorway.

"Are you a relative?" the officer asked.

"I'm his sister—he lives with me. Can I ask what you are writing him a citation for?"

The police officer suddenly looked confused, and his mouth moved silently, his eyes growing cloudy. Ceit stepped into the room, moving slowly, her pale eyes lit from within so that they looked almost as if they were glowing.

"I think you can let him off with a warning, and you'll forget this whole thing happened. You'll leave here and go home and sleep well tonight. You'll wake up tomorrow and never remember you were here. You are a good man. You'll continue to do good work."

The officer nodded and looked at Alan as though he'd never seen him before.

"Yes, I have to leave now," the officer said and walked past Ceit out the door.

The fire behind Ceit's eyes dimmed, and she crossed to stand before Alan, staring at him with a wrinkle of thought forming on her forehead.

"Nice trick," Alan said. "Won't the report from the scene still come back to haunt me even if this guy's memory is wiped?"

"You don't give me enough credit, little brother," Ceit said softly. "The only thing anyone will remember from tonight is that an innocent teenager was cruelly beaten by a man whose body will be found in the canals tomorrow night. He overdosed on that shit you were trying to sell him but not before he told his druggie buddies about the kid he beat with a wrench."

"Really nice trick," Alan responded, defeated.

"The doctor is coming in a minute. You're fine. Your eye will be okay in a few days, no bones are broken. You might lose one of those teeth, but I think that rather serves you right." Ceit stared at him without blinking.

"I can take the bus home," Alan said, his entire body beginning to wilt.

"No, I have a car. I'll be out front." With that, Ceit turned and exited the room.

The doctor took her place, an overworked scrap of a man who smelled of cigarettes and long hours. No bones were broken, his eye would be fine, and if he didn't want to lose any teeth, Alan would have to stick to soup and soft foods for a few days. They gave him another couple aspirin and sent him to the front, where Ceit was waiting behind the driver's wheel of the used Buick that served the cul-de-sac when the bus would not do.

"You need to leave, Alan. You're dying here," she said simply before they drove home in silence.

Later, as Alan lay in bed riding a Percocet wave, he rolled her words around in his head. He was dying no matter what, and no relief would come from leaving.

37

CEIT, 1996

FUCKING ALAN.

Ceit sat at her desk in the dark office. The sun would be up soon, but she had no sleep left in her. When she closed her eyes, all she could see was the tiny boy who cowered in the corner of a dark cave underneath a Salt Lake City suburb. She could see his thin face, his matted hair, his eyes, wide and full of terror and complete trust. She had been a lousy substitute for a mother, Ceit knew that. She felt love and she felt pain, but her emotions were becoming muted. The realm of human existence seemed increasingly inane and noisy. The Night Forest called her more and more. Amon had told her this would happen.

The high whine of the g'nights songs moved her soul more than the tears of the old women who came to her to beg for various things. The soft footsteps of the wood elves, their oversized eyes that could be full of either mirth or malice, these things made her mind and body connect. Alan was lost. The little boy who had clung to her hand and insisted on sleeping with her for nearly a year after they had come back to this place was gone. The little boy who had defied their father and written her countless letters, clandestinely dropping them in his elementary school's out-box when she was locked up in MacLaren Hall, that little boy was dead. In his place was a shell of a man who looked increasingly like their father.

Ceit had known about the drugs for some time. Alan might be able to fool Shona and the rest, but Ceit could see his aura, filled with constantly swirling thunderclouds, and she could see his soul. He ached—the depth of the pain he felt was enough to break even Ceit's remote heart. He blamed himself for their mother, their father. He hated her sometimes, he loved her more often, but he feared her always. As much as Alan tried to mask his thoughts, these things were clear. He had a secret he'd been able to hide from Ceit, and for that she was glad. She suspected it had to do with that silly, stupid girl the old women wanted him to marry. Meg. Meg who kept her eyes downcast and called Ceit ma'am. Meg whose very resolve was as thin as a spiderweb in a windstorm. Still, Ceit did not begrudge Alan's secret nor did she pry too much into finding out what it was. Maybe they would marry, maybe they'd move away. Maybe Meg was made of sterner stuff than she appeared to be. Maybe.

Ceit suspected that Alan would find himself in the ER again before too long. She had been able to change his fate this time, but her machinations with the law were dangerous. There was still a task force who watched the Society. Karen McAlister had moved back to the LAPD special services unit and dropped her a note every so often. They took photos of the cul-de-sac, and they watched Ceit. This would not go unnoticed, and it would take very little for the original police report to resurface. If it happened again and again, Ceit could do very little without putting herself and the rest of the Society in harm's way. It was part of the reason she wanted to blow the entire thing to pieces. They would always be watched; they would always be suspect.

Mór Ainsley had told her once that it was a great burden to know too many things. Ceit had been a very little girl, and her great-grandmother had beckoned Ceit to her, staring in her eyes, so like her own.

"It is in the knowing that we are undone, leanbh. I see all I've done, and I see all you will do—carry it so the others do not."

Ceit had been little, and it had been several years before the Sluagh, before her mother's spirit was devoured by the waking dead. She had remembered and not understood. Now she did. She remembered Noni, deep in Canyon de Chelly, telling her she might bring death and ruin, she might not. Noni had not judged; she had known the ways of darkness and had understood—perhaps better than any save Amon—what Ceit was.

Ceit saw her brother, the little boy he was and the man he was becoming. She saw him running from the cave in the darkness, fleeing an evil created by greed and ignorance. She saw him on their first winter solstice after they'd come back to Sinder Avenue. She saw his face warm and his eyes content as they ate before the fire. She saw him walk the stage at his graduation, the polite smattering of applause that accompanied a figure little known to his classmates. She saw his stiff awkwardness. She felt his fear.

Ceit also saw his body, wasted and worn, torn apart by drugs and neglect. She saw the flesh that clung to his bones and the vacant stare as his dead eyes locked on the night sky. He would not be mourned, not even by her—be it so far in the future that her ability to grieve in a human way would be long gone, or be it that his crimes would be too egregious to warrant tears. Ceit did not understand the vision, but she knew it to be true. Ceit saw the truth, and the knowing would be her undoing.

38

AINSLEY, 1924

"THE MAIN HOUSE WAS GIFTED TO THE SISTERS OF the Sacred Heart some time ago by a very honorable Catholic family. The mother and baby home has been saving souls for two years now, and it is a jewel in our fight against moral corruption. You will be most comfortable there, dear, and the child will have the opportunity to become part of a strong Catholic family. You will find redemption for your sins with us through hard work, prayer, and reflection."

The nun to her right spoke in a low voice into Ainsley's ear. The speech felt as though it had been delivered so many times it could be a recording. The carriage entered the high gray walls through a formidable wrought iron gate that was locked behind them by a man who looked more undertaker than guardian. The road ahead was winding. Ainsley's entire body felt as though it were wrapped in a blanket weighted with hot bricks. She was starting to get a bit of her strength back, but not nearly enough to fight her way out of this place, not yet. The Bessborough Mother and Baby Home,

courtesy of the Sisters of the Sacred Heart, had become a caution-
ary tale even in the two short years it had been opened. The old
work homes, where the unwed and unloved had once been sent,
were the places of nightmares; the mother and baby homes
were supposed to bring relief. Ainsley knew different—all young
women knew different.

It was a place for the good Catholic girls who found themselves
in trouble. Ainsley had never dreamed it would touch her life. The
Society did not carry the same set of values the rest of Ireland
seemed fixated on. Their marriages were not made under the capital L Lord. They were not married in a church or cathedral. In fact,
all the babies born to the Society were bastards in the eyes of the
church. Her father had satiated old Father Gerity enough over the
many years he'd been making his visits for the old fool to believe
that the moral code, the marriages, the births, the baptisms, and
the prayers of the Society were acceptable if not equal to the laws
of the church. Her father had joked about the old priest, what a
damnable fool he was, how easily persuaded. He had no idea that
the Society worshipped the old ways and dedicated their babies to
the fae and forest creatures.

It wasn't for the crime of being an unwed, ungodly woman that
Ainsley was trapped on this carriage traveling up a winding road to
a prison disguised as a manor house; it was for the crime of showing her father that she was more powerful than he. He must have
seen her face in the woods that night with the goat, perhaps he
had, indeed, seen the creature in the barn, he had known the fae in
the old woods were speaking to her. He had been thrown against
a wall with the power of her anger alone. She had embarrassed
him. She had frightened him. Her father was no longer the most
powerful Ceannaire of the Society. His reign would end, and with
it, Ainsley would take his place. Never again would the women of

the Society be run by fear. Never again would they endure abuse and bow to the men of their house. If her father knew the half of it, if he knew of the pendant she wore about her neck—and how easy it would be for her to summon the Deamhain Aeir, to command the púca to tear his flesh from his bones—if he knew, he would not have committed this grievous error.

Of course, the dark thoughts that ran the length of Ainsley's mind were contingent on her freedom. If her father managed to lock her in this place, if these damnable creatures in their black dresses stole her child and broke her will, her father would defeat her after all. Her strength was still mostly tapped, and the attack on her father had sucked her soul dry. Ainsley had not known that would happen; she had not known she was even capable of such a thing.

When she had her muscle and fortitude back, she could run from this place—but to where? The mother and baby home was deep in the woods outside of Cork. Ainsley wondered how far the terrible shack that Bryan had hid her in was from here. The woods were vast. It was the same problem she'd faced in the tiny shed just days ago. Where to run? Would she perish in the forest of cold and hunger before she found safety?

The carriage turned a corner, and the main house rose before her. Three stories, dark and foreboding. Side houses stretched in either direction, and Ainsley could see that beyond the steeples and attic windows there were more structures that stretched behind. A great domed entryway, the doors dark-stained wood with black iron overlay. She felt as though she were arriving at her own tomb. A long black automobile, the sort that Ainsley had seen only in magazines, was parked out front. The horses slowed to a stop before the great doors, and Father Gerity turned stiffly to regard Ainsley.

"I leave you here in the hands of the Sisters of the Sacred Heart. I continue onto the rectory. You will find redemption here, my child. I will continue to counsel your family through this difficult time." He nodded at the nuns, who began to pull Ainsley from the carriage.

"You'll die in flames," Ainsley spat at the old man. The nun who had spoken in her ear as they arrived slapped her across the face so suddenly and sharply that Ainsley saw only blackness for several moments.

"You'll shut your vile mouth." The nun's voice was controlled and terrifying in its measure.

"Do not worry, Sisters," said the priest. "The girl has been subject to the darkness of this world for too long. Her father and family walk the very edge of sin, and she has not been raised to know better. It is our job to save what is left of her soul." The old priest crossed himself and nodded at the carriage driver, who pulled away, leaving Ainsley standing between the two nuns.

"Come," the other nun said. "We will get your intake settled and get you to work immediately."

Ainsley felt a wave of despair wash over her, and her strength once again drained from her limbs. The nuns pulled her up the steps and into the great entry hall. As the doors slammed shut behind her, Ainsley knew she would need to summon more than her courage in order to break from this place.

"Amon... help me," she murmured before the world went black and her unconscious head hit the polished wood floor.

39

AINSLEY, 1924

WHEN SHE WOKE, AINSLEY WAS WEARING A ROUGH linen shift dress with a cloth belt. She looked around, startled and confused. She was on a bed. The walls around her were white institutional tile, and the room was bare save the low cot she lay on. Up high on the wall, a small window let the winter sun flood the room. Ainsley sat up, her belly and head aching in unison. She reached instinctively for the locket with the small mirror inside and found it missing, her neck bare. Her skin grew cold and her mouth dry. The nuns must have taken it. Now she was trapped here without the help of the Deamhain Aeir or any of the fae.

"Hello?" Ainsley called with a shaking voice. "Hello?"

Almost immediately, a door opened and a nun wearing a white habit in the style of a nurse stepped in.

"Yer awake, I see," she said. "We've been waiting on ye to finish yer intake. Please put yer shoes and stockings on and join me in the next room." The woman's voice was rushed and impatient. She glared at Ainsley once again and turned on her heels.

"I had a locket. It's gone, I need it back!" Ainsley cried after her.

"Yer things are with us now. Ye enter this place to rid yerself of yer earthly attachments—the Mother Superior will explain it all to ye." With that, the nun left, slamming the door behind her.

Ainsley felt her hands shaking as she pulled on the dark stockings that had been left next to her on the cot. On the floor were the well-worn leather boots she'd arrived in—the only thing she'd been allowed to keep. The baby kicked and spun in her belly. Ainsley stopped, doubling over until the spasm of pain stopped. The door opened, and a sour-faced nun dressed in the traditional black habit regarded her.

"We haven't got all day, girl. Come along," she said curtly.

Ainsley straightened up and crossed through the door into what looked to be an office. The walls were dark and adorned with paintings of various popes. A large silver crucifix hung behind the wooden desk, framing the nun's head so that it looked as though she had knives jutting from either ear. Ainsley would have giggled had she not been so terrified.

"Sit." The nun nodded at a wooden chair across from the desk.

"Are you the Mother Superior?" Ainsley asked.

"You are not to speak unless I ask a question of you. As you have just arrived and evidently are sickly, I forgive your transgression. Remember it though, girl, or you will be corrected." The nun paused, and Ainsley could feel her entire body trembling. "I am not the Mother Superior. I am Sister Mary Claude, her assistant and the one who takes care of the intake. You are a first-time offender in our home. Your father has signed the paperwork for you to stay with us until your baby is born and we find it a proper Catholic home. You will not lay about here—you will work for the good of yourself and others. We will feed you, clothe you, and care for your medical needs as they arise, but you will not be coddled here, girl.

You have descended into sin, and it is only through penance that you will rise." She paused, monitoring Ainsley's expression. "Do you understand, girl? You may answer."

Ainsley felt a panic much deeper than the loss of the locket rising in her gut, the sick vomitus sting already staining her throat.

"I'm not adopting out my child!" Ainsley's voice was high and hysterical, a counter to the cool, methodical speech of the nun. "My child will go home with me. I'm not—"

"You're not in a position to negotiate. You have been signed into our care, and you will remain here until your child is united with a home that can raise it in a godly environment."

"You can't force me to sign away my child!" Ainsley cried.

"Silence now. If you cannot calm yourself, we will need to lash you. God sees all, and it is, at times, through the spilling of your sinful blood that you are made to listen." She pulled a small stack of papers from the desk drawer and regarded them through her narrow, birdlike eyes. "Your given name is Ainsley Robertson. Our midwife has determined you are in or very near your seventh month. You have eight or nine weeks, give or take, until your child is born. Your new name, while you are with us, is Therese Catherine. That is how you will introduce yourself to the others and how you will be addressed. Your possessions—the bag you brought with you and the clothes and jewelry you were wearing— have been taken for the use of the home. You must abandon your old life if you are to begin anew, my child."

"Damn you all," Ainsley muttered, the anger building in her spine again.

Sister Mary Claude stood, a motion so seamless that Ainsley scarcely saw the movement. In her hand was a long willow switch. With a single movement, the lash landed across Ainsley's cheek, the stinging pain so intense her entire body hummed in sympathy.

Ainsley could feel a line of sticky warmth sinking down her skin.

"Why?" Ainsley murmured as she reached a hand to her cheek and drew away bloodied fingers.

"You'll be taught to respect the Sisters at this home." Sister Mary Claude reached for a small black bell and gave it a single ring. Another Sister in a white medical habit appeared at the door. "A bandage for Therese please, Sister." The woman nodded and disappeared again. Mary Claude sat, settling herself as though nothing at all had occurred. "Sister Dolores will take you to your dormitory and show you where you will work. We eat at six in the morning. You will work until suppertime at four thirty. You will pray, bathe, sleep. You are not here to make friends of the other unfortunate souls. You will not disrespect any person on these grounds, or you will be shown what true discipline is. You will see the midwife and nurses every week. You will eat your meals. Do you understand?"

Ainsley nodded, her cheek stinging with the burning pain of the lash. The baby kicked again, and she instinctively placed a hand protectively across her stomach. The white-dressed nun reappeared and ushered Ainsley back into the examination room, where a line of cloth was set to the lash mark. As yet another nun led her down a dark hallway to the dormitory, Ainsley felt as though her feet were made of lead. She would have to summon her strength and find Amon's locket before she could free herself and the child. She would need to cooperate and not draw attention. She would need to survive.

40

CEIT, 1996

ACROSS THE DESK FROM CEIT STOOD CONOR, HIS face seething and his temper barely contained. Ceit was amused; he knew better than to speak harshly to her. He had meant to come here to plead his case, but the pathetic creature had barely been able to force out a single word.

"Matrarc," he sputtered. "I...I..."

"Silence, Conor." Ceit waved her hand, and the man cast his eyes to the wood floor. He had no shield for his thoughts, and they echoed around the room as though it were a concert hall.

"I know why you are here, and I know why you are upset. You have every right to be so, but you must trust my decision. I am your Matrarc, and this is my doing. It is for the best." Ceit spoke levelly as the hate and fear in Conor's head reached a deafening pitch.

"All due respect, my Matrarc, but to ask my wife and I to move into yet another back house when it is our due to be in my mother's house? Why could we not at least stay where we are?" His voice trembled, and a hint of despair polluted the vocal thoughts that swirled in his head.

"Bedelia's house is set for another course, as is the property the back house is on. You and your wife will move as soon as you can to Ellaine's cottage. She knows you are coming. It is clean, and I believe a bit larger than where you have been living. Ellaine is elderly and needs the help of a healthy pair of hands." Ceit leaned forward. "You will take better care of Ellaine than you did your mother."

Conor snapped his head up and looked Ceit in the eyes. His expression was of shock but also fear. "I don't... I cared for my mother all her days." He choked out the words.

"Stop," Ceit commanded, and the man before her fell silent. "Stop. You left her to rot. You and your wife thought to move into the big house, you thought to hasten her dying. Do you forget, Conor, son of Bedelia of the Old Country, that I can read your thoughts as easily as if you spoke them?"

All color drained from Conor's face. He nodded. "My Matrarc, it is, it is just... Ellaine has her own granddaughter. Will she not live in the cottage?"

Ceit sat back, amusedly regarding the man who shook and trembled before her. To pretend that his outrage, his anger, was all for the sake of justice—it was almost too much to not laugh aloud.

"Ellaine's granddaughter moved to Chicago. She has no desire to return to his place. We wish her well on her journey." Ceit stared Conor down until his gaze once again dropped to the floor. "You may go now. Ellaine is expecting you. I suggest you begin to pack now. I will send Alan and some of the others to help you move your things. Go."

Conor shuffled out, escorted by Alan. Ceit nodded to Alan to close the door behind him, and she was left in blissful silence. She hoped this would be the end of Conor's fussing. He had been raising hell since Bedelia's passing about not being allowed to move into the house. This was the first step in the proper direction as far as Ceit was concerned. The old house and back property would be leveled, the lot left bare. Ceit had signed an agreement to sell all the houses on Sinder Avenue. She would not forcibly evict anyone from the cul-de-sac, but as the elders died off, as the younger ones decided a new fate, the houses would be slowly abandoned over the next few years. Soon enough the entire cul-de-sac would be turned into what Alkhem Developments promised would be an immersive Southern California development. Apartments and lofts on the upper floors, shops, groceries, restaurants, and bars lining the street. Rooftop gardens, fitness centers, and green space. Eco-friendly and environmentally pleasing. The mock-ups they had shown her in the property lawyer's office were a virtual paradise for the young and wealthy. This was prime real estate within walking distance to the water, close to the Venice Boardwalk, and primed to become one of the most exclusive areas in West Los Angeles; Alkhem Development would be patient.

Ceit poured herself a cup of tea from the teapot on her desk. She appreciated the aesthetic of a solidly matching tea set. This one was white porcelain with a Polish blue inlay, a winding pattern that looked like a thousand suns rising and setting. The teacup and saucer matched, as did the little cream pitcher and sugar bowl. There would be things she missed from this side of the veil when her time came to leave it entirely. The Night Forest was its own sort of beauty, but it lacked the creature comforts of a solid cup of black tea from fine porcelain.

Ellaine's light-haired granddaughter had come to Ceit in fear last December, not too long before Alan was set to graduate from high school. She had already finished school and had been working in Venice and living in the back cottage, taking care of her grandmother. Ellaine had raised the girl; her daughter had died in childbirth, and the father had run off shortly after.

The girl had quietly and fearfully asked Ceit if she might take an offer to study at the University of Chicago. "I do not wish to return," she whispered, obviously fearing the worst. Ceit instead smiled and congratulated the girl. Since then, she had kept the news quiet. Ellaine saw it as a sign of disgrace, and the rest of the old ones would have agreed. Ceit saw it as progress—a young woman leaving this place, going out into the world, never to return.

Perhaps Meg might go that route, Ceit thought absently as she watched out the window at Conor shuffling back and forth in front of Bedelia's small house. Quiet, simple Meg, who should never marry her little brother. Meg, who had never looked Ceit in the eyes and never would. Meg, whose head was filled with thoughts of dresses and colors. Ceit did not dislike the girl, but she feared her brother fancied her enough to bind himself to this place for all time. If Meg left, Ceit could move her parents into another of the vacant back houses since they would no longer need so much room. Another house could be sold, another step to dismantling the Society. They might be so indignant about the idea that they would leave entirely. That would be nice. They were of the younger set in the Society. Most of the children who would have been near or around Alan's age had left the cul-de-sac for good— some on the guise of attending college, some to marry outside the Society and move away. Some had just left a note and hopped on a train or a bus or a plane to brighter places. There was a day, back in Mór Ainsley's reign, when they would have been forbidden to leave. They would have been pursued and brought back to Sinder Avenue. Her mother's cousin Aoife had been one of these runaways. Grace Robertson had helped Aoife escape, all under the cover of utmost secrecy. This was not the Society that Ceit sat as Matrarc. The young people were free to leave, encouraged to do so.

Ceit would follow them soon enough. As soon as she could free her brother from this place, as soon as the old ones left her empty houses that could be razed to the ground, she would begin her true work.

ALAN, 1996

THE LITTLE BOY IN THE TATTERED SKY-BLUE PAJAMAS stared at Alan with his great dead eyes. The others appeared behind him, their necks raw and red, their eyes blank and unseeing. They were more vacuous than the little one in front of him. The others were little more than wisps of smoke; they seemed to fade every time they appeared now. Only the little boy in the sky-blue pajamas remained solid.

Alan had woken from his sleep to find the visions filling his room. Outside, the moon was new, the sky pitch-dark. Alan sunk to his knees on the wood floor and looked up at the boy.

"What is it you want?" he pleaded. The boy sometimes formed words. Each visit he seemed more coherent. "Tell me why you are here."

"Takkke yooouuurrr seaaattttt." The words that slipped from the little boy's mouth were wrought with effort, elongated, more hiss than language. Alan felt his skin grow cold.

"What are you saying? What do you mean?" he whispered.

"Ceannaire… Ceannaire," the little boy croaked and began to fade as the crowd behind him disappeared entirely.

"No, wait, I—what do you mean? Ceannaire? I am not the leader here. Ceit, she is our Matrarc." Alan crawled forward as the little boy began to step back, growing more like a dream with each movement.

The figure simply shook his head and pointed one misty finger at Alan before disappearing entirely. Alan fell back to lie on the floor. He stared at the ceiling and tried to slow his breath. The visions came not every night but many. They were terrifying but not for the reasons most would hold. Alan wondered what they meant. Ceannaire was what Grandmother Shona told him his great-great-grandfather was back in Cork, before Mór Ainsley brought the Society to America and became the Matrarc. Ceit had never told him this; he wondered if she knew. She knew everything, so she must have known this history. Grandmother Shona whispered to him whenever she had his ear away from Ceit. She told him stories she had been told by those older than her, those who had long since passed. She talked of a time when a man had run the Society.

"Yer great-grandmother—Mór Ainsley, my mother—was the first Matrarc. She sought to erase the history of the Society. She took it by blood, killed innocents for her title. You can take it back. Yer sister is not the only one who can lift the veil. You see the visions true enough, don't you boy?" she slurred furtively one night as Alan pulled her across the lawn to her house. She drank too much most evenings now and often found herself half asleep on someone's sofa. That time it was old lady Ellaine, whose back house was soon to be occupied by Conor and his unhappy wife. Ellaine was angry. Ceit had driven her daughter away and was now selling off their houses. Ellaine knew what would come of her home when she passed, which was likely to be soon judging by the cough that permanently rattled her chest.

Alan had sighed. His eye was still a swarm of bruises and there was a gap in his mouth from where he had, indeed, lost one of the loose teeth. Ceit had not brought up the incident again, but he knew she watched him. He had sold off the last of his pot and was laying low for the moment. His dealer was getting itchy; Alan was a major client, and if he stopped selling, then it would ripple all the way back up. Alan knew he was risking another wrench to the face before too long. Grandmother Shona had set hot tea bags to his eye and cooed over him until he thought he might vomit. Despite his grandmother's increasing dependence on her wine and cheap booze, she confided in him. She couldn't talk to Ceit; no one could. Alan did not know what to do with her information. He couldn't lift the veil. Even Ceit could not do so until Mór Ainsley was dead. There was one Matrarc, and the days of the Ceannaire were long past.

Still, Alan mused as he lay on his back staring at the dark ceiling. It would be nice to be respected as something other than the Dara to the Matrarc, a glorified messenger boy. He could be a powerful figure here. He would not sell off their homes; he'd let the old ones live in peace. Maybe he could be the Ceannaire. Maybe if he were the only one left, he could lift the veil. Without moving to the bed, Alan closed his eyes and let sleep overcome him. He dreamed of what he imagined Cork must look like, rolling hills of green, cottages dotting a hill, a great river in the distance. He dreamed of a world where his mind was quiet, where the nightmares that haunted him in sleep and waking hours were still. He dreamed of a childhood that had not been torn with anger and fear. He dreamed of a world without Ceit.

42

AINSLEY, 1924

AINSLEY HAD BEEN SET TO SCRUBBING THE TILES IN the washrooms in the morning hours and scrubbing the stains from sheets and blankets in the laundry in the afternoon. Occasionally, she was pulled away to tend to the nursery, a cold and damp room full of bleary-eyed infants. In the next room, toddlers up to age four were held, and the older children were in dormitories at the end of the back house. There weren't many older children; they were orphans already by the time the Sacred Sisters had swooped them up into Bessborough. They attended the local school, filing out every morning in a line to walk against the bitter Irish wind to the diocese school. They returned by supper. Ainsley could see them approach through the narrow slits of windows in the nursery. *What lives they lead,* she thought. What lives any of them led in this place.

Her hands were raw from the borax powder used to scrub the tiled floors and redder still from the lye used to wash the linens. It was a relief when she was called to the depressing depths of the nursery to change nappies and bottle-feed the infants. The mothers were allowed to breastfeed, but many hadn't the milk. The babies didn't cry as they should. Ainsley thought this every time she entered the room. They did wail, but not for long, and all the tiny faces seemed to understand that it was a futile gesture in this forgotten place. The toddlers were shuffled through the hall by stern-faced nuns. They were taught prayer, and they were given tasks. Some were even set in the nursery as companions for the infants. Ainsley couldn't bear to look at the toddlers' pale faces as they slowly rocked the babies in their prams.

Ainsley had three roommates, four narrow cots forced into a tiny cell-like room. Alma was only sixteen and newly pregnant, her belly just beginning to show. She cried most every night. Ainsley sat with her sometimes and held her hand.

"I could have kept it hidden for a time longer, I could've," Alma muttered senselessly into her pillow. Ainsley knew it was true. The girl was sturdily built, and the weight would not have been noticeable for some time. Her aunt had told the nuns and signed the paperwork to admit the girl—an aunt she thought she could trust.

Mary Kathleen was just a year or so older than Ainsley, but she had been at Bessborough for nearly four years, having been sent there before it had officially become a mother and baby home. When her son was born, less than a month after she'd arrived, she named him William. "When they adopt him out and I'm free, William will be easier to track," Mary Kathleen had reasoned. Her scheme had been thwarted though; the nuns had listed him as John on his birth certificate. That would be the boy's name to his adoptive parents, and the chances of his mother ever finding him would be slim.

When John wasn't being shuffled off to prayers or into the yard to get what sustenance could be gathered from the Irish winter sky, Mary Kathleen was allowed to spend most of the day with him. He was not a handsome child; his ears were a good size too big for his face, and he had a strawberry mark streaking one side of his neck. Mary Kathleen kissed his forehead and whispered, "It's his good luck sign. No one'll want him, and when he's a bit bigger, we can run from this place together."

The last girl crammed in the small room was a tiny wisp of a thing named Margaret. She, too, had already had her baby some months ago. The infant lay in the nursery, and Margaret tried in vain to breastfeed the little girl. The baby was as tiny as a child's rag doll, her eyes dull and tired. The nuns clucked their tongues as they passed the pram or when they saw Margaret sitting in the rocker with the infant in the feeding room. They shook their heads and treated Margaret with a measure of care not given to most. The priest had given the baby a blessing of sorts hours after her birth. Ainsley didn't understand the terminology the Catholic girls used, but she surmised it was a sort of thing similar to the last rites. But the baby had held on, and even though she weighed precious more than she did at the start, the little baby clung to some piece of this world. Margaret did not speak much, only to whisper prayers while curled into a ball on her bed at night. Siobhan Elizabeth was listed on the birth certificate, a name grander than the tiny creature could ever hope to be. The nuns hadn't even fussed over it, even though it was distinctive enough that it could be traced if ever that were to come to pass. No, they knew that Siobhan Elizabeth was unlikely to ever leave this place.

The subject of names was big among the girls; they talked about them as they worked when the nuns were out of hearing and whispered potential names to each other during breakfast and supper. Even Alma mused about what she might call her baby—Ellen for a girl, Alby for a boy. Though Ainsley had been here just a short while, she knew they were unlikely to let Alma keep either.

Like Ainsley's, the other girls' names had all been reassigned upon entering Bessborough. The idea was that they were allowed to be here in secret and reenter the world entirely anonymously after their penance had been served. As such, Ainsley had no idea what her roommates' real names were, and they knew her only as Therese. She'd seen a girl lashed across her bare back on her first day in the laundry for speaking her true name, and it had scared her enough to shut her mind to it.

Punishment came swift and harsh in Bessborough. A woman a bit older than the rest, her belly larger around than Ainsley's, had been made to stand facing the wall in the hall for the entire work-day. Ainsley had no idea of her crime, and no one dared speak to her. She stood until she visibly trembled and a thin trickle of urine ran down her leg. Her face was pale, and Ainsley could see her eyes were closed and she was murmuring what could have been prayers and what should have been curses. The next day she was gone, and Alma, who was assigned to clean the infirmary, said the woman had passed out after twelve hours of the torture. Her waters had broken, and the baby delivered early. "What came of it?" Ainsley whispered. Alma just shook her head. Ainsley never saw the woman again. She was presumably freed from this place, or perhaps she'd died as well. No one spoke of such things; no one wanted to know what fate might await them.

"The baby would've likely died anyhow," Mary Kathleen whispered one afternoon as they folded rough bath towels in the laundry. William/John sat cross-legged on the wooden table, pushing an empty matchbook back and forth and making soft automobile noises. Ainsley regarded the child. He had never known a different life. When not shuttled off with the other toddlers, the nuns allowed him to stay with Mary Kathleen as she worked. It would show him the value of labor the nuns had said, which was a load of bollocks in Ainsley's opinion, but if it meant he was allowed to be near his mother, they would all agree.

"How does he know what an automobile is?" Ainsley asked curiously.

Mary Kathleen giggled. "He saw the one they keep out front when they took the children out for their constitutional. Thought it was going to launch straight up into outer space, he did. I had to explain they only rolled along the roads, same as horses. Now he wants one of his own."

Ainsley smiled at the little boy, and he looked up and smiled back.

"Why do you say the baby would've died anyhow?" Ainsley asked quietly, trying to shield her words from William/John.

Mary Kathleen glanced at the child and then, content he was distracted, leaned in.

"There's dysentery run rampant in the infirmary. Heard the Sisters talking of it. Don't let that one out till it passes, tell you what." She nodded to Ainsley's belly.

A nun passed by and cast them a sharp look. Ainsley knew her to be kinder than some, but she'd barely think to lash their hands if she thought they were being idle and gossiping. As she turned the corner and disappeared from sight, Ainsley whispered back, "Does Margaret know? When I was in the nursery last night, Siobhan wasn't there. I figured she was in the feeding room, but..." Ainsley's voice trailed off, her mind growing dark.

Mary Kathleen shrugged. "Can't say. Alls I know is that little one wasn't expected to make it even this far."

"Where do they go?" Ainsley asked and saw Mary Kathleen visibly stiffen. "Where are they buried?"

"It's not something to put too much thought into. Unbaptized bastards and fallen women, where do you think they'd put us?"

Mary Kathleen gave Ainsley a pointed stare and then reached over to wipe William/John's nose with her sleeve.

As Ainsley carried the freshly folded stack of linens down the hall, she shuddered. She knew where the baby whose mother had been made to stand for twelve hours till she collapsed was buried. She knew the Catholics and their beliefs about hallowed ground. The babies and mothers alike would be in shallow graves in a potter's field, no markers or stone angels to guide their loved ones to the site. They would be forgotten and lost until a farmer plowed the field in fifty years and found a cache of tiny skulls. The Society was many things, but Ainsley felt a bit of pride that they did not cling to the archaic notion that children could be "illegitimate." The fae and old gods saw no sanctity in the priest's holy water and meaningless words of baptism.

She could feel the baby inside getting ready. It had spun around entire, so now its feet were wedged painfully under her ribs. Every kick was a torture, and even the bland, boiled food set her throat to burn as it threatened to make a reappearance. *Not yet, little one,* Ainsley thought silently as she stacked the linens in the storage closet. *Not yet.* She had to leave this place, figure out how to find a moment's quiet when she might call the creatures from the wood that the Deamhain Aeir had sworn were loyal to her. She had to find the locket that held the small mirror powerful enough to bring down hellfire on this cursed place. The sprite that hammered at her insides would need to find a peace until then. "Soon, little one, soon," Ainsley whispered.

43

ALAN, 1996

"LABHAIR LINN, SPIRITS OF THE OLD WORLD AND THE new." Máthair Shona spoke the words with a shaking voice, her face pale and her gray hair sticking out at unlikely angles. Alan shifted uncomfortably, his legs already growing numb from sitting on the hard ground. Four others—Ellaine, her equally ancient sister Katherine, Conor, and his dour-faced wife—completed the circle. His grandmother had whispered in his ear earlier that day that he was to come to Ellaine's house at nightfall... and not to let Ceit know.

"You do realize she knows everything even without our telling her, don't you?" Alan had replied dryly. He was tired of the old woman's ramblings. He understood Ceit's frustrations more than she could appreciate. His grandmother had become increasingly unhinged in the past few months. He wondered if she'd ever see a doctor, if it was dementia coming on, or maybe her blood sugar was off and causing her to act paranoid, deceptive. But Máthair Shona just smiled at Alan's words and nodded.

"Not everything, love. Trust me," she replied.

So Alan had swallowed his last remaining Percocet and walked across the way to Ellaine's house, where the audience had been waiting for him in her living room, which stank of sauerkraut and scented candles. Alan suppressed his disgust and obliged them when he was asked to sit on the floor in a circle. It didn't make any sense, but Alan had learned long ago that it was sometimes best just to play along with their craziness and then report it back to Ceit, rather than confront them on the spot.

"We know of the visions you have been seeing," Máthair Shona said bluntly now.

"But... I haven't told anyone, not even the Matrarc," Alan replied. It was true. He hadn't even told Meg, and he felt like he told her most everything now.

"We know," Ellaine had echoed, her sister nodding in agreement.

"You have been shown the visions of those who have passed, those who have left this plane. You have the sight in you, same as the Matrarc." Máthair Shona spoke as evenly as her quaking voice allowed.

"Look, what is this all about?" Alan asked impatiently. "I don't know how you know about the dreams I've had lately, but I'm not all that shocked. Can we cut the theatrics, and sit in some damn chairs?"

His grandmother exchanged looks with the others, and they all slowly nodded. Alan rose first, painfully stretching his legs. He switched on the overhead lamp and sat on the stiff sofa.

"Out with it," Alan demanded, his patience waning. He knew he had about twenty more minutes of buzz off the Percocet, and after that he would have to deal with this lot in real time, which seemed unbearable.

Ellaine shuffled off to the kitchen, and Alan could see her filling a teapot. He looked to her sister. "Katherine, will you tell me what's going on?"

The old woman sat next to him. "Your sister—"

"The Matrarc," Alan interrupted.

"Yes, the Matrarc, she has asked me to move into this house with Ellaine. She's told me to leave my house and move in here." Katherine looked to Alan with exaggerated tragedy, her lips trembling.

"I know this. I escorted you over to talk to the Matrarc—do you remember? I am the Dara. I know the business of the Society," Alan said impatiently.

"Of course, but she cannot—why do I have to leave my house?" Katherine's voice was teary.

"It is the decision of the Matrarc, not mine. However, I don't disagree with it. You are elderly, as is your sister. Your husband is long dead, and you have no children. You have lived alone for years. You and Ellaine should live together, and you have this lot to help you." He nodded to Conor and his wife, who looked like she wanted a hole to open up in the floor and swallow her.

"She means to take all our houses from us!" Conor stated boldly. "She cheated me out of my mother's house—that was our right."

"I'll not stay for this discussion. If you summoned me to complain about our leader, our Matrarc, who is the rightful head of the Society, you need to grow some balls and talk to her yourselves." Alan stood as Ellaine reentered the room with tea service on a brass tray.

"Wait, please," Ellaine said and nodded to the tea. "Hear us out, have some tea."

Alan shook his head. "Fine. No more griping about your Matrarc. Tell me how you know about my dreams."

His grandmother cast him a small smile. "All right, dear boy. All right. No more talk of Ceit. But they are so much more than dreams."

For the next hour, Alan drank Ellaine's tea and listened to stories about Rory Robertson. Shona had only secondhand tales, having been just an infant when he'd been alive. Ellaine, however, had been twelve years old when she'd left for America with Mór Ainsley. She had been friends with Alan's great-aunt, Maire.

"You look like him, you do," Ellaine said with a smile. "He had a grand, booming voice."

"He beat his wife and daughters," Alan said firmly. He knew these stories. Even though he had been young when he'd first heard them, he remembered his own mother talking of her great-grand-father and the stories she'd heard of his temper.

"Aye, he was imperfect. But he was a leader through and through. No one was ever removed from their cottage in the old country, no one was forced out," Ellaine insisted.

"So what is this for?" Alan sighed, tired. He wanted nothing more than to go home and sleep off the drags that the Percocet had left him with. "None of you are being forced into the street. When my sister took over the responsibilities of the Matrarc, she saw what state the Society was in. I loved Mór Ainsley as much as anyone. I don't remember her well, but I remember she was always kind to me. And I know—I know for a fact—that when my sister had to step in and take over the business of the Matrarc, you were all nearly out on the streets anyhow." He pointed at Shona, who looked flustered. "In the years before we came back to this place, you nearly drove the money into the ground. We are barely making the taxes and utilities as is. My sister, our Matrarc, has worked her ass off keeping these houses you all claim as your own. She's moving you in closer because we cannot afford to keep things the way they have been. We cannot. So you can live with your sister, and you two"—Alan turned his glare to Conor and his wife—"you two can stop your bitching."

The room was silent and stunned. Alan stood to leave.

"I don't know what you know about my dreams. You've told me some romantic stories about what a wonderful man my great-great-grandfather was, and you've complained about your Matrarc. I'd watch it if I were you. I don't know why you think me disloyal enough to listen to your prattle, but do not make the same error again." He started for the door. "Grandmother, I trust Conor can see you home."

Instead of going straight back, Alan walked to the end of Sinder Avenue and toward the beach. He needed to clear his head, to hear nothing but the ocean. The old ones were up to something, that was obvious, and a nagging voice in his head told him exactly what. It was treason, and he had no idea what Ceit would do if she knew. He laughed out loud—she already did know, more than likely. In truth, Alan did not know Ceit's true intention for selling off the homes in the cul-de-sac. The money was an issue, it was true. But he suspected there was far more to it than just that.

As he reached the water and crossed the sand, Alan kicked off his sneakers and let the icy ocean water wash over his bare feet, soaking the cuffs of his jeans. Did Ceit know his own treasonous thoughts? There were times, such as tonight, when faced with opportunistic idiots like Ellaine and Conor, that he would defend Ceit to the end. But other times, in the quiet such as now, when only the waves breaking on the shore and the occasional screech of a night bird filled the air, that he remembered his father's blank eyes, remembered the last time he'd seen his mother. Really seen her—not the shell that was left after her illness or possession or whatever the hell happened to her. He had been seven years old, and she had been so pale, but she'd given him a small smile and mouthed that it was okay as his father had closed the door to the bedroom. He also remembered the cold stone blackness of the cave, the taste of the rag that had been shoved in his mouth after he'd been snatched off the street. He remembered being tied with rope and lying hidden under a pile of blankets in the trunk of a car as they drove and drove and drove. Alan remembered the monster made of fire that screamed its way down the twisting corners of that cave as he ran for the dim moonlight. He remembered that he'd peed himself and how he was embarrassed to tell—how that was the worst thing in his head as the police gently questioned him and the doctors shone lights in his eyes and asked him if he was hurt. All these horrors had occurred over only three years—he had lost his mother, seen his father disintegrate before him, lost his home, his core, the ability to feel safe ever again—but it was the stain down the crotch of his pants that was the biggest grief.

Alan remembered these things, and he knew the cause of it all. He knew that Ceit was the root of all his sufferings, his nightmares then and now. He knew that he would never stop hearing the screams in his ears as long as she walked the earth.

CEIT, 1996

CEIT SAT ALONE BY THE DARKLY GURGLING BROOK that ran through the Night Forest. It was not safe for anyone but her and Amon. The creatures with the sharpest teeth and blackest intent tended to live in the shadows that surrounded the icy water that sprung from the bowels of humanity itself. Amon had told her it smelled of sulfur to him, but to Ceit it carried the scent of rich earth and soil just planted. She found it calming here, and no one—not the g'nights or the curious wood elves—would bother her here. Even the Asrai, the mercreatures who lived in the inlet fed from this brook, would not dare venture this far into the forest.

She had seen the source of the false visions of the little boys. Ceit knew it was her grandmother and the other elders who were summoning them. It took all their strength, and she had seen the effects already wearing Máthair Shona thin. The old woman was acting erratically. Alan said she was drinking most every night. Ceit wasn't surprised. Neither Shona nor the other elders possessed any natural magick. Whatever skills they were using to conjure the visions were hard won and took a great deal of energy to control.

The thing she could not see, the part what was blocked to her, was who was receiving these visions. It must have taken an incredible amount of energy from the elders to conjure the mist that surrounded the recipient while also conjuring the images of the dead boys with their marred necks and black eyes. The one who was seeing these horrors was also adept at hiding his or her thoughts; the mist alone would not be nearly enough.

Ceit had not confronted Shona or the others. She kept thinking they would reveal their hand eventually, but it was not happening fast enough. Amon, for all his supposed all-knowing power, was also blocked. He feigned shock, but Ceit knew that he was but a facet of her—he was no more powerful or insightful than she was. It was why Amon had pushed her to hone her abilities when she was a child, why as a teen, when she was back in the Society, he had hounded her to practice her craft, develop her skills. His strength was dependent on hers. She had not always known that, and now that she did, it was empowering. As a teenager, living in that house alone with her brother, acting more mother than sister, Amon had been her only guide. He had been a father, a mentor, the only one with whom she was entirely honest.

As she thought on him, Ceit heard his footsteps in the undergrowth behind her.

"Hello, my liege," he said softly, his voice gentle.

"I was just thinking of you, Amon," Ceit replied, indicating the spot next to her on the smooth river rock. Amon joined her, his preternaturally pale skin nearly glowing in the gloom.

"Have I ever told you about your great-grandmother?" Amon asked.

Ceit smiled a bit, glancing at Amon. "Of course you have. Do you have a new story?"

"Not really," Amon said. "You are older now—in human years,

of course—than she was when we first met. You look so much like her. Funny, your grandmother and mother went a different direction."

"My mother was lovely," Ceit replied, giving the demon a sidelong glance. "My grandmother is, well, culpable for many things, but her outward appearance is a bit out of her control."

"No doubt, my queen, no doubt. But you did win the genetic lottery, as did Ainsley Robertson. You have more in common with her than anyone else in your line, though your line does go back and back and back."

"I think you must have a point in there somewhere, Amon. This false flattery rings thin on you. What is it you came here to tell me?" Ceit looked the demon full in the face, his eyes of no particular color containing galaxies.

"Only that you have a coup forming, not that you don't already know that. If you do not address it, they will continue to try to persuade whomever they are pursuing." Amon, even though not human, had perfected his range of empathetic human expressions. The one he used now was a mix of concern and urgency.

"Let them," Ceit said with a bit of frustration. "The magick they are conjuring for their illusion is slowly killing them all. Shona has aged ten years in as many days, the others too. Let them drive themselves into the ground as they play their games. If they die, when they die, I will sell their houses and leave that cursed place all the sooner."

"This is true, and if it were so simple, I would say your plan was sound," Amon said carefully. "But someone is receiving these images, someone who has the ability to block us both. That someone may be a bigger threat than a bunch of old women and men creating hallucinations."

"What I do not understand, Amon"—Ceit dipped a bare toe

into the dark brook and flicked the water skyward—"is how whoever this is can prevent me from seeing their thoughts. They can keep the mist surrounding this fiasco intact, and yet they do not see the falseness of the visions? I do not know who is receiving them, but I do believe they think them true."

"Dear one, you have not yet learned the secret of mankind itself? It is not about truth—it is about perception. We believe what we want to see, not what we are shown. You have to ask yourself who it is that wants to believe something. Who is lost and looking for an answer? Who would see a row of little dead boys and believe their voices were for them? Who needs to feel as though they can see what others cannot?" Amon stared at her unblinking.

Ceit nodded. She knew in her heart what the demon was telling her. She knew there was one who walked this world lost and searching for sight. She knew that the void they looked to fill had been largely of her making. She shivered and pulled her knees to her chest, leaning to rest her head on Amon's bony shoulder as she watched the night creatures slide through pitch-black water.

45

ALAN, 1996

MEG SMELLED OF VANILLA AND APPLES. SHE SHIFTED away from him in her sleep, and he pulled her closer. A soft sigh escaped her lips, and her body molded to his. Alan knew they couldn't stay like this much longer. Meg would need to wake and sneak back to her own bed. He should have woken her, but instead, Alan lost himself in the scent of her hair and feel of the skin on the back of her neck. She stirred slightly and rolled onto her back, her eyes fluttering open.

"Oh Jesus, what time is it?" she murmured.

"Late. We need to get you back," Alan whispered.

"In a minute… just a few minutes," she whispered back and rolled over to face him, eyes inches apart. "Just a few minutes."

"You are a bad influence," Alan said softly, a smile on his lips. "You need to get out of here before your father crucifies me in the middle of the cul-de-sac."

"He won't. He thinks we're getting married," Meg said with a lopsided grin. She leaned in and kissed him, her lips tasting slightly of raspberry lip balm.

"You want to test that theory?" Alan said with mock reprisal. His hands ran over the flesh of her back.

"Have you thought about it?" Meg asked.

"Yeah, I've thought about it. I think about it every day, every hour, every minute."

"So all good then, right?" Meg propped herself up on one elbow. "Move with me downtown, or screw FIDM and LA—let's just go to New York in January, or San Francisco, or Chicago, or anywhere."

"Why are you choosing the coldest possible spots for January? Are you trying to convince me or kill me?" Alan said with a smile.

Meg caught him in a pointed stare. "I'm serious. Let's leave. I have only a few weeks left of school. We can leave. I have a little bit of money, so do you, so let's get out of here."

"I love you," Alan said softly and leaned in to kiss her. She received it and then pulled away, studying his expression.

"But you won't leave." She stated it as fact rather than as a question.

"You don't want me, Meg, trust me. You need to get out of here, but I can't leave," Alan said, his heart slowing with every word.

Meg shook her head and leaned in, kissing him deeply. "You don't get to tell me what I want. And you can leave—you just feel like you can't."

"You know why," Alan said sadly.

"Your sister?" Meg answered, an edge to her voice.

"Your Matrarc," Alan answered simply.

Meg sat up, wrapping the bedsheet around her. "Not my Matrarc. I'm leaving this place, and you could too. She doesn't need you, Alan. She doesn't need anyone."

Alan lay on his back staring at the ceiling as Meg quickly dressed and slid out the window. He watched as she walked as casually as possible to her house and let herself in the back gate. Alan knew she would be climbing through her bedroom window in a moment.

It was useless to try to explain it; Alan didn't even have the words. Ceit did not need him. He did not need her either. The role of Dara was perfunctory, and Ceit would manage fine by herself, as she had before he had turned eighteen. No one would stop him from leaving, and in fact Ceit would support it. So how to explain that he couldn't leave because he was already broken, his spirit already mired in the blackness of the Society? Alan saw his father's lost face when he closed his eyes. He saw him on that last day before he left their rotten shell of a house for Los Angeles to go after Ceit. When Alan had left for school that morning, his father had been passed out on the couch, his face sticky with his own vomit. Alan saw his father as he was now, haunted and destroyed, his eyes eternally open and terrified. Boyd Healy Robertson stared into a never-ending void and saw nothing outside of the darkness. Alan wondered how long it would be before Meg would have to pull him out of a bottle of whiskey. Maybe he'd just go mad first and try to stab her like his father had done to Ceit and the others at the children's home so long ago. Maybe he'd succeed, and her blood would stain the floor of their New York City apartment. He was broken and no use to anyone but the Society. It was here and only here that he could keep the voices from devouring him entirely. Alan closed his eyes and allowed himself to dream, a vanilla-scented pillow and the feel of her fingers in his hair. It was an illusion, but it was enough for now.

46

AINSLEY, 1925

SIOBHAN ELIZABETH LAY IN AN INFIRMARY PRAM, HER tiny face pale and her perfect miniature fingers slowly twitching as though dancing to music only she could hear. Ainsley stood in the doorway watching Margaret gently rock the baby. She'd been here for three days straight. The nuns had given up trying to make the girl leave. She leaned in and sang a low song to the child.

I see the moon, and the moon sees me,
Shining through the leaves of an old oak tree.
Oh, let the light that shines on me
Shine on the one I love.

Margaret's voice was thin and tired. The girl hadn't eaten or slept unless forced by the nuns since the baby had gone ill. If she closed her eyes, Ainsley could hear her own mum singing while she rocked infant Maire. Nearly overcome, Ainsley pulled herself away from the doorway. She was supposed to be on her way to the laundry with a cart of soiled towels. If she lingered here any longer, the nuns would draw the switch across her hands. She already had several angry red lines from the previous week's infractions. They knew she wasn't a Catholic; her name might be Therese here, but her past was no secret to the nuns or the other girls. How the girls knew, she had no idea. She suspected the Sisters of the Sacred Heart were bigger gossips than they'd ever admit to being.

As she pushed the rattling cart down the hall to the laundry, a sharp pain crossed her stomach, making her stop and double over.

"Oh…" Ainsley moaned and immediately clamped a hand over her mouth. If the nuns heard or if they thought it was her time, she'd be shuttled off to the midwives to be monitored. It wasn't time yet; it was far too early. This was just a cramp. January had brought a new year, but Ainsley had at least another month, maybe two, before it would be fully her time. She'd been farther along than she'd expected when she arrived here, and Ainsley couldn't help but wonder if she'd ignored the early signs. Although, she knew the answer to that clear enough. She hadn't wanted to see anything awry—a missed monthly, a bout of the sick. She'd ignored it all until her belly started pressing against the waist of her skirt.

Ainsley repeated the mantra to herself: just a cramp, just a cramp. It couldn't be time, but the nuns in the infirmary who worked as midwives had already told her she was likely to deliver early—the stress, they told her, the poor diet and the time in the cabin was likely to make the baby arrive before the ninth month. The prognosis chilled her; she needed that extra time. She had finally formed a plan to try to get her locket back. It was risky and likely to land her standing in the hallway for twelve hours, or lashed across her palms until she bled, but it was worth whatever punishment might befall her if she was able to get the Deamhain Aeir's locket back and summon him to her. She understood now that all the fae, the púca, the night creatures that had appeared to her in the woods as she hid in Bryan's foul little shack, all these needed an invitation. The only way to get their attention in this place was to call the Deamhain Aeir, take the deal he offered. Her throat closed as she thought of it. Not only the child she carried but her entire line would belong to him if she dared to catch the moonlight in the reflective silver of the tiny mirror. But what of her and her child if she refused? Or was not able to cry for help? Her daughter—she knew it was a girl in her heart—would be signed over to a good Catholic couple, and she'd never see her again. Would they let her leave after? It was what she had been told: after the baby was adopted, she was free to leave this place. But Ainsley had seen more than a few girls whose babies were long ago adopted still toiling and scrubbing the floors. They still owed the Sisters for their care, they had been told, and would be released when the debt was paid in labor. Ainsley suspected her debt would never be repaid and she'd rot here.

The cart delivered, Ainsley set back off down the hall, trying to look as busy as she could, her belly relaxing and tightening as she walked. It was nothing, she told herself, just the tension. She was looking for a particular nun, someone she hoped might help—a novice nun named Sister Agnacious, who would bring Ainsley salve for her hand when the others weren't minding her. One night she'd brought four fresh apples to Ainsley's cramped sleeping quarter. She hadn't said a word, just handed them over with a smile and left. Alma had cried all night for the kindness. This wasn't Sister Agnacious's doing, Ainsley knew, but she was complicit in keeping all the women there, complicit in selling off the babies whose mothers were largely forced into signing them away.

Ainsley had met only one girl who had signed the papers willingly. She was so young, fourteen years old. Catherine was the

name given by the nuns. Her baby had been born shortly after
Ainsley arrived, a healthy baby boy who she had let the nuns name.
He had been adopted out quickly, and still Catherine remained
at Bessborough. She was unnaturally cheerful, and she talked
about how blessed her son was to be with such a good family, how
blessed she was to be in a good home and serving the Lord. Ainsley
often fought the urge to smack the blessings right out of her fool
face. Maybe it was the fire that came with expecting that made her
temper rise, but she couldn't stand to see the girl's smile or hear
how the Lord had shown upon her on any given day.

"She has nowhere else to go," Mary Kathleen had stated simply
one day when Catherine was in an especially blessed mood in the
laundry. "I heard it told she was sent here from Belfast, and her
father told everyone she was dead. She can't go back, and where
else could she be?"

Ainsley supposed she should have more mercy on the girl, who
was a child herself and likely to stay so long at the mother and baby
home she'd become a nun herself.

Ainsley shook off her residual frustration about Catherine and
concentrated on looking like she was exactly where she had been
told to be in case anyone took notice of her. Her hopes lay in Sister
Agnacious being willing to steal more than a few apples from the
kitchen. She had seen a storage room by accident when she was
cleaning the washrooms reserved for the Sisters at the end of the
main building. The door had been ajar. She'd snuck a look before
anyone had seen. It had appeared at first to be all paperwork, but
she'd seen the sleeve of a dress hanging out a box, and she realized it must be the things they took from the girls as they admitted them. All Ainsley's things, including her clothes, suitcase, and
locket, must be in there or nearby. But it was locked the next time
she'd passed by.

Ainsley had no way of stealing a key without being noticed. She knew this well. But there was one who might help her. It might backfire as well, and she could find herself in Sister Mary Claude's rectory office, subject to her ever-changing collection of switches. But it was her only hope and well worth the risk.

Sister Agnacious couldn't have been more than twenty; she still had a childish smattering of acne across her cheek, and her eyes were full of innocence. The young novice was tidying up a playroom where the prospective parents would meet the children they were buying. It was meant to look like a proper nursery, so different from the cold stone and metal chambers the children actually dwelt in. No, this room would have convinced even the most discerning adoptive family that the Bessborough Mother and Baby Home was a place full of love and life. Colorful paintings of animals and flowers adorned the wall alongside an ornate silver cross. There were hardback children's books, dolls with eyes that opened as they were placed upright. A stuffed teddy bear sat in a rocking chair. Sister Agnacious jumped to see Ainsley in the doorway and nearly dropped a handful of wooden blocks.

"Therese, you frightened me. Is everything all right? You aren't to be down this way. Sister Angelica is in charge of me today, and she'll have the skin of your hands if she sees you." Sister Agnacious stopped and placed the blocks in a wooden basket before crossing to Ainsley and taking her hands. "Oh dear, this looks as though it might be a bit irritated. I'll bring you more salve when I get a chance."

Ainsley smiled at the young nun and took her hand. "You are kind, thank you." She took a deep breath and began. "I need something else, and I have no right to ask it of you."

Sister Agnacious began to speak, but Ainsley held up a hand and gave her a begging look. "I had a locket when I arrived. It was a gift from my mother—and her mother before that. The Sisters took it off my neck when they admitted me."

The nun's face immediately fell, and she started to speak, but Ainsley interrupted again and spoke in low, rushed words. "I won't wear it, I swear. I will keep it hidden from sight, no one will know. When I am released from this place, when I go home, my mother will cry buckets if it's lost forever. Please, Sister."

She felt no remorse for the deception, but there was a twinge of guilt for the task she was asking of the novice.

"Therese, I… if they catch me, I could be sent away," Sister Agnacious whispered.

"I understand, I do. And I hate that I ask it of you, but you are the only one who can help—the others don't understand. Please…"

Ainsley felt a tear form in the corner of her eye. It was sincere; without the nun, she had no friends outside her fellow prisoners.

Sister Agnacious nodded, looking past Ainsley to see if anyone was approaching. "Okay, I'll try," she said. "I think I know where they keep the belongings. Some get sold, but they only do that at the summer market so it's likely still here. What does it look like?"

Ainsley's hands shook with adrenaline as she described the pattern, the four letters inscribed on the brass surface. "Inside is a mirror," she said. "It's precious to me. I pray it has not broken."

Sister Agnacious took both Ainsley's hands in her own. "I will pray for that as well and for the day you leave this place and begin your life anew in the blessings of the Lord. I pray for that every night for you and all the girls."

Ainsley choked her response. Prayer was, to her, a pile of goat droppings, but the young nun was sending her love in the only way she had of summoning an ancient healing energy. In that capacity, it was made of the same light and goodness as the fae and forest folk that Ainsley followed.

"Thank you, Sister," she replied.

As she scurried down the hall, her belly again stabbed with pain. She paused, one hand on the wall, to catch her breath. These were too far apart to be labor, much too far apart. And according to the midwife, who she had just seen, it was far from time. *You need to wait, my daughter,* thought Ainsley.

She lingered at the entry to the infirmary, where Margaret was still singing softly to her dying baby.

Over the mountains, over the sea,
Back where my heart is longing to be,
Oh, let the light that shines on me,
Shine on the one I love.

Ainsley could see that Margaret's face was wan and pale, but her eyes were dry. She knew her child was not long for this place. It would do no good to offer comfort; she had made her own peace with the truth of the situation. Ainsley's hands surrounded her belly, and she whispered the song they sang in the Society to her unborn daughter.

I sing of the fae and the wood and the vine,
And the night that lasts forever.
The ghosts of your loves and the ghosts that are mine,
Will linger there forever.

Her child could not be born in this place, not here. She needed to flee these people and the dead god they bowed to.

47

AINSLEY, 1925

AINSLEY PUSHED THE BOILED TURNIPS AND TINNED beef around her plate. Her mouth tasted of vomit and everything burned on the way down her throat. The other girls called it the water qualm; the nuns in the infirmary said it was ulceritis. Whatever it might be, Ainsley could barely take a bite. Next to her, Alma studied her worriedly.

"They'll be angry if ye don't finish, they will," she whispered.

"I can't," Ainsley whispered back. "I feel like the baby's kicked my gut into my throat."

Alma's already pale face cooled a couple of shades more, making her look more ghost than girl. She was just starting to show proper now and had suffered few of the expectant symptoms so far. She trembled every time any of the girls complained about the cramps or indigestion or the pains that could shoot right up from outside in. Sister Maura leaned over Ainsley's plate, inspecting her progress.

"Therese, is there a problem?" she asked curtly.

"Sister, I don't feel well. I feel as though I'll be ill. I can hardly swallow." Ainsley looked up hoping for mercy.

"Child, these are the gifts of the Lord. There are plenty of hungry souls in this world who would eat what you leave," Sister Maura said, her voice patient.

"I'll take what she can't finish." Alma spoke with a hurried intensity and looked up at the nun. Alma was forever hungry, the modest portions far below what she was accustomed to on her family's farm.

"That's not entirely what I meant, Alma, but I suppose I can look the other way on this occasion—just make sure there is no waste." Sister Maura winked and strode away, hands clasped behind her back.

Alma looked to Ainsley in shock. Ainsley pushed the plate toward her.

"Go ahead. I'm done." She smiled.

Alma grinned back and placed Ainsley's full plate over her own empty one. Between mouthfuls, she looked up and whispered, "That was unexpected. I think sometimes they're not so bad."

Ainsley did not reply but instead surveyed the room, looking for Sister Agnacious. She hoped Alma was right. She hadn't seen the nun since this morning when she'd caught her in the nursery. Her belly had continued to cramp and release all afternoon, but nothing that looked to be a pattern. The midwife had told her that she was to pay attention when the cramps came at regular intervals, and to tell the Sisters right away. These cramps weren't regular, but they felt as though her belly was on fire, a queer mix of nausea and pain that passed in a moment but left her shaking.

Ainsley raised a hand, and Sister Maura walked back to them and nodded.

"I need to use the lavatory," Ainsley said quietly as a wave of pain washed across her stomach.

"Of course. Are you having contractions?" Sister Maura knelt down to Ainsley's side and placed a hand on her stomach, which was hard as a rock. "It feels as though you might be. We should take you to the infirmary."

"Please, the lavatory, I—please," Ainsley whispered, the pain already receding.

The nun stood and nodded. "As you will, but when you return, I think it's best to send you down to at least check."

Ainsley limped to the stairs at the end of the dining hall. The lavatory was just a few steps up. She felt as though she were going to faint, but she couldn't do that here. It wasn't time yet; it couldn't be time. They had said she had two more months, at least one. Ainsley needed those weeks to find the locket and gain her freedom. Her baby could not be born in this place. As she reached the steps and took the handrail, she felt a rush of warm liquid, as though she'd urinated on herself.

"Therese, stay there—I'm coming." Ainsley heard Sister Maura rushing across the dining hall, and her strong arms caught her as she stumbled back. The other girls were murmuring, and Ainsley heard several audible gasps. Another set of arms took her from the other side, and she looked around, her gut cramping and releasing, the waves of pain and nausea almost overwhelming.

"I'll help, Sister." Ainsley looked to see Margaret at her side. *They must have driven her from the nursery in an attempt to make her eat*, Ainsley thought confusedly. The two of them helped Ainsley walk past the other girls, some of whom reached a hand out and patted her elbow or skirt, whatever they could reach.

"You'll be all right, love!" a voice called as she rounded the corner down the hall to the infirmary. Ainsley groaned; she was many things, but all right was not one of them.

"It's not time!" Ainsley nearly shouted the words in her frustration. "They said another month! Maybe two!"

"Calm yerself, love," Sister Maura said patiently.

"Babies don't care much for what doctors have to say," Margaret said from the other side.

"Your little one is proof of that, Margaret," Sister Maura said and hoisted Ainsley up a bit straighter. "Now, here we go, almost there. Come, let's get her into the birthing room. I suspect that's where she's headed anyhow."

Ainsley found herself laying on crisp white linens in a brightly lit examination room. There was a tray of shining steel tools against the wall, contraptions that scared Ainsley even to look at them. The midwife entered, followed by two novices who were training for the duty. Margaret was still holding Ainsley's hand. Her eyes were troubled, and she leaned in.

"I'll pray for you and the little one," Margaret whispered. "I know you don't follow the church, but it's all I know to do. Think of it as a blessing."

"It is a blessing, it is. I—thank you." Ainsley pushed out the words before another contraction gripped her body and she fought the urge to scream.

"All right, everyone out. That's you, dear," the midwife said, looking to Margaret.

And at that, Ainsley was left at the mercy of the Sisters. They draped her with a white sheet as the novices pulled her linen dress over her head and replaced it with a hospital gown of stiff cotton.

"Must keep everything as clean as we can, right? Okay then, where are we?" When the midwife reappeared from under the draping sheet, her face was a mixture of concern and surprise. "Well, you're beginning to crown," she said. "You've been in labor for some time—you didn't think to tell anyone? What were you going to do, have the baby in the washroom?"

"It's not time… it's not time," Ainsley moaned.

"It most certainly is," the midwife said curtly. "Now stop your carrying on. This is the pain the Lord hath blessed us with to wash you of your sins."

"Gabh transna ort fhéin," Ainsley muttered. Her lower back was aching as though it would break in two.

"Shut your pagan mouth." The midwife's voice was sharp and held the edge of a warning. "We'll not have that devil language in this place." Even though Ainsley knew they could make things far worse for her, she couldn't stop the old language from spilling out.

"Loscadh is dó ort." She felt the power of the Society in her words, the old language, the Gaelic she had been raised on, the curses her mother had muttered at the old priest as he rode away after every visit. She was not part of this world; she held no reverence to their crucifixes and holy water.

"I'm warning you, girl—I'll have you gagged if you can't shut your cursed mouth." The midwife barked the words as she wheeled the cart full of shining steel tools to the bedside. The novices looked uncertainly at each other and rushed about the room in a frenzy of activity that made Ainsley dizzy to watch.

With a deep breath, and full understanding of the consequences, Ainsley leaned up and caught the midwife's eyes. "I don't believe in your sins. Yer a jailer, and you claim your work in the Lord's name. Go ndéana an diabhal dréimire de chnámh do dhroma."

At that, a paralyzing contraction washed over her, and she felt the sensation that her body was being ripped in two.

"Yer lucky yer so far along, girl, and I don't have the time to deal with yer foul mouth. You need to push—the baby's head is on its way out."

The midwife settled her novices to her sides, and the three of them guided Ainsley as the gut-wrenching pain washed over and over her in waves. There was no earthly way to tell how much time had passed. Ainsley felt as though every bone in her body was melting with exhaustion. The pain became a being of its own, its own universe. Ainsley longed for her mother, her sister, the women of the Society. When a child was being born, the women would rally and gather together. They had herbs to ease the pain, and she would have been given willow bark to chew to ease the cramps. Nothing was provided here—no morphine, no comfort. Ainsley's throat felt raw and red, and the novices still refused her even a sip of water.

"C'mon, girl, yer baby is like to die in there if we don't get it out. Curse me if it helps, but I need ye to rally." The midwife cast a stern and solid look at Ainsley, and she knew that despite her curses and anger, she had to stop fighting the woman for the sake of her daughter.

"All right, I see the shoulders. Keep at it," the midwife commanded.

Ainsley felt the sticky discomfort of blood and knew she and the child were in danger if they didn't deliver soon.

"We've got it now, girl—we've got it. One more and we… there we go."

Ainsley felt an immediate rush of relief. The contractions and searing pain didn't disappear, but they lessened to a sharp ache. None of it mattered though, as above the din of confusion and chaos a thin, high wail filled the air.

"A girl. A bit small, but her lungs sound strong and true," the midwife declared. "Girls, clean her up and let Therese hold her. She can have a bit of time. She's earned it, even if she is a pagan."

Ainsley leaned up to see the young nuns washing the mysterious and angry little figure with wet cloths. "Sister… I…" she began.

The midwife waved a hand at her. "Please, girl. I've been birthing babies for forty years. You think yer the first one who's told me the devil will make a ladder of my spine? The Lord forgives us in our pain. There you go." She stood back as one of the novices wrapped the red-faced creature in a white blanket and gently placed her in Ainsley's arms.

Immediately, the baby calmed, staring at Ainsley as though she were a wonder of the world. "Hello, cailin beag. Hello, little one," Ainsley whispered. The creature looked more fae than human with its wrinkled cheeks and great slate-gray eyes.

"Those'll change soon enough," the novice said softly. "Light as they are now, I expect she'll favor you."

Ainsley smiled and looked up at the young nun. "Thank you," she said simply, and the novice nodded in return.

"You can have a bit of time—we need to get you to a proper bed and cleaned up besides. You can stay with her, and if yer milk comes in, all the better."

Ainsley scarcely heard her. She was staring into the face of her infant daughter, a love she never knew existed beginning to take root. For months she had thought this creature a sprite, a trick of the fae, a monster. It had only been in the softest of times that she had allowed herself to think of it is as a child—*her child*.

Ainsley ran a finger down the infant's cheek. She alone had created this—she as the child's sole parent, the sole source of life. There was no father, no nuns, no jail, no cold white-tiled walls of the birthing room. The universe that had been built of pain had cooled to a peace found only in the old woods. No one else existed in this moment, just Ainsley and the sprite that was greater than any forest magick.

48

CEIT, 1996

CEIT SAT ON HER THRONE AS THOUGH CARVED FROM stone. She did it on purpose; the old ones who surrounded the table were visibly shaking. Ceit needed their fear, needed them to quake before her. Amon was right in this matter—it was past time to put an end to their games. Ceit had thought it a useful tool for their own unraveling. It was assured that if they did keep conjuring the visions, they certainly would put themselves in their graves. Shona had a grave-like pallor already; her teeth were brown with neglect and her hair stringy and unwashed. The others were in equally poor condition. Ceit regarded each of them with a long stare, intentionally making them squirm before she moved her gaze. She'd had to summon them herself since Alan had disappeared. While on one level Ceit saw it as a good sign that he might be rebellious enough to split from the cul-de-sac entirely, it was also an annoyance. He needed to hear this. Ceit was positive he did not know of the old ones' machinations. She was nearly positive it was he who had been receiving the dreams and waking sights of the dead little boys. She had wanted him here for this meeting in order to be sure. *It has to be him,* she thought darkly as she stared down Katherine, who had a line of green snot slowly leaking out her nose. Ceit turned her gaze with disgust.

"Matrarc… we… can I ask why?" Máthair Shona began hesitantly.

Ceit did not say a word back to her, only raised a hand and, with the slightest effort, caused Shona's water glass to fly from the table and smash against the far wall. It was a parlor trick, but it had the desired effect. The old ones gasped, and Ellaine started murmuring what sounded to be prayers.

"Who are you praying to, old woman?" Ceit asked coldly.

"Pardon, Matrarc. It's a little song that they used to sing in the old country. I remember it from my childhood. It calms me some," Ellaine said softly, her voice shaking.

"Then sing it for us now and calm us." Ceit's words were intentionally even, no hint of anger in her voice. She was not as angry with them as she was tired, tired of cleaning up their messes, tired of wading through their superstition.

"Oh, Matrarc—I'm sure I can't." Ellaine tried a casual laugh, but it came out as a hacking cough.

"I'm sure you can. Let's all hear it. I need you calm," Ceit replied.

"Oh, all right." Ellaine looked to her sister and then back at Ceit. In a thin voice she intoned:

I sing of the fae and the wood and the vine,
And the night that lasts forever.
The ghosts of your loves and the ghosts that are mine,
Will linger there forever.

"It's nice," Ceit said. "Mór Ainsley used to sing it as well. Do you feel better?"

Ellaine's eyes darted back and forth from her sister to Conor.

"I... I—"

"I expect not." Ceit cut her off. "I'm wondering if you know the truth behind that song? No? My great-grandmother used it as a call to the forest folk and the fae of the old woods. She said if it were sung by the right person at just the right time, it would lift the veil between this world and the next for all time, permanently. Can you imagine? The ghosts of your loves and the ghosts that are mine walking among the living? Riding the bus? Sitting at your dinner table? That was the power of that chant." Ceit paused, waiting for her words to sink in. She took a long draught of the Diet Coke in front of her. "Of course, nothing is like to happen when you sing it. In your voice, it is just a children's song, a charming little bit of the old Irish countryside. You don't have any real power, do you? Any of you?" Ceit cast a long look at each of them.

"Matrarc... if you please, you summoned us—what is it you need from us? I can see you are angry." Shona spoke softly and rapidly.

She thinks to control this situation, Ceit thought, smiling. But her eyes remained steady.

"A little dead boy," said Ceit. "Several little dead boys actually. But one in particular is most troublesome. He is wearing blue pajamas, and he has bruises around his neck. His eyes are black, and he is as consistent as smoke, less actually. What is your intention? You are haunting someone with this vision, this cheap magick trick, but what is your intention? The effort to conjure the sight is almost more than you can bear. You're all falling apart at the seams." Ceit flicked her fingers at Conor, and a fine powdering of his already thinning hair snowed down on the table. He gasped in fear and surprise. "Pardon me," Ceit said with a small smile. "That was petty, and I abhor pettiness."

"Matrarc." Shona thumped the table with her fists to punctuate her words. "The visions of the boys come from a higher place. We are but the messengers—"

"Bullshit. Do you forget who I am? What I am?" Ceit raised her hands, and as she brought them down, the table flipped to its side, broken glass hitting the walls. "Do you think I haven't known of your game for months now? I am the Bandia Marbh. I am the Goddess of Nightmares. I rule the night that lasts forever from your nursery song. You think to conjure visions and torment one in my name? It ends now."

Conor and his vapid wife had already run for the front door, and Ellaine was helping Katherine up from the floor where her chair had tipped over.

"My mother did not resort to scaring others!" Shona stood tall and faced Ceit, her eyes uncertain but her shoulders straight and strong. "She never used her rank to—"

"Your mother, my great-grandmother, didn't have the power to do so," Ceit interrupted. "She was gifted, true, and she was your Matrarc, but that was all she was ever going to be. You weren't given a tuppence of what she was born with. You are a weak, cowardly old woman. You tried to be rid of me years ago—all of you did— and I proved myself stronger than whatever childish ambitions you aspire to. You will stop your conjuring, you will cease to send your visions out, and you will keep your head down and do as you are told. This is my only warning."

Ceit flicked her hand the other direction, and the table righted itself, the chairs sliding back into place. With another nod of her head the broken glass began scooting toward the center of the room as though being drawn from a magnet. As it collected, it swirled upward into a tornado funnel that danced in the lamplight. The old ones watched in horror and wonder.

"Go now," Ceit said firmly. As they turned to the door, Ceit released the spinning cyclone, and the shards of glass flew to the entryway, expertly dodging the old women and man, embedding themselves in the door and wall. "Now," Ceit repeated. The old ones scurried out into the night.

Ceit sighed and crossed to the kitchen to collect the mop. She had lost her temper. She had meant to make a more clearheaded warning, but this would do. If she could not have their loyalty, she would have their fear. As she cleaned up her mess, Ceit softly sang the song that she had half forgotten.

> I sing of the fae and the wood and the vine,
> And the night that lasts forever.
> The ghosts of your loves and the ghosts that are mine,
> Will linger there forever.
>
> Let's call to the wind, to the sun, and the rain,
> And the night that lasts forever.
> Out beyond the veil is the blackest of nights,
> Your soul gone to the nether.
>
> The dead never sleep and the night never breaks,
> You're alone until forever.
> With teeth that can bite and the claws that will tear,
> Your soul it will not weather.

49

ALAN, 1996

"YOU'RE SURE ABOUT THIS, MAN?"

"Yeah, totally sure," Alan replied, tired of people second-guessing him. This guy was one of his regular pill customers, and he had been all over Alan's ass about his diminishing supply. But tonight Alan was offering something better than pills. He had a wad of money—a few hundred in twenties—all that was left after he'd paid rent on Meg's apartment. He'd meant to save it, but *fuck that*, he figured. He needed to prepare.

"Never thought I was going to sell this shit, like never, man. Here you go."

The man went by different names—Randy sometimes, Rick others. He could have been any worn-down relic on Venice Beach. It was hard to discern the homeless from the rest of the beach rats. He'd tried to sell Alan a handgun a year ago; God knew where he got this shit. Alan had turned him down. He didn't want a gun— then or now. They scared him, truth be told. Alan knew how fast his moods shifted, how fast his anger could rise. A thing such as a gun... the very idea made gooseflesh rise to the surface of his skin. No, no gun. But he had a need for something else, and he'd heard Randy/Rick bragging about it on the boardwalk. He was a damn idiot, and Alan half thought he'd have been picked up by the police before Alan could make the deal.

"So it's a little rusty, but you can totally polish that shit up. See here where the blade is a little scuffed up? Just take a little metal cleaner and buff it out. But be careful man—this baby is sharp as fuck. Contraband shit, cool right? This bad boy belonged to the rebels in the Salvadoran war, probably killed some motherfuckers with it. Real deal right here." Randy/Rick nodded his head vigorously as he spoke, adamantly agreeing with himself.

Alan regarded him coldly and examined the machete. He could have gone to any of the knife stores, or even the mall, but Alan had no desire to even tempt the idea that someone might track his purchase. The Society was still interesting enough to the forces that the purchase of a large knife would likely demand attention. Besides, Randy/Rick had been hounding him. This was a good way to buy him off peacefully—give him more money than this thing was worth, part ways.

"I don't care about its history," Alan replied coldly, his patience waning. "How much?"

"Three hundred," Randy/Rick said with a half grin.

Alan looked at him for a moment. "Three hundred? One helluva a knife, huh?"

"Dude, I told you—this is Salvadoran contraband shit right here. That's probably blood on the blade, genuine shit." Randy/Rick's mouth started twitching, and Alan sighed.

"Fine, whatever, real Salvadoran blood. Great." Alan handed over three hundred dollars. Randy/Rick grinned, his eye flicking to the side.

"Good on ya, man! Let me know if you open shop again. I'm

loyal to local business owners!" Randy/Rick laughed and loped off down the boardwalk.

Alan was left holding the sheathed blade. He tucked it awkwardly into the belt of his jeans and started off toward home. There was a time when he would have roared that asshole down for this. If he was telling the truth and this machete had been used in the Salvadoran Civil War, then he had, effectively, profited off the deaths of thousands. But the time for a moral compass was gone for Alan. He thought of his father, he thought of the scar that still ran the length of Ceit's shoulder and arm. He thought of the little boy in the sky-blue pajamas. He thought of their mother and the broken memories he had of her.

Meg was back at the apartment downtown. He'd told her he would be back tonight, but he needed to stash the knife under the house with the rest of his hidden things, and he was sure to run into Ceit. She'd needed him for something tonight, but he'd blown it off. Fuck that, Alan thought. Dara was no more than errand boy, and he was done running her errands. Meg had decided to leave in January. She'd already made the train reservation. She'd bought two tickets, nonrefundable. "Come with me," she'd pleaded. Alan had been silent.

Her parents were getting suspicious. They'd found her gone one night, and she'd spent the week listening to them rant because she wouldn't rat him out. It was getting close to her graduation though, and she'd be eighteen. She would be free, and Alan breathed easier knowing she was leaving this place, with or without him. Alan had been increasingly glad he'd signed a month to month lease on the studio apartment. They had been using it more and more. It was too dicey to keep going from his house to hers. Ceit was certain to know, and her parents weren't fools, not to mention all the prying eyes from the rest of the cul-de-sac.

The apartment had become their space, their sacred circle. Alan almost told her about the veil, what it looked like on the other side, the mercreatures with their pointed teeth and mesmerizing eyes. Meg had never seen it, since she wouldn't be initiated into the fold officially until she was eighteen. Alan had seen it only that night his mother went ill. He and his father were allowed in for reasons he still did not understand. It was a woman's space; he and his father were a virus in this world. Or were they? It was a nagging thought that his great-great-grandfather had been Ceannaire, that a man had lifted the veil and run the Society. Alan, and Ceit as well presumably, had been told it had only ever been women, Matrarcs. What if it had only been one woman before Ceit? And what if that woman, Mór Ainsley, had taken her position through death and murder and blackness? What did that mean for Alan? Could he lift the veil and walk the Night Forest? Could he call the winds and hear the thoughts of others if he tried? The little boy told him yes, he could.

Alan turned onto Sinder Avenue and ducked behind the house to the little hollow crawl space where he still kept a few pills. He slid the machete into the space, tucking it back so that a curious hand would not reach it. As he rounded the side of the house, he saw the old ones being ejected from the front door. Máthair Shona was cursing and frantically shaking something from her hair. Ellaine and Katherine were crying and holding tight to each other as they crossed the lawn. Conor and his wife were already well down the sidewalk, practically sprinting back to their back house. He thought to call out to his grandmother and then stopped himself. This was Ceit's business, and her business it would remain.

50

AINSLEY, 1925

AINSLEY WAS ALLOWED ONE DAY IN THE INFIRMARY, and then she was back to the laundry. Every bone in her body ached with the effort it took to lift the heavy bags into the cart, and the crank wheels for the washers were murder. Her breasts were ripe to burst when her milk appeared out of the sky on the third day. Sister Maura had promptly taken her to the nursery and sat her down in the aged rocker.

"Yer lucky, you are. You can help the others—we don't have near enough formula."

With that, a wan-faced infant was placed in her arms, and the novice midwives set to pulling Ainsley's uniform dress down over her shoulder and fixing a blanket to drape over her exposed breast.

"But this isn't... this isn't my daughter," Ainsley said in shock. She hadn't seen the infant after the first day in the infirmary. She'd shown up at the nursery every day only to be told it wasn't on her duty roster and to move along. The aches of recovery were mixed with a stabbing horror that she might never see the child again if she didn't figure a way out of here soon.

"Well, aren't you the smart one," Sister Agnes, the nun in charge of the nursery, clucked. She was a heavyset matron who looked more footballer than nun. "This little one was born the day before yours, and he's rejecting the formula. You'll feed him, and the next, and perhaps yer own too. The Lord has blessed you with milk, child. It's yer duty to give."

Ainsley started to object when the novice nun gave her already aching breast a swift smack that made tears form in Ainsley's eyes.

"Why… what?" Ainsley moaned.

"Got to get the milk to rise," the novice explained apologetically. She then reached out and pinched the nipple in a vise grip that made Ainsley's whole body contort with pain.

"There we go," the novice declared. Sister Agnes nodded with approval as the novice situated the infant to the nipple. Ainsley was paralyzed with the horror and wonder of it all. He puckered his tiny lips and began to suck, and Ainsley suddenly felt relief on the skin of her breast that felt ripe to burst.

"All right, there we are," Sister Agnes said.

In the end, Ainsley found herself cradling the pale, underfed infant in her arms as though he were her own while the novice midwife kept watch.

"Not all the girls have milk, you know," the novice said softly when they were left alone for a moment. "Yer lucky, she's right about that. This one, we were—are still—so worried for him. But he's eatin' now, and that's a good sign. You did that, yer savin' him."

Ainsley nodded. "His mother? Can't she be here for this?"

The novice shook her head. "What's the use of it, upset her more?"

"Please, can't I see my baby? I still have plenty left," Ainsley whispered, indicating her other breast, and the novice looked up and down the nursery furtively.

"This little man is done anyhow, nodding off, see?" The novice reached down to take the sleepy infant, his mouth slack and his belly full.

"What's his name?" Ainsley asked softly.

"Thomas Eugene." The novice rocked the baby back and forth.

"How British," Ainsley said with a smile, and the novice laughed.

"Wait here," the novice said quietly.

When she reappeared, she held a fussy, red-faced infant in her arms. Ainsley immediately felt a pull from the bottom of her gut. Her daughter—her perfect, tiny daughter. As the novice placed the baby in her arms, Ainsley maneuvered the other breast free. She saw the baby's eyes were beginning to clear. The novice had been right; they were setting to the pale blue-green that matched Ainsley's own. The infant stopped fussing and stared up at her.

"Hello, little one. I'm back, love," Ainsley whispered.

As the infant nursed, Ainsley leaned back in the rocker and gently stroked the baby's tiny forehead.

"You haven't named her," the novice said. "They'll let you keep the name you choose if it's proper, even if it's British." She winked at Ainsley.

"I don't have a name yet," Ainsley said softly. "I didn't think she was quite real, you see."

"Well, they'll choose one quick enough, so if you want any say in the matter, I'd make up my mind," the novice said slyly.

At that, Sister Agnes reentered the room and surveyed the scene. "Well, what's this then?"

"Thomas was done, and I didn't see the harm," the novice said as she rose.

"The harm, Sister Claire, is that there are infants in this nursery who won't feed on the formula, and there's this one who will. She's no need to nurse—this is a vanity. But it's started now, so finish her up. But you know better, Sister."

"Yes, Sister Agnes," the novice replied.

The exchange was no more than a mist through which Ainsley held her tiny daughter. Names—what name could she give? Maire, after her sister? Or Colleen, after a story she'd heard once about a warrior girl who fought the British. Branwen, a strong and noble name. She suspected that whatever she gave to the child, it would be changed to Mary or Katherine on the birth certificate anyhow.

"We're leaving here, little one." Ainsley leaned down so only the infant could hear her words. "We're leaving this place."

51

AINSLEY, 1925

IT WAS SEVEN DAYS FROM THE BIRTH OF AINSLEY'S daughter that Sister Agnacious crept into the nursery as she sat in the rocker, Thomas Eugene in her arms and her own baby in the pram next to them. He was pinking up nicely, his cheeks growing rosy and his eyes bright. Ainsley had met his mother, a sickly-looking girl who couldn't have been more then fifteen who worked in the kitchen. She'd clung to Ainsley and cried when she'd told her she'd been made his wet nurse. She kept thanking her until Ainsley couldn't stand the sound of the words any longer. She was being forced into this role, but it wasn't the fault of the baby or the mother. If Thomas's mother had proper food and wasn't made to work twelve hours a day, perhaps she'd have her own milk and she could nurse her child in front of her own hearth.

Sister Agnacious silently observed Ainsley for a moment, a curious expression on her face.

"What a blessing," she said softly, crossing the room to sit next to Ainsley.

"Sister, I haven't seen you since we talked." Ainsley fought to keep her anticipation at bay.

"Not for lack of trying," Sister Agnacious said with a small frown. "They've been running me ragged. Scarcely had a moment alone, but I did manage to get away." She gave Ainsley a half smile, ripe with secrets.

"You found it?" Ainsley felt her heart lifting. On her chest, Thomas pulled away and started fussing. Ainsley held him over her shoulder and gently patted his back until a tiny burp emitted from his mouth. She exchanged the babies in the pram so her unnamed daughter was in her arms.

"I think so." Sister Agnacious pulled out the bronze locket with the intertwining symbol and the AMON engraving.

"Oh yes! Oh, Sister, I'm so grateful!" Ainsley felt tears rise in her eyes.

Sister Agnacious put a finger to her lips and glanced over her shoulder. "I don't know a thing of what yer talking about. Don't let it be seen—they'll lash ye, I know they will. Then they'll start looking for who found it for ye."

Ainsley nodded. "Of course." She paused, afraid to ask. "I haven't wanted to ask the others, but you work in the infirmary, yes?"

Sister Agnacious nodded. She reached out to take the little girl's hand and cooed softly at the infant.

"Margaret's baby, little Siobhan, is she... ?" Ainsley could scarcely bring herself to ask. The one night she'd been allowed in the infirmary, the infant had not cried a bit. Margaret was there until she was ushered out, and still the infant lay quiet and still.

Sister Agnacious shook her head. "She's holding on, she is. But not much longer. She won't eat, and she hardly moves. Margaret won't hardly leave her side."

"Can I nurse her?" Ainsley leaned forward, her daughter unin-terrupted in her meal. "They've been bringing all sorts of infants for me to wet-nurse, why not her?"

"I suspect they don't want to waste the milk," Sister Agnacious said sadly.

Ainsley felt a coldness run down her spine even though she held the key to her and her daughter's freedom in her hand. For the last four days, she'd been made to nurse two other babes besides Thomas. She was allowed access to her daughter only as a cour-tesy. Sister Agnes had finally relented and said the presence of her child made her milk fuller. Why not that infant? Ainsley knew that Sister Agnacious was right—the nuns saw no use in saving a dying child, even one who seemingly refused to let go. *She is fighting this place harder than any of us,* Ainsley thought angrily. Little Siobhan Elizabeth was working to fill her grand name.

Sister Agnacious slipped out the nursery and down the hall, leaving Ainsley alone with the infants. Her daughter lay in her arms, belly full and cheeks a perfect rose. *She sleeps as though the world is in the right,* Ainsley thought. All she had to do was catch the sun or moon in the reflection of the silver mirror and this could all be over. The Deamhain Aeir would rescue her. Perhaps. What if he proved himself a liar and the moonlight in the mirror was no more than that? What if she was trapped here for good? Her daughter would be taken, and she would spend the rest of her days scrubbing stains from sheets and borax off tile. Her milk would dry, and she'd become an old woman in this place. She'd die here and be buried in the potter's field on the forest's edge.

Or what if the Deamhain Aeir did appear? What if he were an honest deamhain? Not just her soul, which she cared little for, but her daughter's and granddaughter's and on and on and on—they would all belong to him. Amon had said that one of her line would be born to take a role in the darkness to come, one would be the ruler of the Night Forest, the leader of the dead and darkness. Would it be this little one? Or would Ainsley be long dead before the one Amon spoke of would appear? What did it make her if she sold her daughter or granddaughter away to the deamhain? Was she so very different than the nuns who hid behind the walls of the Bessborough Convent? Could she determine her daughter's stars? Or her granddaughter beyond that? Could she rob another little girl of her voice in the name of freedom?

She rubbed the bronze locket and placed it in the deep pocket of her uniform dress. What life could she offer her child anyhow? The Society was done with her, she had no money, and no one would take her in. Finn was long gone, no more real than a nursery song now. She had no interest in him. So what would become of them? Was it a selfish notion to keep her daughter from the family that might adopt her? Would her new parents be wealthy? Would they teach her to play the piano and buy her iced milk in the park on Sunday afternoons? Would they take her away from this cursed country with its dead god and go to America? Would she grow up with a clipped American accent and no memory of the suffering inflicted on her before her birth?

Ainsley closed her eyes and fought tears. She had told herself for so very long that this is what she wanted: the locket, the deamhain, freedom from this place. Now that it was within her grasp, she wondered if she'd ever feel free again.

52

CEIT, 1996

IT TOOK JUST UNDER FIFTEEN MINUTES FOR THE HOUSE to be reduced to a pile of rubble. Bedelia's old bungalow, with its termite infested walls and uneven foundation courtesy of the Northridge earthquake, was no more than a pile of stucco and wood. Ceit had stood on the other side of the street and watched with an impassive face, knowing full well that the others were peeking from behind their curtains at the spectacle. Alkhem Developments had wanted to hold off on the demolition until all the houses were in their possession, but Ceit had asked it as a favor. Neither the lawyer nor the real estate agent had understood, but Ceit had a definite motive for her request: she needed to send a message.

Since her meeting with Shona and the old ones, they had lain low and the visions of the little boys had not been conjured. They were growing weaker by the day, their efforts to block their thoughts increasing futile. Ceit knew they met in Ellaine's living room, under what they thought was a cloak of silence. There they talked of a day when Ceit would no longer be their Matrarc.

They talked of their new Ceannaire. They told stories of Ceit's great-great-grandfather, who, from what Mór Ainsley had told her as a child, had run the Society with fear and violence. But those memories had changed in Ellaine's and Katherine's minds. Shona had been too young to remember him except as a story told by others. But Ellaine and Katherine had been children when they'd left Cork, and the stories they spun now about the Society as it had been differed greatly from what Mór Ainsley had told.

The bulldozers set about the task of lifting great chunks of the house into the back of an enormous truck. Ceit wanted the lot to stand empty, a reminder of her power and intentions. The old ones were so far unsuccessful in their attempts to recruit any new members to their coup. They had approached Meg's parents. Meg's mother had been born into the Society and was as dim as Meg appeared to be. Her father had married in, a rare occurrence but not unheard of. It had all happened well before Ceit's time, and as such, she did not know the circumstances that led to Mór Ainsley trusting the man enough to join the Society. But in the fashion of a true convert, the man was twice as zealous as anyone in the cul-de-sac.

Ceit glanced to the end of the street to see Alan walking from the direction of the bus stop. He'd been agitated lately. The normally strong veil he kept over his thoughts and emotions had broken a bit. Ceit could see inside his head with unusual clarity at times. Darkness and anger swirled there. He thought of Meg more than Ceit was comfortable. She had realized in one rather shocking moment that the two of them were intimate—and much closer than they let on. Ceit did not care for it; Meg would bind him here. Alan stopped and stared at the demolition site.

"Like what you've done with the place," he said dully.

"The first of many steps to come," Ceit said simply.

He crossed the distance to stand next to her. "How many more?"

"All of them, little brother, eventually," Ceit replied. Alan had not been privy to all her business dealings with Alkhem Developments, even as Dara. Ceit had wanted to keep this close to her chest.

"And the old ones? And me? If I marry Meg, the way Grandmother is frothing at the mouth for me to do, wherever will we live?" His voice was mildly sarcastic, and Ceit fought her annoyance.

"If you truly choose to marry the girl, then you will live wherever you please, away from this cul-de-sac, away from the old ones, away from all this. The Society is at its end, brother." Ceit caught a flash of emotion from Alan's tumbled brain; it was screaming fear that raced from every corner of his thoughts. He spoke and acted calmly, blithely even, but inside he was being torn apart. Ceit immediately felt the weight of her love for him. She loved very few people on this plane; Alan might be the only one when she really thought on it. His pain was caused by her, had always been caused by her.

Alan sighed and stared at the bulldozer piling up broken planks and drywall.

"And you have that right? The right to bulldoze a thing that was in creation long before you were born?" Alan asked, his voice weary.

"Yes," Ceit said gently. "I do. Mór Ainsley should have done the same. Instead she brought it to this place when she should have burned it down and left it on a hillside in Cork. But she was afraid, although of what I am not sure." Ceit paused, studying Alan carefully. "You're not happy here. You wish for so much more. I know about you and the girl."

Alan cast her a slightly surprised look, then stared back at the destruction. "I supposed you would know. You know everything, don't you?"

"No," Ceit replied, "I don't. But I know that the guard you keep over your mind is slipping. I know you've been sent false images, false dreams. I know that Meg may not be as dull as she appears, but I know you are cast for so much more, brother."

"You don't know her," Alan snapped, and Ceit let the words land without reacting. "You all think she's some kind of idiot 'cause she's quiet. None of you know her." Color rose to his cheeks. "And you know nothing of my dreams. None of you do. I know that before you, before Mór Ainsley, there was a different sort of Society. I know that you aren't the only one who is special—you aren't the only one who can see past the veil." He spat the words out; they dripped venom.

Ceit stood quietly. "Alan. You see a group of dead little boys. One wears blue pajamas and has bruises around his neck. He talks to you and has vacant black eyes. He tells you things. He is getting more and more transparent every time he appears. You have not seen him for some time."

Alan turned and loomed over her, his hands and lip trembling. "You're reading my thoughts—you saw them there. You can't stand that I have my own visions, my own calling." His voice was controlled hysteria. Ceit saw the blinds move on the bungalow next door, and she knew that Máthair Shona was listening, along with whomever was in her kitchen.

"No, love, I'm not. I saw the ones who sent these mirages to you. The boys are a false vision. There are those who want you to betray yourself, to betray me." Ceit felt a well of emotion opening up—Alan's face was full of so much pain.

"Fuck you. I don't need an invitation to betray you. I'm fucking sick of it. I'm done. Find someone else to run your damn errands and open the door. Fuck you." Alan had a fine line of drool on the corner of his mouth, and it made him look the way he had when he was small, a tiny little boy lost in the world, clinging to Ceit as his only family. Ceit reached out to take his hand, but he pulled away, his eyes wild. Abruptly, Alan turned and ran back the way he'd come, back up the cul-de-sac and off toward the beach.

Ceit took one last look at the construction site and then turned to go inside her house. Aware that nearly all the windows on Sinder Avenue had peeping eyes who had witnessed the scene, she raised her arms over her head and murmured a summons to the rain. Instantly the skies darkened overhead, and the clouds unleashed a torrent. The construction stopped, and the workers ran for cover. Ceit stood in the walkway, her arms outstretched and her face to the sky. With a nod of her head, the rain turned to hail that pounded the rooftops around her. Satisfied, she went inside and out of the damp.

53

ALAN, 1996

ALAN DREW A BREATH AND STEADIED HIMSELF BEFORE entering the hospital room. His eyes were dry and red, his throat raw. He knew he looked to be a patient himself and would be treated as such if he were unable to pull it together. Ceit was full of shit; she was using her fucked-up mind tricks to mess with his head. He'd been sloppy and let his thoughts slip. He would have to be more careful. He wanted quiet, he wanted to pretend his life hadn't been torn out from under him.

His father had been carefully bathed, his hair washed and a clean shirt pulled over his head just for his arrival. Alan knew the staff had noted his schedule and tried to keep up appearances. He also knew that if he were to arrive on a Tuesday afternoon instead of Wednesday, he would find Boyd Healy in a stained hospital gown reeking of a week's accumulation of sweat and filth. His coma was what was termed "persistent and irreversible" in the words of the medical people and their charts and IV towers. Boyd had been moved here—the same Inglewood long-term care facility where his mother had died—after about a year in the medical ward of the state prison. He would never be free, but Folsom needed the cell and Boyd Healy Robertson would never wake up, or so they kept telling Alan.

No one knew he came here. Máthair Shona had an idea but had long ago decided not to care. Ceit would never know. Alan told her what she needed and nothing more. It had been this way since he was a child, even before his mother became sick. Alan had always known the danger that lay in letting Ceit Robertson too far into your head. Even back then, the old ones had stared at her as though she were made of shards of finely sharpened glass. Perhaps she was.

His father lay still in his bed, staring blindly ahead. The nurses had long ago explained to Alan that his father's blinking and occasional muscle twitches were nothing more than involuntary muscle movements, responses in the brain that were hardwired to function even after the capacity for higher thought was destroyed. Higher thought. Alan grimaced as he took a seat by the hospital bed and stared at Boyd Healy. Higher thought. Who knew what was going on in his father's mind. The report of what had happened to Boyd had been sketchy at best. He attacked people at the group home where Ceit had been living in Los Angeles. He had fallen and hit his head—or maybe it was the stress, or an aneurysm, or a psychotic break, or maybe, maybe, maybe. Maybe it had been something Ceit had done. She had never told him, and he hadn't asked.

The afternoon that Boyd disappeared, Alan had arrived home from school to find a pile of crumpled dollar bills on the table and a social services officer on the doorstep. Alan relunctantly let the man in, and the two of them put old soda cans and dirty paper plates into a trash bag while the man cautiously asked Alan questions about his life, his father, his sister, his school. After a bit, when it became evident that Boyd wasn't going to return home before dark, the man called someone and another car pulled up. Alan spent the night sleeping on the couch of a house that smelled like dog. A foster home, they'd called it. The woman who answered the door took his bag and tried to be nice. The man who had helped Alan clean the living room explained things to her that Alan wished he could unhear. Alan laid curled up in a ball on the sofa, and as he closed his eyes, he saw the image of a serpent and the unearthly glare of his sister's eyes, and he knew it was her fault. Whatever happened to take his father away lay squarely on her.

By his count, Alan had been given two periods of normal. The first was right after his mother had died and he went to live with Cousin Aoife. Aoife had been fun, more like a teenager than an adult. She made him ramen noodles from packets for dinner and let him watch movies on HBO on the weekend. She showed him an album of photos of his mother when she was younger and told him stories about the way things used to be. She told him how she had left the cul-de-sac when she was old enough to get away and how she went to college. Aoife told Alan he was going to be okay, and he believed it. It hadn't lasted though; the year passed, and it ended.

The second period of normal was after the terrible foster home and their scratchy couch, after his father had been sent to Folsom, after his sister disappeared. Alan had gone to live in a big house with a trampoline in the yard. Joy and Michael Crawlings had a dog and a bike in the garage that fit Alan perfectly. They didn't ask him about his sister—they didn't even know about the cul-de-sac. They treated him as though everything had always been normal. He almost let himself believe he could stay there forever. They sent him Christmas cards for years, and he stuffed every single one in the bottom drawer of his dresser, unopened. Eventually, the cards stopped; everyone gave up sometime.

"Alan?" A familiar voice spoke softly from the doorway.

Alan turned and offered a smile to Mariane, her hair considerably grayer than it had been eight years ago when his mother had died in this same place. Mariane was the one responsible, Alan knew, for making sure the dandruff was cleaned from Boyd's head and his teeth were brushed every morning. She did her best even in a place that was willing to let Boyd rot.

"Hello," he said simply.

"You're done with school then?" she asked, leaning against the doorway.

Alan nodded. "For a while now—guess I haven't visited in too long." He gestured to his father. "He looks good. Thanks for cleaning him up."

Mariane grimaced. "I wish we had more staff. He deserves a bath more than once a week."

"I'm not sure he does, really," Alan said softly, his voice neutral. Mariane didn't flinch; they had this conversation often.

"Young man," she said as she always did. "What we do for others in this life isn't about what they deserve—it's about what we can give. You can make yourself crazy weighing what people deserve."

Alan gave her a half smile. "Not sure what I have to give."

Mariane crossed the room and placed her strong hand full of lines and rivulets on his shoulder. "Well, that's why we're here. Besides, you come here when you can, you sit here with him. You do fine."

With a firm pat, she exited the room, leaving Alan alone with his father. On the table next to the bed sat a small framed black-and-white image. His father smiled broadly, and some invisible source of wind blew his mother's hair across her cheek, almost obscuring her face caught in laughter. On her lap sat baby Alan, maybe six months old, and to the side stood Ceit. She must have been three, almost four in this picture, and she stared at her family with a slight crease in her toddler brow as though, even then, she thought herself outside this world, outside this little piece of normalcy.

"You were right about her," Alan whispered to his father's still form. "You were always right."

54

AINSLEY, 1925

"YOU'VE GOT TO COME, YOU'VE GOT TO."
Margaret's voice jarred Ainsley from sleep. She felt drugged.
Between the regular hours in the laundry and the time she was
expected to put in at the nursery, she felt like a dishrag wrung to its
end. Her nipples were cracked and bleeding. The nuns had refused
any salve or cream for the irritated flesh, saying it was her penance.
The scratchy fabric of the linen dress felt like fire. She grimaced as
she sat up.

"What is it? Margaret? What time is it?" Ainsley asked
confusedly. The moon was just starting to fade and dawn was not
far away.

"Late. Please come, please... and quiet—we can't wake the
Sisters." Margaret's voice was frantic.

Ainsley followed Margaret down the hallway to the infirmary,
where Ainsley guessed she had been camped for the night.

"It's Siobhan, she's having trouble breathing." Margaret stood
over the pram, her face lined with worry.

"We should call Sister Agnes, yes?" Ainsley said, looking at the baby's pale face. She was gasping for air, and her lips were an unhealthy color that bordered on blue.

"No," Margaret said forcefully. "She'll do nothing—they all think she's as good as dead." Margaret turned to Ainsley. "Nurse her, at least try. You've got to. They say you turned Thomas Eugene from the edge. You're a miracle they say, you've got to try. Please, the nuns haven't allowed it. They think she's as good as dead... please, Therese, please." Margaret started crying, a soft, hiccuping sound.

"All right," Ainsley said, pulling up a chair. "Hand her to me." Ainsley pulled down the shoulder of her dress, wincing as the fabric scraped the raw, irritated nipple. Margaret's eyes grew dark with concern when she saw.

"Jesus, I don't suppose they've given you any relief for it," she said softly as she handed the infant to Ainsley.

Ainsley shook her head. "It's my atonement, don't you know?" She winked and looked down at the baby who was fighting for every breath. "Margaret, I don't know if she'll take to it, she's so—"

"Just try, please just try," Margaret said, her voice breaking.

Ainsley brought the infant's lips to her breast, but there was no reaction. The tiny little girl lay as though half in this world and half in the other. Ainsley, swallowing her pain, gently massaged her breast and opened the baby's tiny mouth, managing to get a few drops of milk past the child's lips. The infant stirred slightly, and Margaret knelt before them.

"Please, love, please try," Margaret whispered.

Then, as though a miracle had opened before them, the sickly little girl began to suckle. She latched on, and the joy of it overrode the pain. Ainsley felt tears rise to her eyes, and she looked to Margaret, who was openly weeping. Ainsley sang softly to the child as she drank.

I sing of the fae and the wood and the vine,
And the night that lasts forever.
The ghosts of your loves and the ghosts that are mine,
Will linger there forever.

The blue tint disappeared from the baby's lips, and she opened and closed her hands, as though pumping the milk through her tiny body.

"That's pretty... what is it?" Margaret whispered as she leaned against Ainsley's leg and stroked her daughter's tiny foot.

"A song we sang back where I come from," Ainsley said softly.

"I hope you get back there, if that's where you want to be—you and your daughter," Margaret said.

"And you. May we all take leave of this place," Ainsley replied as she switched the baby to her other breast, the child drinking as though she'd not eaten for weeks.

"My real name is Niamh."

"I'm Ainsley."

The two girls smiled at each other and sat in silence as the sun cast its first light in the sky.

55

AINSLEY, 1925

THE NUNS DECLARED IT DIVINE INTERVENTION, AND on the day when Siobhan Elizabeth was moved from the infirmary to the nursery, all the girls were called to the chapel for a special Mass. Typically, Ainsley sat silently during the forced attendance at Mass, but this time she whispered a prayer of sorts in her head. She prayed for Niamh and Siobhan to be free of this place, prayed that one day she and her daughter, still unnamed, would find themselves on the deck of a ship—but not to England, no. That dream was done with. She prayed to go to America, where the church did not hold such an iron grip on its people, where she could raise her girl to be strong.

Ainsley had continued to sneak into the infirmary at night to feed Siobhan. The ironic part of her being in the nursery was that the infant was now on the regular rotation of babies that Ainsley was expected to feed. Her milk was so full that her breasts ached as she spent her mornings in the laundry. By the time she was released to the nursery, they were ripe to burst. Her own daughter was kept nearby; Sister Agnes was still convinced that having the infant near was the only reason Ainsley's milk was so strong. The nuns whispered about her, she knew. It was said her milk had healing powers, that she could clear a child's croup or indigestion. It was said that the dysentery outbreak had near to died off after Ainsley had started nursing the infants.

"You've got to name her." Sister Agnes sighed with frustration as Ainsley sat in the chair, rocking Siobhan Elizabeth. The little girl had gained more weight than Ainsley had thought possible for an infant in such a short time. Her face was pink and her eyes clear. She had little blonde curls beginning to sprout. She looked like a doll in a store window. Sister Agnes carefully swapped out Siobhan Elizabeth for Ainsley's own daughter, who was beginning to favor her more and more. Her eyes had settled on light blue, cold and crisp as the sky in winter. Her hair was wispy and light colored; in truth it looked like she and Siobhan could be sisters.

"If ye don't name her, I'll do it for ye," the nun said in an exasperated tone. "We have to finish the birth certificate. Can't believe it's gone on so long already. I can go over a list of approved names if ye want."

"I don't know her name yet. Soon, I promise," Ainsley replied.

"A good solid name will help her to be adopted. I'll bring ye the list." The nun muttered as she left the nursery.

Ainsley shivered—she knew as well as anyone that it was only a matter of time before a new batch of adoptive parents arrived and children disappeared with them. William had been adopted a week ago. Mary Kathleen had left the next morning, her face stained with tears. She had been so convinced that the strawberry mark and his ears would drive all the prospective parents away. But a couple who ran a farm out near Limerick showed up and adopted four little boys. It was a fair bet they were set to be trained to work the farm. They took the three oldest boys from the school-age children and William from the toddler room. Mary Kathleen had to walk her son down the long hallway to Sister Mary Claude's office. She was allowed to give the child a hug and then was told to leave and go back to her work, and that was that. She'd never see her boy again, and it was likely the child had gone into a home that prized him more for his labor than his heart.

It would not matter what name she gave her daughter. If a good Catholic couple came in looking for a baby, they were likely to change the name and never tell the child where she'd come from.

Ainsley kept Amon's locket near as she worked. She had sewn it into the lining of her uniform dress so it would not fall out of her pocket by accident. At night, she lay awake, knowing the key to her and her daughter's escape was so close, but the price so very high. It was selfish, she thought sometimes, selfish not to take the offer made to her. It was also selfish if she opened the locket and caught the moon in the silver reflection. It was selfishness and ignorance that had brought her to this place; maybe that was what she needed to escape it.

56

ALAN, 1996

THE ELDERS SAT IN A CIRCLE ON VENICE BEACH. ALAN huddled against the low wall that ran alongside the walkway. The sun had set about an hour ago, and the wind was whipping across the water and seemed to be trying to tear his bones straight out of his flesh. There weren't many tourists this time of night, this far from the main drag of the boardwalk, but curious locals stopped and pointed, clearly wondering what was going on. A few hundred yards down the beach, a drum circle beat into the night, and eventually, the curious lookers would be drawn away or lose interest. A cop rode a bike back and forth, slowly taking in the scene, but after deciding that there were no drugs—at least not hard ones—he, too, lost interest and disappeared to survey the drum circle.

The elders took no notice. They chanted and swayed back and forth, their wool skirts and wraps lifting in the fall wind.

"Oscail na geataí dúinn."

The gates weren't opening though. No matter how many nights they sat out here at the place where the Matrarc would lift the veil, it still would not rise for the old women. Alan had come along at his grandmother's request. Máthair Shona had sat level with him, locking her eyes on his.

"The power that lives in your sister lives in you as well," she had said. "Come and chant with us, ask for the forgiveness of the goddess, ask for the veil to lift for us, for the power of the Matrarc to be broken."

Alan considered the old woman's request.

"What you suggest is treason." He spoke carefully. The elders had never seen Ceit's full power, they had never seen her demon familiar devour a person whole, and they had never seen the darkness that she was capable of summoning. "If you had seen what I have seen, you would not speak so lightly of betraying your Matrarc. You might remember what came of your last efforts."

Still though, he had come. Conor had also accompanied them. He wore an aged wool cab cap and a moth-eaten wool jacket. He looked like he was an extra in a time traveler movie. Alan had stifled a laugh when he'd seen the man. Men were allowed to accompany the lifting of the veil only under the most dire of circumstances, but this was no true lifting of the veil; this was a mutiny, and one that was sure to fail. Only the Matrarc could lift the veil. These old women were conjuring no more than theatrics.

"Damn fools," Conor had muttered all the way here. Alan nodded in agreement.

"They are going to get themselves arrested if someone doesn't shoot them first," Conor proclaimed.

What Conor proposed to do about either scenario was a mystery to Alan, but still, it felt good to have someone else who knew what it was to be forever fated to be a spectator to the magick the women of the Society held to be true.

"Oscail na geataí dúinn," the group now wailed to the night sky.

Behind him, Alan heard two voices—more curiosity seekers.

"Holy shit. I know what this is," a female voice whispered excitedly.

"Classic Venice Beach. That's what it is," the other voice, male, replied.

"No, I mean yes, that's totally true, but this is—this is that cult group!" The female spoke low but with an intensity that made Alan cringe.

"I prefer the other cult, the one with drums—they have pot," the man whispered back.

"Shut up." She giggled. "No these guys are that group, you know that kid that disappeared a few years ago? That woman who died before that? Crazy shit."

"Is it now?" Conor's tenor rang across the beach. Even the old women stopped their chanting and stared in his direction. The couple let out frightened squeals of surprise, and Alan could hear their footsteps moving farther away.

"We're not a sideshow act here for your amusement," Conor hollered down the walkway at the couple. Alan was filled with an unexpected rush of gratitude for the older man's diligence. He had heard them and done nothing. The gawking, the stares—he had become numb to all of it.

Conor sat down on the wall and looked down at Alan.

"They were talking about you and your mum, you know," Conor barked as the old women, their chanting over for the night, began pulling themselves off the sand and slowly moving back to the walkway.

"It's you and your kin that made us a circus act, boy," Conor muttered. "You could at least tell them to shut the feck up when you hear the gossip."

With that, he stood and strode off among the old women who were now awkwardly ambling toward the cul-de-sac. Máthair Shona turned to give him a questioning look, and he waved her on.

Instead of following, Alan walked down to the water's edge. Staring out over the ocean, he reached out a hand and ran a single finger down the veil that hung invisible to the eye between this world and the next. He could feel it: a taut, pliable thing, but impossible to tear or pierce with a blade. No, it could be lifted only by the one who had the ancient blood of the Matrarc running through her veins.

And even then, it was not a surety. Máthair Shona was her mother's daughter and still locked out from the next world. Alan's mother was also denied the legacy of her birth. Only Ceit could do it, and she was set on dismantling the world that gave the old women a reason to exist. Alan closed his fingers and the veil slipped away into the night sky, taking on the consistency of the sea spray and cold wind. Ceit had never given a care to the chaos she left in her wake—as was typical. His father had known. Alan cringed as a shockingly cold wave lapped up over his sneakers, soaking the cloth material and socks underneath.

Alan gave one last glance to the ocean and turned back to catch up with the old women on their way back to Sinder Avenue. They were his home, and if they needed him to pierce the night veil, then he would find the way. Ceit was the Matrarc and entirely mortal. The next time the Sluagh were called, they would not miss their mark as they had so many years ago with his mother. No, this time, the Sluagh would find Ceit in an unfamiliar place—a state of uncertainty—and they would rip the flesh from her bones and feast on her damned soul. Alan paused in the doorway to the little house. It was time for the power of the Matrarc to be cast among all the people of the Society. No more sitting in the shadows for him and the other men. No more cowering and false reverence as the women gave his sister. No, end times would begin soon.

57

AINSLEY, 1925

AINSLEY WRAPPED HER ARMS AROUND HER KNEES, HER breathing ragged and shallow. Her entire body ached, and her head spun. A dark cloud of grief enveloped her, and there was no escape. Her arms tingled with the gravity of the loss, and her breasts ached, the milk spilling through the linen uniform dress. Ainsley opened her mouth, but instead of an animal wail rising from her gut, she emitted only a high-pitched hum—a dying siren, an empty shell. Anger, pain, hope, love, compassion, all these things were lost to her. Only hate and grief remained. She pulled into herself tighter so that she might disappear completely. But it didn't work, and she remained a ball of agony, lowly sobbing on the washroom floor.

The couple had entered the nursery with Sister Mary Claude and Sister Agnes. They were prim—neat leather shoes with a tiny heel and a stylish hat for the lady, a brown tweed suit with a gold striped tie for the man. He had a streak of silver in his dark hair, and she was younger, with golden hair neatly coiffed behind her neck. They had gone to the pram next to Ainsley, where Siobhan

Elizabeth lay gurgling and pulling at her toes. The infant looked up startled, her doll's mouth caught in a perfect O shape. Ainsley watched the couple melt instantly, and she filled with dread. They couldn't just take the baby; Niamh wasn't there and wouldn't be until the night. They had to tell her—they had to be stopped. Speechless, Ainsley watched the couple lift the little girl into the air and the woman cradle her to her chest. Oblivious, Ainsley's own daughter finished her meal and pulled away, fussing slightly.

Without taking her eyes off the couple holding Siobhan, Ainsley lifted her girl to her shoulder and gently patted her back. When the little burp emitted, the couple looked to her as though they had been entirely unaware that there had been anyone else in the room. Ainsley quickly covered up and stared at them wide-eyed, her heart pounding.

"Pardon this," Sister Agnes said hurriedly. "Mr. and Mrs. Quincy, this is one of our girls, Therese. She's been integral to boosting little Siobhan's health."

The couple nodded, and the man turned his head to Sister Mary Claude, asking her something or another.

"We don't normally take our prospective parents to this part of the home, but as it is Siobhan's feeding time, we thought you might not want to wait to meet her," Sister Agnes offered by way of apology. She was obviously flustered by the state of indecency the couple had walked in on. Ainsley couldn't care less if they saw her bare breast. This woman in her trim dress with her dainty hands that had never known a day's work couldn't feed Siobhan. The baby would wither and die in this woman's care.

"Why, they look as though they could be sisters," the woman murmured, and Ainsley felt a stab of panic in her chest.

"They're not," she snapped.

"Therese!" Sister Agnes cast her a warning look, and Ainsley knew her hands would be lashed at the very least when the couple finally left. "Pardon the girl—she's not in her right head."

Ainsley felt a wave of anger rising in her, and she opened her mouth to speak as Sister Agnes stepped in front of her. "Well, all right. Why don't we go spend some time with little Siobhan in the sitting room, and we'll talk further?" She turned to glare at Ainsley.

As the woman exited the nursery with Siobhan Elizabeth, the man shook his head and said to Sister Mary Claude, "That name, it's... not fitting."

Ainsley bit her tongue to not yell after them the words that rose in her mouth. She needed to get to Niamh and fast, and if she found herself in the discipline office, she would not be able to tell her that the baby was being taken.

"You can, of course, name her anything you please—a good Catholic name perhaps," Sister Mary Claude said lightly as they turned into the hall.

Ainsley dreaded leaving the infant, but she needed to tell Niamh. Placing her daughter carefully in the pram, she nodded at the novices and straightened her dress before walking calmly to the door. It wasn't until she was sure the nuns and the couple were out of sight that she bolted to the laundry where Niamh was working. All the girls looked up at Ainsley's entrance, but the nuns overseeing the room were mercifully distracted so Ainsley was able to scan the washtubs for Niamh.

"You've got to come—they're taking Siobhan," Ainsley whispered desperately. "They're in the sitting room. You've got to hurry."

Niamh's face paled by two shades, and she dropped the sheet she'd been scrubbing. She didn't say a word, but ran for the door.

"Margaret!" a nun at the end of the room yelled.

"She's ill—I'll check on her," Ainsley called back. The nuns cast her annoyed looks but went back to their business.

Ainsley found Niamh in the hall, standing stock still.

"I can't stop it—they won't stop it. I can't... can't..." Niamh murmured. "I just want to see her. I have to see her."

"Niamh, you—we have to try. Tell them she's sickly, tell them she's ill-tempered, say anything. Make them change their minds!" Ainsley whispered desperately as they hurried down the hall to the sitting room.

Niamh stopped and turned to Ainsley. "It's no use. I knew this would happen. I thought I'd lose her so many nights, I already mourned her, you see. I think I said goodbye every night I sat with her. I just want to say it one more time—I need to see her." She turned and crossed to the sitting room door. It was slightly ajar and Niamh thrust it open, but instead of commotion and drama, there was silence. Niamh turned to look at Ainsley, her face wrenched with confusion and grief.

"It's empty. They're gone, " she said softly.

Ainsley felt her spine grow cold and her head began to throb. Without saying a word, she turned and ran back down the hall to the nursery. She burst through the door to see the novice uneasily folding baby blankets. The pram where she'd left her daughter was empty. She stared at the novice, who looked up. Her expression was torn, her voice soft as she said, "They wanted twins, you see, but we have none. Your girl and Siobhan, well, they look to be sisters. They took both girls."

Ainsley felt the floor drop out from under her, and her body was caught in a spinning vortex. She didn't hear the words the novice said next, her eyes compassionate and apologetic. She didn't hear anything but the screaming cyclone that echoed in her ears.

Sitting on the floor now, she didn't know how she'd found her way to the washroom, or how long she'd been there—only that the day had fled and been replaced with the night. The world had gone black after she'd run to the window to see the long dark automobile pulling out the drive and Sister Mary Claude standing guard at the door. The screaming echo of her loss resounded in her ears. The world would never be quiet again, her soul would never be whole. She had sat so many nights with the solution right in her pocket, weighing God and universe and fae and right and wrong. She'd sat and tortured herself and asked impossible questions, and now the path was clear. She didn't give a damn about her soul— all she wanted was her daughter back. The existential shite she'd allowed to roll around in her head had robbed her of time, and now it was like to be too late.

A narrow beam of light shown down through the slit of a window high up the stone wall. The thin fabric ripped easily as Ainsley pulled the locket from its hiding place. Her heart felt heavy and dead as she opened the brass latch and caught the patch of errant moonlight in the silver reflection.

58

CEIT, 1996

THE MOON HUNG FULL IN THE SKY AS CEIT STOOD ON the shore overlooking the water that on the other side of the veil was the Pacific. Here it had no parentage, no name, no end. It wrapped the world entire and plunged to bottomless depths. The Asrai leaped out of the water, twisting and contorting their long tails, their bony and clawed arms reaching for the sky. They could smell the blood that was to come. Ceit was not sure where the blood would flow from, but the Asrai knew things that had yet to happen and were never wrong.

Ceit stood alone on the beach. She had not invited the old ones to the monthly lifting of the veil. They had cried and begged, and Ceit had closed the door on them. They were not worthy of this place; their treasonous thoughts were as easy to read as if they'd been written in a book. They were angry. Another razed patch of land stood in the cul-de-sac. The house where Katherine had lived was now a cleared lot of dust and debris. The giant trucks with their noise and chaos would arrive tomorrow to haul it away, leaving an empty space, a hole where her great-grandmother had bred the superstition and mindless tradition that ruled this place for far too long.

And another would be soon to follow. Ceit had seen in Meg's mind a plan: train tickets, a new city with skyscrapers and lights. She wanted Alan to follow her, and finally, Ceit saw she had been wrong. The girl wasn't holding Alan back; he was doing that on his own. Ceit had also seen that Meg would leave with or without him and soon, probably as soon as she graduated in a couple of weeks. An early exit from school, and an early start to a new life. Ceit felt a bit abashed that she had so misjudged the girl. Perhaps she was simple, but likely not, and the girl was able to dream bigger than Sinder Avenue. Her parents could be moved into Shona's back house then, and another step could be taken toward destroying this cursed place.

Ceit closed her eyes and sang the song that could, if she wanted it to, unveil the night forever. Tonight, however, all Ceit wanted was the noise and chaos of the Night Forest. She wanted to lose herself in the cacophony, the madness of the realm she had been born into this world to rule.

I sing of the fae and the wood and the vine,
And the night that lasts forever.
The ghosts of your loves and the ghosts that are mine,
Will linger there forever.

Let's call to the wind, to the sun, and the rain,
And the night that lasts forever.
Out beyond the veil is the blackest of nights,
Your soul gone to the nether.

The dead never sleep and the night never breaks,
You're alone until forever.
With teeth that can bite and the claws that will tear,
Your soul it will not weather.

The wind howled across the dark water, and the Asrai screamed in delight. A flock of bats sailed from the woods, skimming the surface of the water as a two-headed monstrosity that might have been a dolphin in the waking world swam in a slow loping pattern among the rabid Asrai that thrashed their tails and clawed at the water's surface. From the woods beyond the night ocean, Ceit could hear the storm of insect and bird, a scale-tailed monster reaching for the moonlight. It was revelation, a celebration that Ceit brought to them tonight. Soon she would be coming home— no longer would she treat this realm as a distraction. Alan would find his path, and soon she could shutter her ties to the waking world entirely.

59

AINSLEY, 1925

"I'VE WONDERED, DID I OFFEND? IS IT MY MANNER? I feel my interactions with your sort are so limited that I never know quite what to say or not to say."

Amon leaned against the washbasin. He was dressed in the exact brown tweed suit and gold striped tie that the man who had stolen her daughter had been wearing.

"I wait and wait. You seem to like this sort of incarceration, and who am I to judge? You go from allowing that half-wit to squirrel you away in the middle of the woods to allowing your father and the priest to lock you up here. Where will you be jailed next?" Amon smirked slightly and looked around the washroom. "I can see the allure. This is just so medieval, and that was a splendid era for my kind. Yours... not so much."

"Did I summon you here to mock me? You said you'd help!" Ainsley stood on unsteady legs, an anger growing in her gut that threatened to devour her whole.

Amon shot forward with unnatural grace so that he was inches from her face. Ainsley could smell ash and burning things.

"I need to know if you're ready to fight. I can do my part, but you will need to rally. I cannot set things right for you unless you are ready to allow yourself to be who you truly are, and that is not a pretty little girl from the countryside. You are dangerous and wicked and powerful beyond your imagining. You can be a savior for your people, or you can suckle orphaned babes until your breasts wither and your body dissolves to dust. It is your choice."

Ainsley closed her eyes and saw a vision of flames. Screams rang in her ears. She smelled her daughter's sweet baby scent of soap and milk, and she heard Maire's voice as she sang softly going on about her work. She saw the rolling waves of the Atlantic, and felt the motion beneath her feet. She opened her eyes.

"I'm ready," she said simply.

Amon smiled, his pointed teeth reflecting the moonlight.

"Well okay, asal dona. It's time to work."

60

ALAN, 1996

ALAN LEANED UP AGAINST THE CONCRETE WALL OF the drainage ditch where he had woken. The machete was strapped across his chest, under his jacket. Alan vaguely remembered being on the boardwalk several hours ago. He had taken a handful of pills. He hadn't been sure what they were, a gift from one of his suppliers, a bribe to get him back into the game. Alan had accepted the token, but he did not intend to go back to dealing. No, he expected he wouldn't last much longer. He had a plan, and there was no return to normal life involved.

Ceit would be on the beach. The moon was full, and it was the night when she led the old ones through the veil for their monthly chanting and wailing. She would be in bed by dawn; these nights drained her, and she slept like one already dead.

Alan rubbed his aching temples and stared up at the sky. The air smelled of standing water and rotting things. He saw his father's face on that last day, the day that Boyd Healy Robertson tried to set the world right. Alan hadn't known what his father's intentions had been on that day so long ago, but he did now. Now, Alan understood the method to his father's madness.

"But it didn't work out so well for Hamlet," a voice whispered in his ear.

Alan rocked back and forth. The pills had given him the shakes, and he felt as though he would vomit.

The little boy in the sky-blue pajamas and the others hadn't appeared in weeks. Alan had called to them, begged for them to reappear. They had a message for him; they alone could tell him what his destiny was in this place. They knew he had the same power to lift the veil that Ceit possessed. They knew that he could lead. They knew that the title of Matrarc had been won in blood and death, and it could be won back the same way. Ceit had told him that the visions were false, that they were being sent by the old ones. Alan had walked away from her that day with her words ringing in his head. Ellaine and Katherine telling him they knew of his dreams, his own grandmother nodding sympathetically. Ceit said they were using him, manipulating him.

"She's right. The boys are false," the voice hissed, snakelike. It seemed to reverberate from the center of Alan's head, echoing in both ears.

"Shut up! She's not! I saw them! I heard them!" Alan screamed to the night sky. Next to him a pile of rags moved and a dirty face appeared, disoriented and half-conscious.

"Chill, brother—you want the cops down here?" the figure grumbled.

Alan nodded, his hands shaking wildly.

"Hey, you got more of that?" The man lurched forward into a lumbering crawl. "You got more? I got this, I can trade ya." He pulled a filthy half-empty bottle of Jack Daniel's out of his coat. Even in the darkness, Alan could see things that had no business being there floating in the brown liquid. He felt a wave of nausea overcome him, and he vomited down the front of his jacket. The sour stink of it caused the man to immediately fall back.

"You gotta get it together man, you gotta pull it together. Hey, you got more? You got pills? Oxy? I have pain this doesn't touch." The man smiled, revealing a rotten, gapped mouth. Alan started to reply but then slammed back against the concrete in terror. From between the chipped and missing teeth, a snakelike tongue darted out and tested the air, then shot back into the foul depths. The man smiled, and his eyes caught the light from the streetlamp overhead. Alan swallowed a scream as the pupils glowed blood red. "I got pain brother. You have pain? Maybe we can help each other. You got more?"

The man's scratchy voice then morphed into a silky whisper. "I can take your pain, brother, just let me take your pain." The snake-like tongue darted out again, and the man clawed his way forward. His filthy hands were talons, his fingers razors.

Alan screamed and pulled at his jacket, reaching for the machete underneath. The first strike of the knife was met with resistance, the flesh unwilling to accept the blade. Alan raised the machete— the blade that had slaughtered a thousand Salvadoran women and children—over his head and brought it down again and again and again. Black-red blood sprayed upward. Finally the monster, the demon, the horror disguised as man stopped moving, stopped gasping, stopped fighting.

"I am but mad north-north-west," the disembodied voice hissed into Alan's ear.

Alan stood, wiping the gore off the blade onto the demon's rags. He looked to be a man again, face lined with age and the elements, his eyes open and staring. All demons looked to be man. Returning the machete to its sheath, Alan turned toward Sinder Avenue.

61

AINSLEY, 1925

THE GRAND FRONT DOORS OF THE BESSBOROUGH Mother and Baby Home blew open as though the locks had been made of sand. Amon stood to the side, a pleased look on his face.

"My lady," he said, gesturing to the door.

Ainsley hesitated. "The others... the other girls..."

"Are outside your control," Amon finished for her. "You summoned me to help you. Your child is part of your line and part of my deal. The other souls in this place are not our concern."

Ainsley felt a stab of guilt, but she knew he was right. She could not save the others, or their children. Sister Mary Claude burst from her office and stood in the hall, gaping at the open doors.

"Therese!" she barked. "What is the meaning of this?"

"Sister, if I may," Amon said from the shadows. Ainsley looked over to see him dressed in full vestments, gold crucifix around his neck, a rosary at his waist. Ainsley almost guffawed to see him, but he cast her a look.

"Sister forgive my dramatic entrance. I am the new clergy in service of Father Gerity. I need the girl to come with me." He spoke in a silky, seductive voice, totally incongruous with his look. Sister Mary Claude's face was growing red and patchy. She was as angry as Ainsley had ever seen.

"Father, it is utterly inappropriate for you to be here, and you cannot take the girl. She is in service here at the home. Therese, you are to go back to your quarters immediately." Sister Mary Claude spit as she talked, the outrageousness of Amon's request overwhelming her.

Amon looked at Ainsley. "I asked nicely—it's all I can do." With that, he reached one pale hand toward the nun, his palm facing her as though he were pushing her back. Sister Mary Claude cast him a furious look and started toward the doors. With one swift motion, she was lifted a foot in the air and thrown back to the far wall. She landed with a sickening crunch and lay still. Ainsley stared at the motionless form and then at Amon, who was already heading for the door.

"Well?" he asked in an impatient tone.

"She's..." Ainsley stared at the thin trickle of blood that escaped from under her robes.

"Dead? Maybe. If not, she's taken quite a spill. She's not your concern. Come." Amon strode through the open doors, and Ainsley followed on unsteady legs. The winter air was biting, and she had no coat. The thin material of the uniform dress gave little protection. She shivered in the midnight air.

"All right, next the child. They're on a train on their way to Dublin as we speak. Your daughter, who they're planning on naming Bernadette"—Amon shuddered—"I hope you have a better idea, silly girl and your no-name baby... I digress. They are on the rails as we speak." Amon looked up at the sky and then reached his hands to the stars. He muttered something that sounded like a chant, and the ground started trembling.

"Canaim na fae agus an t-adhmad agus an fíniúna."

A stone cross that hung over the home's gaping entry fell and shattered as though it were made of glass.

"Agus an oíche a mhaireann go deo," Amon intoned.

The deamhain looked back at Ainsley and lowered his hands.

"That should do it," he said briskly. "Come, no time to waste." He trotted toward the convent's long black automobile. Behind them, a rising chaos was starting to manifest. A scream that indicated Sister Mary Claude's body had been found rose like a high-pitched siren. Ainsley ran after Amon, knowing that more would surely die if anyone were to try to stop them. The deamhain had little regard for human life, and he was impatient. The car started without a key and the deamhain drove faster than Ainsley imagined the automobile could naturally travel as they barreled out the winding drive and away from the stone prison.

Ainsley held her breath, her fingers grasping the leather seat beneath her.

"It's your first automobile?" Amon asked. His tone was such that they might be heading off to a summer picnic. Ainsley nodded.

"What was that you said back there? What did it mean?" Ainsley asked. "Where are we going now?"

"So many questions. You have to trust me. The words I spoke back there are words you know, although you may not know the old language. What is the song you all sing in your Society?" Amon looked over at her as the automobile seemingly drove itself.

"I sing of the fae and the wood and the vine, and the night that lasts forever. The ghosts of your loves and the ghosts that are mine, will linger there forever." Ainsley spoke the words in the same cadence Amon had. The deamhain nodded, grinning with sharpened teeth.

"Yes, that's the one. You will learn the true power of that rhyme. If you learn to channel your strength through it, you can accomplish great things."

"Is that what you did?" Ainsley asked, her whole body shaking with cold.

"I stopped your child's travels. Now we must go fetch her," Amon said simply. "You can close your eyes if you wish. I can travel through time without such archaic contraptions, but you cannot, and I rather need you with me, don't I? Still, I can cheat a bit—we'll be there in no time." The deamhain winked and turned back to stare straight ahead. The trees and dark woods were passing faster and faster, and Ainsley felt dizzy.

"What if they see us?" she asked, feeling unconsciousness overtaking her.

"They won't," Amon said as the world went dark.

62

CEIT, 1996

CEIT LEANED WEARILY AGAINST THE FRONT WALKWAY of her little bungalow on Sinder Avenue. The sun would be up soon, and the sky was already lightening. These nights drained her but not in the way she expected. It was no effort to lift the veil, and the Night Forest soothed rather than aggravated. The exhaustion came with returning to this space. Ceit was becoming increasingly intolerant of the weight of this plane, the emotions and thoughts that constantly swirled and became easier to read with every passing year. When she was a child, she had only intermittently been able to clearly read the thoughts of others. Now one had to maintain a powerful veil over their minds to keep her from seeing and hearing every ill intent, every fear, every hope, every passing idea.

The time was coming. It may be years off, but the day was coming when this cul-de-sac would be razed to the ground and the Society would be but a memory. Ceit could wait years if she knew the ending would be complete; she had already waited this long. A black cloud hung in the corner of her mind. Alan. He was more powerful than he gave himself credit for. The wall he had built around his mind had been strong and impenetrable until recently. Ceit caught bits and pieces—images, words, fears, but mostly a great and terrible void, a blackness where a little boy had once existed. Alan hadn't been home for several days. Meg had even come asking about him, but Ceit had no answer. She felt the cold of the night air and suspected he was sleeping on the streets. She felt a numbness that replaced hunger and thirst and knew he was filling his body with the pills and weed he kept under the house. His eyes were dull and unseeing. He refused to listen to the truth of the visions he had been sent. And why should he? Ceit stretched her arms to the sky and rolled her stiff neck. He wanted to believe that he was the chosen one, that he was special. All creatures of this world wanted that; to tell them otherwise was inhumane.

"Your mother had ideas about leaving this place," a voice from behind Ceit said softly. Ceit turned to see Máthair Shona in her nightgown and robe, her feet bare.

"Hello, Shona," Ceit said simply.

"The years you were gone—after my mother died, after whatever became of my Grace—all those years, we were denied the lifting of the veil during the full moon." Shona crossed to sit on the front step of Ceit's home, staring at the empty space that used to be a house across the way.

"You're leaving out the bit where you refused my care and tried to exile me," Ceit said, sitting next to her. The old woman smelled of cinnamon and freshly baked bread. It was a welcome change from the mildew stench that had clung to her for weeks now. Ceit regarded her curiously—she had bathed, her hair was neatly tied back, and her face was haggard but her eyes were clear. Her thoughts were full of memories of Ceit's mother, Grace, her hair loose and catching the sunlight, a little girl twirling in circles on the sidewalk, laughing.

Shona turned to look directly at Ceit. "For all you know, there's much you do not."

"The rot you've been feeding Alan? My great-great-grandfather, the Ceannaire? I know well of him. He beat his wife and daughters, your mother. He locked Mór Ainsley in a mother and baby home. He was a wicked man, and he was ultimately powerless. He could not lift the veil or call the fae—he ruled the Society with fear." Ceit met Shona's eyes and waited for a reply.

"He was all those things, it's true," Shona said, her light eyes catching the rising sun. "But he wasn't powerless. Neither is your brother. You have my grandfather's wickedness in you—I saw it when you were first born. You may not have killed or beaten, but you have the same capacity for cruelty that he did. My mother did too. Perhaps I do as well. We are a cursed line. Only my sweet Grace escaped that dark pit of a soul that was born back in Cork. My mother told me when I was a little girl that she had had to make a deal to leave Ireland, that one of our line would be the Ceathrar Marcach, the bringer of end times. You are olc. You are legion."

"Very Christian of you, Shona. I thought we were more enlightened than that. There is no devil or god. There is nothing neither good or bad, but thinking makes it so. Shakespeare even knew that. I am not legion. I am the Bandia Marbh, and my time in this plane is coming to a close. My last task is to make sure that Alan is settled and free of this place. He deserves that. When you rejected me, you also denied him. He was as sweet a child as my mother, your Grace. You thrust him out on his own, you allowed my father to pollute him, you tore his mind and heart in two. You talk of devils and horsemen and the apocalypse, but you are the evil that was born in Ireland. Mór Ainsley told me stories, too, and I know the cost at which you came—the blood that was spilled to save you." Ceit stood and turned abruptly; the old woman's smell of rot had returned, and Ceit was weary.

Shona shot to her feet. She swayed slightly, holding on to the handrail. "Leave us be. Let Alan be the Ceannaire like his great-great-grandfather was. He is kind and smart. He will take care of us. You can go wherever you like, but leave us be."

Ceit spun on her heels, locking eyes with the old woman. "The time for the Society is past. It should never have left Cork. It breeds superstition and fear. My father was driven mad by it, and it opened the doors to allow the Sluagh to kill Mór Ainsley and my mother. It's rotten and dangerous. The sooner you all die off and these houses demolished, the better."

Shona laughed, a manic cackling sound. "You think the Society can be destroyed that easily? Wait until we die? Build a mall? You are many things, girl, but you are foolish to the core. You think my mother, your great-grandmother, didn't try to leave the Society in Cork? She paid the highest price trying to raze this place to the ground. She knew you were the Ceathrar Marcach, the darkness that was promised. She knew the deal she had made, and I know I was not worth the price!" Shona's voice rose to a fever pitch, and lights began popping on in the houses down the way. Always listening, always waiting—the old ones heard everything.

"What are you saying, old woman?" Ceit hissed. "You are speaking in riddles. You came out here to tell me something, so out with it."

"You are the reason my Grace is dead. You are the reason my mother is gone. The Sluagh were sent after you, but you were too strong for them even as a child, so they attacked my Grace, my sweet girl, and they ate her alive." Shona clung to the railing, her face pale and her eyes wild. Figures appeared on the doorstep of Ellaine's house.

"Who sent the Sluagh after me? Was it you, Grandmother? Did you manage to conjure the Sluagh and call the Rabharta the same way you and yours summoned the vision of a little dead boy? What did you do!" Ceit roared down, the entire house shaking. The front window shattered outward, glass spraying the lawn.

Shona fell backward, her high manic laugh coming out in choked sobs. "Me? No, you little fool. I did nothing to harm my daughter. I do not have that power, never have. It was Mór Ainsley who knew you needed to die. She knew you were the reason our line was cursed, you were the deamhain my mother spoke of that haunted us. You are the beginning of the end of creation, and she knew you needed to be destroyed."

The house rocked back and forth on its foundation, but Ceit stood firm. She raised her arms over her head and a rain of hail and rock began to fall from the sky. "You lie, old woman. Mór Ainsley has spoken to me from the next world. She was my guide as I escaped the prison you tried to lock me in."

"Little idiot," Shona spat from the ground, her hands covering her head, trying to protect herself from the pelting rain of ice and rock. "The same demon that seduced my mother has been whispering in your ear since you were born. It will tell you anything to keep you loyal. I may not have the powers that you inherited from the old country, but my eyes are open, which is more than I can say for you."

The rain abruptly stopped, and Ceit tried to control her breath. All across the cul-de-sac, lights were on and figures looked from windows or stood on their front steps.

"I will end this place. I am patient. I will wait until every last soul that claims allegiance to the Society is dead or scattered in the wind. You will never see the lifting of the veil again. You will never stand on the beach as the tide rolls in on the night ocean. The time for this place is over."

Ceit turned and strode back into the house, slamming the door behind her. The house was in chaos, broken lamps and overturned chairs. Ceit did not see any of it. The old woman's words rang in her ears. Amon—had it always been Amon? The visits from Mór Ainsley when she'd been locked in MacLaren Hall, when she'd been hidden in Canyon de Chelly? Was she so trusting that she never looked further than what she wanted to believe? Ceit emitted a dark laugh. Perhaps she was not so different from Alan. They both needed to believe they were more than what they were. She held the bronze locket that Amon had given her so long ago in her hand, opened the tiny latch, and caught the dawning sun in the silver reflection.

63

AINSLEY, 1925

THE AUTOMOBILE FLEW INTO THE DAWN, AND BY THE time Ainsley awoke, they were on a paved road and the rising sun was a blur. The horror of what Amon had done at the convent was beginning to settle in. Sister Mary Claude's crumpled form flashed in front of her eyes. Ainsley shivered and wrapped her arms around herself.

"Good morning, little one," Amon said from the driver's seat. "We'll be at our destination any moment—we made exceptional time thanks to a little preternatural boost. I have to say, it's downright primitive the way you creatures operate."

"Sister Mary Claude..." Ainsley said softly.

"Is likely dead. Would you like to send some flowers? A card perhaps? You wanted away from that place, and she was in our way. I have no time for it. You need to let go of this notion that all life is precious. The bulk of it is far from precious, and even that worth salvaging isn't all your philosophy claims it to be. You kill goats and sheep and whatnot in your little shitepile of a village, yes?" Amon cast her a sidelong gaze.

Ainsley nodded. Her entire body was numb.

"Those creatures have parents and children. They feel pain and fear. They mourn the passing of those you murder. Do you carry that weight?" Amon asked, not even pretending to watch the road, the automobile guiding itself.

Ainsley felt a rush of outrage. "That's not the same thing at all. Those are animals... We—"

"Have established dominion over them? They serve you, they feed you, they are nothing but a tool to you. You need to understand, little one, that with very little exception, all of mankind is your goats. You and your line have dominion over them, and one day the one will arrive who will rule us all. So allow yourself to release useless emotions—you do not need to feel regret, remorse. You've heard the saying 'the lion does not concern himself with the opinions of the sheep'? Well, you are the lion, my dear, and far more dangerous than you know. You want your daughter back, yes?" Amon glanced back at the road and swerved the automobile suddenly and expertly, avoiding a dark blur that could only have been another traveler.

Ainsley nodded. "But how do we get her from the adoptive parents? They took her and Siobhan—"

"The others do not concern me. I am here to retrieve your daughter, who you'd best name before I do. I have one in mind, but you won't like it." He grinned and his milk-pale face seemed to split in two—two rows of sharpened teeth catching the dawn.

"What did you do to stop them?" Ainsley asked suddenly, her spine growing cold.

"They were on a train, it needed to be stopped. This thing on wheels we're in will move only so fast, even with my help. Much farther and they'd have been inconveniently far away. Much more work." Amon looked back at the road. "We're just arriving upon it right now. Ready to see your child?"

Ainsley looked ahead. There was a mass of stopped automobiles and people out in the heath all looking toward a spectacle of some sort off in the distance. Women were holding their hands to their mouths, looks of shock on their faces. Amon stopped the automobile on the heath with the others and got out.

"Coming? We're on foot for a bit." He started walking. Ainsley jumped out and followed after him. The others gathered at the side of the road did not seem to see them at all. Ainsley had no idea what she was looking at—up ahead, a mass of twisted metal, incongruent parts, smoke, and the smell of burn, coal, and something else that made the hackles rise on the back of Ainsley's neck.

"What did you do?" she asked, stopping in the heath, staring in horror at the growing realization of what the words Amon had spoken at the convent had meant.

Amon turned. "I stopped their progress. Come, lion, let's not get too sentimental about the sheep." He turned and seemed to glide rather than walk through the rough grass and weeds. The passenger train that had been carrying her daughter, Siobhan, and the prim couple was in pieces, derailed and destroyed.

"You killed her," Ainsley whispered in horror. "You killed my baby."

Amon turned and glared. "Give me some credit. There was one survivor, a miracle really." The rail workers and men and women in white jackets with red crosses swarmed the scene. None saw Ainsley or the deamhain. Ainsley stumbled into the wreckage, her heart broken—little Siobhan, all these innocent people. She looked down and saw what was left of a young woman's face; her chin had been torn away and her eyes were dead marbles, staring to the sky. Ainsley felt vomit in her throat, and she stifled a scream.

"Here we are," Amon called from a distance. Ainsley blindly followed him, people around her shouting commands, pulling bodies from the wreckage. Amon stood over a pile of what looked to have been leather train seats. Underneath the wreckage, a soft whimpering could be heard. Ainsley immediately lunged at the debris, pulling away fabric and metal. The flesh on her hands ripped and her blood mixed with that which stained what had been a first-class travel car. Finally she saw a pale pink hand. It was smeared with dirt and grease, but it was opening and closing, grasping for the surface. As Ainsley pulled the last piece of twisted black metal away and revealed her daughter's face, the tiny creature blinked at the sun overhead and started to wail. Ainsley pulled the child into her arms; her heart was racing, and she realized her face was wet with tears. The child seemed untouched, which was, quite frankly, impossible, given the extent of damage that surrounded her. Ainsley inspected every inch of her child—no scratches, nothing but a bit of grime. The child wrapped her hand around Ainsley's hair and gurgled.

"Where's Siobhan? Where's the other baby?" Ainsley demanded. Amon stood to the side, watching impassively.

"You don't want to find her, little lion, trust me. The train derailed, worst accident in the history of the passenger line to date. With the exception of a few poor souls who were in the very rear car, there were no survivors. I'm sad to say those unfortunates will pass soon enough from their injuries. Grievous harm." He looked around and then started walking back to the car. "Come, we're done here."

Ainsley clutched her child to her chest. All these people… Niamh's tiny, perfect miracle baby. She had only been comforted by knowing Siobhan was going to a home where she'd be cared for. This was Ainsley's doing; this was her fault.

"Fault, blame, cause." Amon turned and cast her an impatient look. "How do you know this accident wasn't going to happen without my interference? Trains derail, accidents occur. Perhaps I just saved the child. Maybe I slowed the train, or delayed their departure so the crash would happen here, but that does not mean it would not have happened."

"Is that true?" Ainsley whispered, her voice thick with horror. "It was going to happen anyway?"

Amon walked back to her and held out a hand. "Come, we need to leave this place. I can mask us for a time, but eventually our presence will be known. And you have other business to attend to." Ainsley took his hand, unnaturally smooth and cold as ice, and stood on shaking legs. Her daughter cooed quietly and pawed at her face.

"We all die, little one. All these souls would die one day, maybe today. Maybe just twenty miles up the line, maybe in their sleep. Maybe they'd step out in front of an automobile, maybe their heart would burst while they ate their dinner. You can feel guilty, or you can accept that nothing is given without a price. This child"—he pointed at the baby with distaste—"will forever wonder if she was worth the price that was paid for her retrieval. Even if you never tell her, she will have a nagging memory of this day and will forever feel unworthy. Nothing to be done about it. We all carry a weight. You will need to accept that this mediocre child is but a cog in the machine, a tool toward a greater reward. You will never forget what you have seen and have yet to see today. You will always question if you should have thrown my locket into the jacks or if you are worth the sacrifice."

Ainsley shook her head and started walking back to the street. She couldn't stay here in the midst of the smell of burning flesh and metal. It couldn't be, it wasn't true. The deamhain spoke in riddles, half-truths. Would the train have derailed anyhow, taking her daughter with it when it did? Was Amon's only interference to shield her daughter? Or was it a lie he told to keep her sane?

As she approached the automobile, Amon stood next to it, holding the passenger door open. The crowd had grown, and still no one appeared to see them. A bucket brigade had arrived, and the trucks were lumbering their way across the heath to what was left of the train.

"Come. It's time to go home. It's time to take your seat as Matrarc of your people. You will not need my help for much longer. I feel you coming into your own already, little lion." Amon nodded at the car. Ainsley sat and pulled the door shut. As much as she loathed to take any more help from the deamhain, her little sister was waiting for her, her mother. The women of the Society needed to be freed from their Ceannaire.

The automobile flew past the crowd; no one looked back. Ainsley held her child to her breast and softly sang in her ear.

I sing of the fae and the wood and the vine,
And the night that lasts forever.
The ghosts of your loves and the ghosts that are mine,
Will linger there forever.

64

ALAN, 1996

ALAN WOKE WITH A POUNDING IN HIS HEAD, AND HIS hands felt entirely numb. His face was pressed up against cold steel, and he was laying on some sort of metal surface. The air smelled of urine and unwashed bodies. Alan opened his eyes to see another pair inches from his face.

"Ha ha! He's awake! Ha ha!" the figure yelped. The breath that emitted was beyond foul; it stank of dead things.

"Cool it, Charlie," another, more authoritative voice called from a distance. The sound of footsteps followed. "Good morning, sleeping beauty."

Alan looked around at white clinical walls and the flimsy curtain that separated the tiny nook he was in from a noisy and chaotic hallway. A light bright as the sun shown in one eye and then the other.

"Sorry about that. Can you sit up?" the voice that was presumably not Charlie asked briskly.

Alan tried to rise, but his head felt as though it were on fire. Painfully, he pushed himself up and saw he was on a metal cot in an examination room. With a groan, he recognized the ER where he had been not so long ago. The man who he guessed to be Charlie had an unkempt if recently cleaned beard halfway down his chest, and he wore a set of green scrubs. He sat on his hands on a cot on the other side of the room.

"Sleeping beauty, sleeping beauty, sleeping beauty! Ha ha!" Charlie screamed and bounced up and down.

"Charlie, goddamn it, shut up."

Alan turned to see a forty-something man with tired rings under his eyes and a stethoscope around his neck. "I'm Dr. Evans. That's Charlie. Ignore him. Busy night means you get a roommate. Can you tell us your name? The police brought you in, no ID. You've been given IV fluids, and we patched a few scrapes. You tested positive for opioids, which is what is making you feel so awesome now."

Alan had an aching memory of the previous night—he had done something, a voice in his ear, a demon. "The police... what happened?" he whispered, fearing the answer.

Dr. Evans looked at a chart at the foot of the cot. "You were found naked on the beach. A nice citizen called 911 so you wouldn't get pulled out with the tide. Any memory how you ended up there?"

Alan shook his head.

"Well, no matter. You didn't have any ID. We can keep you here long enough to get you some breakfast, and you can call someone to come get you. Do you have someone to call? If not, we can get you a bed at the shelter downtown. We have cab vouchers." Dr. Evans looked at Alan, and his expression softened a bit. "You can't be more than eighteen. Your folks know where you are?"

"My folks are dead. I live with my sister," Alan said. His mind and body felt empty and drained.

"Well, I'm real sorry to hear that. Let's call your sister, shall we? I can get you some help, outreach programs—opioids will melt your brain by the time you're twenty if you let them." Dr. Evans nodded. "I'll have a nurse bring you a breakfast tray."

"And me!" Charlie screamed.

"And you," Dr. Evans said without looking back as he exited out the curtain.

Alan lay back on the cot. A nurse brought two trays of flavorless food and a cup of strong coffee.

Charlie ate with vigor and then stared at Alan's untouched food.

"Go ahead," Alan said, indicating the tray. Charlie jumped up and grabbed the food, greedily shoveling it into his mouth. In between bites he looked up at Alan.

"You got more?" he asked, and Alan was thrown back to a foggy memory—the Venice canals, an old man, the air smelling of vomit and blood. He jumped and slammed against the wall.

"More food, more food, more food, more food," Charlie sang as he chewed a dry piece of toast, bits of barely chewed bread spraying the room. Alan shook his head in horror, as Charlie laughed.

"Okay, Charlie. You are out of here. Let's get you back to the home, all right?" A nurse entered the space and moved the tray out of Charlie's grasp. The man grinned and looked to Alan.

"Somebody told me they thought he killed a man once. I was the only one actually invited to the party, I was!" Charlie squealed and swayed back and forth.

"Okay, Charlie, let's go." The nurse looked back at Alan's shocked and pale face. "Don't mind Charlie—he's a little crazy, but harmless. Aren't you, Charlie?"

Charlie pulled away from the nurse and stared at Alan. His erratic and constantly moving eyes locking on Alan for a long moment. "The eyes of T. J. Eckleburg see all. You can't hide in the valley of ashes."

Alan shook his head. The too-bright lights overhead were pulsing, and cot felt as though it were spinning. "What—who are you?"

"That's enough, Charlie." The nurse pulled him out of the examination room.

Alan closed his eyes and tried to remember what the pills had blurred. In his head, a silky hiss resounded in his ears, and he knew he was damned.

65

AINSLEY, 1925

AS THEY FLEW DOWN THE PAVED ROAD INTO CORK, Ainsley cradled her daughter and tried to block out Siobhan's face. She tried to forget Niamh's lost expression as she stood in the hallway at Bessborough. She, alone, was responsible for the child's death, no matter what the deamhain said. Ainsley knew the price that she had paid for calling Amon and accepting his deal. She had no choice now but to follow through, collect Maire and her mother, and leave this place forever. She couldn't leave them in her father's house. Ainsley knew she would spend the rest of her life atoning for the choice she had made.

The automobile screeched to a stop, and Ainsley lurched forward, clinging to the child. She glared at Amon, who did not wait for a response and had already opened the door. He stared up at the sun, which sat at midmorning, a weak light that brought no heat to the frigid day. It would snow soon; Ainsley could smell frost in the air. Around her, people bustled to and fro going on about their business.

"Can they see us?" Ainsley asked hesitantly as she climbed out of the automobile. She still had only the thin linen dress from the convent, and the cold air cut deeply.

"It's not so much a question of seeing as it is remembering they saw you." Amon started walking toward the dirt road, too narrow for anything larger than a horse and carriage, that led out of town and wound around to the River Lee and the grassy hill where the Society waited. Ainsley scurried after him. "They might acknowledge you in a moment, but we are like a passing shadow, nothing they can put their fingers on or be sure they saw. You are like a memory."

Ainsley trudged after him. She had walked this road many times but never with an infant and never without a proper coat. She was shivering uncontrollably when Amon finally turned around to stare at her.

"Fragile little creatures aren't you," he stated impassively. "Here." He flicked his hand slightly, and Ainsley instantly felt warmer. Though no coat appeared and the weather had not turned, she felt insulated nonetheless. The baby quieted as well, and Ainsley found it tolerable to keep putting one foot in front of the other. As they marched to the hill where the cottages of the Society dotted the landscape, Ainsley looked down at her child. *She need never know*, she thought fiercely. The child need never know what had to happen to bring her here.

"What happens after this?" Ainsley asked.

Amon looked back but did not stop walking. "That's quite up to you. I have ideas, but you are perfectly capable of taking care of yourself—as soon as you allow yourself to acknowledge your skills." He stopped, and Ainsley was grateful. The walk was long and largely uphill; between the scant meals she had eaten and her overall exhaustion, she felt as though she might faint. Plus her daughter was fussing, and her swollen breasts told her the infant needed a breakfast herself.

"I need to rest, and the little one needs to feed." Ainsley sat on a tree root a few feet off the road just in case anyone decided she was more recognizable than just a memory. As the child suckled, Amon looked on with a look that was part disgust and part wonder.

"You are strange creatures—so like an animal and so far from the gods," he murmured, although his voice was not unkind.

Ainsley looked up. "What do you mean 'skills'?"

Amon crouched before her so he was eye level. "You need never bow to another again. You need never cower. You have been a victim in your life, and you have been in need of rescuing. You need to decide when you are tired of your life being decided by lesser mortals. Remember, little lion, you need never concern yourself with the sheep again." He looked around him and nodded to the last clinging leaves on an elm tree. "Can you make them drop? Think of your intent, let them go… Know your dominion over them."

Ainsley adjusted her daughter, who was already starting to nod off, and then stared at the dead leaves, hanging on by just the thinnest bit of sinew. She stared and stared.

"You're trying far too hard. Just let them fall. Pull them into your mind, and let them go," Amon whispered.

Ainsley closed her eyes and centered herself. When she looked again, she imagined the leaves going in and out of focus. A sharp pain penetrated her eye, and she winced. The leaves floated gently to the ground with the winter breeze. Amon smiled, his thin lips becoming nearly invisible.

"That's a start," he said quietly. "You cannot force anything to happen that is not already in existence. You can only work with what is before you. Feel the hum of the leaf or stone or drop of water, allow yourself to move through it, not upon it." Amon looked at the sky. "Time to keep walking."

As they trudged up the dirt road, ever closer to Ainsley's home, she caught sight of the old woods and knew they were near. "Amon," she said quietly, and he glanced back. "The púca appeared to me when I was trapped in the cabin. It helped me escape Bryan, and it would have killed my father and his men. But I sent it away. I rejected it."

Amon chuckled. "If there's a more sensitive creature than you mortals, it is a púca. You may have wounded its feelings, but it will return to you. All the fae and forest creatures are under your dominion. You have yet to know how to call them to action, but they hold allegiance to you. There is one in your line, many years from now, who will hold dominion entire over their realm, and they recognize your noble blood. All you need do is summon the púca. It will return. It appeared as a horse?"

Ainsley nodded, a bit surprised. "How did you—"

"Drama. The púca is nothing if not dramatic. A giant black horse is quite the showstopper." Amon paused. "Here we are."

Ainsley looked up the swell of the hill and saw the edge of the little cottage where she had lived her entire life. Relief was overwhelmed with another emotion though—the place stunk of rot and death. She could see it almost dripping off the eaves. The air that was normally sweet with elder and dog rose was thick with the stink of decayed flesh. Amon wrinkled his nose. Ainsley did not wait but instead bolted up the hill, clutching her child to her chest. As she approached she heard the keening wail of the Caoine. With horror, she realized Father Gerity was sitting in a wooden chair outside the door to her cottage. A younger priest was nearby, fidgeting nervously.

"Well, what is this, what is this?" Father Gerity muttered, struggling to stand.

Ainsley looked around wildly. "Who has passed? Why are they singing the Caoine?"

"What are you doing away from the home, child? What sorcery is this?" The priest's face was flushed, and the younger priest rushed to assist him.

"Amon!" Ainsley called, and the deamhain was instantly by her side.

The priest shrank back, falling over the chair. He crossed himself and muttered in Latin.

"Auferetur daemonium diis placet legione venit..."

"May I?" Amon was practically salivating.

"Not yet. I need to know who they are mourning." Ainsley glared at the priest, and the chair he had been sitting in flew back into the side of the house, slamming against the stone frame.

"That's the way," Amon whispered, never taking his eyes of no particular color off the terrified priests.

Ainsley held her child in one arm and pushed the door to the cottage open with the other. A cloud of blowflies swarmed out the open space, and Ainsley shielded her child's face in the folds of her dress. The stench was unbearable. They were on the last day of the Caoine, which meant the women of the Society had been wailing to the fae for seven days and nights already. The men would not be far away; her father, their Ceannaire, would be hosted in another's cottage, away from the reality of death, away from the rot and decay. Ainsley's skin was cold despite the layer of warmth Amon had shielded her with. The infant stared up at her with her pale-blue eyes, frightened and curious. All Ainsley could imagine was her mother's face—how had she passed? Had her father finally beaten her to death? Had she fallen ill? She could be cold and nearly as cruel as her father, but there were times when they were left alone that she had been allowed to soften her gaze, tend to their scrapes and bruises, listen to their stories. Ainsley could hear her mother singing baby Maire to sleep, her voice tender and soft. Her mother had been a good woman, and away from this place she could have been again. A collective gasp and barks of complaint rose from the room. It was dark inside, and Ainsley's eyes were bright from the daylight. She could see nothing save what appeared to be a thousand lit candles.

"Máthair!" she cried.

"Ainsley? Oh God, Ainsley!" A voice from the back of the room rose above the din. Her mother shoved through the crowd and clung to Ainsley's shoulders. She looked down at the infant, her face clouded in confusion. "How?"

Ainsley felt as though she had been carved from ice. "Who passed, Mother?"

Her mother started quietly weeping. "She had a fever, and I thought it had broken. We treated her with elm bark and apple vinegar. I thought she was recovered entirely. I wanted to take her to town, to the doctor, but your father... he said it was in the hands of the fae. We left the offerings, but it took her in the end. I prayed to the fae, I..."

Ainsley felt the world turn to a blur around her. "Why is the priest here, Mother?"

"The Father... he has come to collect the body. It is a sin, he says, to bury ours here in the heath. Your father—"

Ainsley waved a hand and silenced her. She knew exactly what had happened. Her sweet, soft sister with her dancing eyes and the curls in her hair was dead. No one summoned a doctor, no one took her to town to the hospital. They let her die, and her father had called the priest so that Maire would not even be buried with her people, in her homeland. She would be in a cold grave, a potter's field for the unbaptized, perhaps surrounded by the bones of the infants and unwed mothers that had not survived Bessborough. The world around her screamed past in a torrent of pain, but Ainsley steadied herself—she could not mourn, not yet.

"No," Ainsley said softly. "No. She will be buried on our land. The priest is leaving."

Ainsley turned to the old man, who was on his feet again and murmuring Latin nothings while the younger priest supported his weight. She stared at him, thinking of leaves falling from the tree and the chair slamming back against the stone. She imagined Father Gerity on the day she was torn from her sister's arms and taken to Bessborough. She imagined the priest's watery eyes as he left trails of saliva on her mother's best china teacups. She heard his voice as he muttered to her father that she was spoiled, ruined, and damned. She felt the wretched brush of his paper-thin fingers as he clasped her wrist. She saw Sister Mary Claude, broken and left in a heap of vestments and crucifixes on the floor of Bessborough. She could have saved Maire—she could have saved her from the superstition and the fear. Maire would be running from the barn now if it weren't for the old man and his dead god. She pushed with her mind, the infant in her arms becoming increasingly agitated, until she let loose with a wail that matched the Caoine.

Behind her, the great black muzzle of the púca snuffed at Ainsley's neck. She turned and leaned her forehead against the chest of the beast. The baby in her arms wailed and clung to her chest. Ainsley looked up and could just see the monster's eyes, shining black coals that descended forever. She nodded.

"Scrios iad," she whispered.

With a bleating scream, the púca tore past Ainsley. Her mother jumped out of the way as the great black horse, whose head nearly reached the height of the cottage, charged the two priests. The younger of the two ran for the woods. Father Gerity stood on shaking legs. He held up his gold crucifix.

"Salvum me ac tenebras!" he shouted as the púca, the nightmare horse of the old world, trampled and tore. The women had all run from the cottage and past the grisly sight. The púca reached down and, with its great teeth, tore flesh from bone.

The child in her arms screamed hysterically, and her mother fell to the ground unconscious. Ainsley stared at the horror and understood for the first time what she was. She was a creature of the old darkness. Softly she sang into her daugher's ear.

Let's call to the wind, to the sun, and the rain,
And the night that lasts forever.
Out beyond the veil is the blackest of nights,
Your soul gone to the nether.

The sound of thundering footfall turned her head. Her father—Rory Robertson, Ceannaire of the Society—raced toward her, his face red and patchy, his eyes full of fire.

"Cailleach dhochreidte!" he roared.

"Hello, Father," Ainsley said softly. All fear of the man she had loathed her entire life was gone; only hatred and anger remained. But for him, his jealousy, his rage, his violence, but for his black soul, Maire would be alive and Siobhan Elizabeth would not be lying cold under the twisted wreckage of the train. But for, but for, but for.

"You know what needs to be done, little lion," Amon whispered in her ear, and Ainsley stared into her father's eyes. The púca paused at the gristle and bone that had mixed with the earth beneath its hooves. Her father stared up at the monster, and a look of deep fear washed over his face.

"Ordaím thú," he said with a shaking voice.

"You are no longer Ceannaire of these people, Father," Ainsley said quietly. "The fae and forest creatures do not heed your commands. They never did, and you know this. You cannot lift the veil. The fae and forest hold allegiance to a new Ceannaire."

Summoning an ancient knowledge that was more instinct than learning, Ainsley lifted her free arm, the infant in the other calming and staring upward in wonder.

"Glac leis." Her voice was strong and clear.

The púca reared back, its hooves shaking the earth entire as they landed. With a screaming huff, the púca charged forward, biting the back of Rory Robertson's neck. The man screamed and flailed his arms and legs. The púca shook him violently, and the man lay still. With a last glance at Ainsley, the púca charged off to the old woods, the limp form of the last Ceannaire of the Society disappearing forever into the Night Forest beyond the veil.

Ainsley felt her entire body grow solidly numb. She leaned to her daughter and sang softly.

The dead never sleep and the night never breaks,
You're alone until forever.
With teeth that can bite and the claws that will tear,
Your soul it will not weather.

66

ALAN, 1996

THE CAR SLOWED TO A STOP IN FRONT OF THE BUNGA-
low on Sinder Avenue, and Alan opened the door.

"Pack your bag, meet me at my house. We'll leave immediately," Meg ordered, her voice frightened.

"Meg," Alan replied, looking at her eyes and their barely
contained panic. She had miraculously answered the phone call
Alan had made from the ER and had shown up in the Society's
old Buick, her face pale and frightened. The doctor left him with a
handful of drug outpatient treatment handouts that Alan tossed in
the trash outside the ER. Alan still did not remember what he had
done in the hours leading up to ending up naked on the beach—
he only had a nagging surety that it would eventually find him. All
he knew was that he was convinced beyond measure of what he
had to do, what he must do.

Meg wanted him to run. She wanted him to pack a bag and
hop an Amtrak out of Union Station to New York, or anywhere.
She was scared. Her parents had been talking about Ceit, and

she knew trouble was coming. Alan couldn't leave with Meg—he could never leave. He had a faint memory of the machete covered in blood. Maybe it was a dream. He knew though that he could never be trusted again. He was broken, and his heart was soured. He saw demons everywhere, heard whispers in his head. How long until he saw Meg's blue-gray eyes grow red and sharp, her tongue turn to that of a serpent? How long until the murmuring in his head told him to cut her, harm her? She needed to leave, and Alan needed to stay and finish what had to be done.

He said none of this, only nodded. Meg pulled the car into Máthair Shona's driveway, and Alan watched as she ran to her house. The gaping hole next to it where Katherine used to live made Alan's temples ache. Ceit was destroying his home. The last place where he remembered his mother when she was well. The last place where his father had been sane. The only home he could not be sent away from. Ceit was a plague—she was the plague of darkness that had been foreseen. She was the locusts and flies combined. Ceit was the end of their world and the reason for his emptiness.

The door to his bungalow opened, and Ceit stood in the frame. Her face was impassive, but Alan could see worry in her eyes. Without saying a word, he walked past her into the house. He went to his room and pulled a duffel bag from under his bed. As he shoved the contents of his drawers into the bag, Ceit moved to stand in the frame of his door. She watched as he zipped the bag and turned to face her.

"Why pack, little brother, if you have no intention of leaving?" she asked gently.

Alan felt like his body and soul had been shredded. He swayed back and forth and finally lost the strength to stand. Collapsing back on the bed, he folded his face into his hands, racking sobs shaking his body. He cried for all the confusion and loneliness he had felt since that day in this house so very long ago. He cried for his mother and his shell of a father. He cried for his grandmother, never respected, never seen as enough. He cried for Meg. He would never again smell the vanilla-sweet scent that lingered on the back of her neck; he would never again wake next to her, her hair intertwined in his fingers.

Ceit sat next to him. "You *can* leave, Alan. You can. I can see only a bit of the trouble you are in—you are blocking it still. But you can leave this place. You have always been free."

"I don't know what I've done," Alan choked and looked up at his sister. "I don't know."

"If you open your mind to me, I can see deep within—I can see what it is you have forgotten." Ceit sat next to him and gently brushed his filthy hair away from his face.

Alan took a deep, heaving breath and stared at his sister's face. Her eyes were so pale they hardly held a color at all, and her hair, her face were ageless. She could be ten years old or one hundred. She would always look this way. As he stared, a small earthworm, no longer than a dime, crawled from her ear and inched its way down her neck. Alan watched in stunned horror as an army of tiny brown worms spilled from her nose, eyes, ears. He fell back, a scream caught in his throat. Ceit's expression was confused, her eyes concerned. As she opened her mouth, a thousand black worms dripped down her chest. He reared back, scrambling off the bed and out the door, leaving the monster that was Ceit standing alone. Her legs and arms were now serpents, the fanged heads waving wildly. As he ran from the house, the little boy in the sky-blue pajamas appeared. His eyes were no longer black as death, and the bruises, purple and yellow, around his small neck were gone. He looked up at Alan and smiled; his teeth were perfect and white. As Alan watched, the boy multiplied, once, twice—a thousand little boys dotted the cul-de-sac. Alan threw his head back and screamed, a Caoine wail, grief for the life he had been denied.

67

CEIT, 1996

"YOU'RE SURE?" CEIT ASKED INCREDULOUSLY. MEG nodded her head vigorously. Ceit had gone to the drawer where household cash was kept and counted out what was sure to be more than enough for Meg to buy two Amtrak tickets. As she handed the money to the terrified girl, Ceit could hear her frantic thoughts racing through her head.

"I shouldn't come to the hospital with you." Ceit answered Meg's question without her having to ask it. "He called for you, but you need to bring him back here. I'll help you with money or whatever you need, but you should get him on a train tonight. Get him out of town. He's done something beyond imagining, and it hasn't been found yet, but it will. He's sick. He needs to leave this place."

Meg looked uncertain. "But my parents?"

"I will handle it all," Ceit said. "Do not tell him I had any part in this or he will reject it. He loves you and will follow you away from this place. Take him."

"Matrarc... what did he do?" Meg whispered.

Ceit closed her eyes and saw a foggy image of a small bridge. She smelled vomit and blood. "I do not entirely know. He has blocked it from even himself. Get him back here, get him cleaned up, and then leave with my blessing."

Meg nodded, and Ceit watched as she drove off in the Society's beat-up Buick to pick up Alan from the ER. She wondered if it would work. Alan's mind was a raging storm, a cyclone composed of equal parts anger and fear. If he left with the girl, would she be safe? Would Alan be prone to fall back into this madness and harm her? There was a way to watch over the both of them; she would need to pull a familiar from the Night Forest, task it with taking care of her brother and Meg. In the past, she would have had to call on Amon for this magick, but now she far exceeded what Amon could provide.

Amon had not denied the charge that Mór Ainsley's visitations during those terrible years when Ceit had been exiled from the Society were false. He had looked Ceit in the eyes and dropped to a knee.

"I have been tasked since the dawn of this time with bringing you home. By the time I found your great-grandmother so many years ago, I had been searching for the rebirth of our leader for centuries. The Night Forest has lain in the shadows for too long. I knew that with you, our Bandia Marbh, the time is coming for that which was promised."

Ceit considered this. "The stories, the blood on your hands, Amon…"

"I once told your great-grandmother a story about lions and sheep. She had your spirit but not your talents. Neither of you need bow to the sheep again, and you never need hold guilt for what nature would take in its time and of its own accord. This place, this time, this body is finite."

Ceit sent the demon back to the Night Forest. She wanted quiet. She wanted to unravel what Shona had told her. Ceit knew then that she might have saved Mór Ainsley from the Sluagh at the end, but the darkness had devoured her soul long before. She had summoned the killing fae with the intent of destroying a child and had to watch as it ate her own granddaughter from the inside out. She'd never let on; she'd never expressed any emotion at all during those terrible days. But Ceit now knew that the stoicism had been masking a horror that she had never anticipated.

Ceit sat in the old Barcalounger that now lived in her office and waited for Alan to return. As she heard the car pull up and park in Máthair Shona's driveway, followed by Meg's frantic words, she knew this would likely not work.

She rose to her feet and slowly walked to the front door. Opening it, she stood in the frame, assessing her little brother. Alan's entire being was like static. He was not making connections between any of his thoughts. The veil he had wound so tightly around his mind for so many years was starting to come undone, and Ceit could see further in than perhaps she ever had. It broke what was left of her human heart. Since childhood, he had masked his thoughts from her. He had become exhausted trying to keep her out and had convinced himself that she plotted against him. She saw their father in his eyes; all the fear of imagined threats that had haunted Boyd now lived in his son.

His words were confused, his mind bursts of sound and sharp, biting memories. As he packed his duffel bag, loudly proclaiming in his head he was never going to leave with it, Ceit felt an over-whelming wave of grief. He was lost to himself now. The little boy who had held her hand as they walked to school so many years ago—years before the Sluagh and the troubles, happy years—that little boy was dead. A shell had replaced him, and the face didn't even match entirely. Ceit did not fully know what he had done last night, but she caught stronger and stronger glimpses of it as she stood in his doorway.

"If you open your mind to me, I can see deep within—I can see what it is you have forgotten." Ceit reached out to feel his soft, wavy hair one last time. It was matted and stuck to his head, but in her memory, he was grinning up at her, a tooth missing, and his eyes were clear and happy.

His face shifted and contorted with fear. Ceit pulled away and immediately took Amon's locket from her neck, summoning the demon. She needed Amon to intercede, put on a mask that would comfort Alan—an old teacher, a neighbor, something familiar. As Amon appeared, Alan began to shake with fear and disgust. He scrambled off the bed and ran from the house, and Ceit saw him turning in circles in the cul-de-sac, a dark cry escaping from his lips. Amon looked to her for what was being asked of his presence. Ceit had no answer. Her last task on this plane had been to care for her brother, and now he was beyond what help she could provide. Meg appeared on their front steps, a bag over her shoulder and her face slack with shock. Faces peeked out from behind curtains, watching the spectacle.

"What did he see, Amon?" Ceit asked.

"He saw me entering this waking world, and his mind is slipping. He saw you as those who fear you will see. He saw a monster." Amon stood beside her. He smelled of burned wood and early dawn.

"He killed someone, didn't he?" Ceit asked, knowing the answer.

"I cannot see much more than you—his thoughts are too muddy—but where he has veiled his memories from you, I can see a bit. He did kill someone, a homeless man. They'll find him soon enough, and the police will take Alan away. It would be a mercy to take care of him before they do." Amon turned to Ceit.

"Perhaps, but I cannot," Ceit said. "I do not have dominion over this world, and I will not overstep my boundaries."

Outside on the street, Shona walked from her bungalow, slowly approaching Alan. She spoke, words Ceit could not hear and did not care to decipher. Alan collapsed into the old woman's arms and allowed himself to be led back to the bungalow. The door to Shona's house closed, and Ceit turned to Amon.

"I will finish up my affairs here. My time in this world is ending. We will be going home soon."

Amon grinned, his thin lips revealing bright white razor-sharp teeth. He was more animal than man, more beast than mortal. Soon he could drop this visage altogether and be as he was intended to be: a shadow, a wind, a terrible impulse, a wicked nightmare. Ceit, too, could untangle herself from this mortal body, and her spirit— which could be taller than the mightiest trees of the Night Forest, as miniscule as the dust on the backs of the g'nights—would be free. She could lead the creatures of her domain and put the concerns of man behind her.

68

AINSLEY, 1925

AINSLEY SAT ON THE EDGE OF THE OLD WOODS WITH her daughter in her lap, the child cooing and grasping at loose strands of Ainsley's pale hair. They had buried what was left of Maire as the sun set. The women of the Society had gathered around, already treating Ainsley as though she were their Matrarc. Her own mother had kissed her hand and stared up at her with haunted eyes. Ainsley knew what had transpired was not her fault. She had been trapped for a lifetime, a foot hovering precariously over her neck. Some of the men had already set off; they knew without asking that those who still carried allegiance to Rory Robertson were not welcome here any longer. The stars shone overhead, and Ainsley looked down at her child.

"I asked the fae to make an elixir once, to take you from me. I'm rather glad they are unreliable," she whispered.

A voice wrapped around her ear. "A changeling perhaps, trade for a fae creature, a bundle of sticks, a mass of stone and moss?"

Ainsley laughed. "I think not." The owner of the voice, the wood elf, with its skin the color of a birch and unnaturally large eyes that shone with the dancing spirit of the glow flies and fae rings, peered shyly from behind an elm.

"No. I think I will keep her. But I suppose I will need to name her," Ainsley said softly.

"You are leaving us," the wood elf said, its voice wrapping around on the night breeze, seemingly coming from everywhere and nowhere.

Ainsley nodded. "I must. I am taking the women and any who recognize my place as Matrarc. We will sail to a new land, where children are not ripped from their mother's arms, where a dead god does not rule with superstition and fear. So tell me, little one, how do we honor you in this new place? How do I reach beyond the veil in a land that is far from the old magick?"

The wood elf crept closer and knelt on the edge of the ancient forest. Behind it, a crowd of curious faces—the old nanny goat, insect and animal alike—gathered, and the night wind carried their instruction and warnings, guidance and love. Ainsley rocked her child and listened to what would be her future.

69

ALAN, 1996

ONE MATCH, TWO, THREE, FOUR, FIVE, SIX—ALAN lit the little sticks and flicked them back onto the dead grass of the little bungalow on Sinder Avenue where once a monster had eaten his mother and killed his grandmother. One, two, three, four. The voices were a constant roar, the silence worse. A monster, a monster, a thing already dead that could no longer die. Only one thing to do now. One thing, one, two, three, four. Ceit had smelled of ashes and cinder as the worms poured from her mouth. She had smelled of things long destroyed and land that would never grow a blade of grass again. She smelled of pestilence and boils, blood and the fire that brought the lightning.

Alan had gone house to house, stopping at the sites where great bulldozers sat, ready for the next day's work. It had been there he had found the gasoline, a can left by a worker ready to fuel the iron monsters on the next workday. But that would never happen. No more work, no more, no more. One, two, three, four. Already the cul-de-sac was rising in flames. He could hear the screams and shouts of Katherine and Ellaine as they stood in the street, decrying the fire, blaming Ceit. Not her fault, not her fault, mine, mine, mine. Alan laughed hysterically. Only this house remained. Ceit was nowhere to be seen. She would not stop this; she wanted it, so maybe it *was* her fault, maybe, maybe, maybe.

One match, two, three, just the right one and this house, too, would start to smolder, the smoke would rise from the old wood and it would burn, burn, burn.

"Alan!" A voice cut through the thick fog of his brain. He looked up to see Meg, his Meg, his bride, standing before him, her face smeared with soot, her eyes wild. "Alan! What have you done?"

"Free, little bird, free," he murmured. "My sister used to sing a song to me when I was a little boy. Do you want to hear it?

The dead never sleep and the night never breaks,
You're alone until forever."

"Alan, you're not making any sense. We need to get away from this place!" Meg's voice was low and pleading. Already, Alan could hear the wail of sirens in the distance, a Caoine for a lost people, a death wail for a little boy who died in a cave in Salt Lake so many years ago.

"Fear killed him, Meg!" Alan cried and then laughed at his joke. "Fear. That is what killed me."

"Alan, you're not dead, and we can still leave. Come on, now!" Meg held out a hand, and Alan remembered that if he kissed her on the inside of her elbows, she would sigh as though all was right in the world. He could taste her skin, her lips. An overwhelming scent of apple and vanilla filled his head.

"I'm dead, love, but I will come. We will leave this place forever. Dead, dead, dead." He stood and took Meg's hand. Her parents stood in the cul-de-sac, their house engulfed, the others too lost and unmoored. One last match, one, two, three, and the house with the Barcalounger and its dark wood floors and unceasing memories of pain began to disappear in smoke and flame. Alan walked away from Sinder Avenue, his bride pulling him along by his hand. He had destroyed the monster; he had slayed the dragon, and now he was the Ceannaire.

70

CEIT, 1996

THE REVELRY ON THE SHORE OF THE NIGHT WATER
was deafening. Ceit spun and twirled with the creatures that had
charged the shore in celebration. Asrai jumped from the ocean,
twisting in delight; the g'nights swarmed and danced. All manner
of fang and talon reached to the forever moon and gave thanks. All
those under her dominion screamed their delight. Amon was now
a creature of the wind, his human form abandoned. He wound
around her, caressing her bare skin. Ceit allowed all the sensations
she had denied her human form to overwhelm her. She was home.
The time would come when the Night Forest and the waking
world would meet, but tonight they would dance and bathe in
the moonlight, time dissipating around them and the stars forever
keeping watch.

71

AINSLEY, 1925

THE WIND ON DECK WAS SHARP AND BITING, BUT Ainsley paid it no attention. Most of the Society were down below, many ill, not accustomed to being on the sea. All the women and children and a few of the men, husbands and brothers of the faithful, had pledged their fidelity. The cottages on the hill outside Cork sat empty, and they would crumble in time. The memories of their lives in Ireland would all eventually crumble. Ainsley had a vision of a far-off place, a peaceful ocean away from the angry Atlantic; they were bound for America.

Her daughter gurgled in her arms, and Ainsley looked down at what she had deemed to be an imp, a trick of the fae when she grew in her belly. She felt Maire's hands on her swollen stomach and felt a pain in her heart that she had been left behind in the heath.

"She's lovely, miss. Getting a bit cold up here for the child. Might want to get below before you catch a chill."

Ainsley looked the sailor in the eyes. He was kind and a bit fearful of her, as it should be.

"Her name is Shona Maire." She smiled and started below deck to join her people, singing softly as she went.

I sing of the fae and the wood and the vine,
And the night that lasts forever.
The ghosts of your loves and the ghosts that are mine,
Will linger there forever.

EPILOGUE

From the Desk of Cooper Carlson—*LA Examiner*

AND IN LOCAL NEWS TONIGHT, THE STRANGE CASE of the Sinder Avenue cul-de-sac fire in Venice Beach. Missing persons, destroyed property, and the seeming end of a mystery that has lived in the heart of Venice Beach for generations. Sinder Avenue was home to the Society, a religious order of sorts. The community grew around them since their arrival to the area in the 1920s. A source of interest to some, ire to other, the Society existed as an anomaly, a reminder of a different era. Though not without its controversy, the group had seemed to go quiet in recent years and might have been forgotten about altogether if not for the events of last week.

As has been reported, the cause of the blaze was arson, the motivation and perpetrator as yet unknown. There were deaths at the scene—an Ellaine Cullen, from an apparent heart attack, and Shona Robertson, from burn injuries and smoke inhalation. Still missing is Shona Robertson's granddaughter and by all accounts leader of the Society, Ceit Robertson. At just twenty-one years old, Ceit Robertson was in a position of spiritual and financial leadership within the group, a responsibility that came with the title "Matrarc." Ceit Robertson's brother, Alan Robertson, sought medical attention for minor injuries at an area hospital following the fire, and has subsequently disappeared as well. Alan Robertson, as you might remember, was the subject of news himself as a child when he was taken from a foster home in the LA area and, in a highly publicized case, found to be held by a Satanic cult in Utah. He is considered a person of interest in both the arson and the disappearance of his sister. If you are listening to this broadcast tonight, Alan, there are people who need to talk to you. You might be the only one who has the answer to this puzzle.

So the mystery of the Society and Sinder Avenue remain. This is a sad story in all regards. The disappearance of a young woman, the deaths of two elderly victims, a broken young man seemingly chased by tragedy, and the end of an era for Venice Beach. To deepen the mystery, our office has learned that the land was sold to Alkhem Real Estate Developments in the weeks leading up to the fire. So what does it all mean? Sooner than you can imagine, the cul-de-sac that since 1925 has been home to this anomalous group will be transformed into a branch of the revitalized Abbott Kinney district. Will anyone remember the Society as they sip their lattes and microbrews on outdoor patios? A piece of Venice Beach history burned in that fire, and it shall never be reclaimed. So as I sign off, listeners, I raise a glass to the Society, forever embedded in the strange quilt that is Venice Beach. This is Cooper Carlson reporting for the *LA Examiner*, good night and Godspeed.

ACKNOWLEDGEMENTS

IT'S BEEN A STRANGE YEAR TO LAUNCH A BOOK, AND I am more grateful than ever for all the love from the team at Turner Publishing for their continued belief in my work and tireless energy. Todd Bottorf, Stephanie Bowman, Heather Howell, Kathleen Timberlake and many others—thank you for your energy and positivity.

I owe an eternal debt of gratitude to my editor, Kathy Wieskamp Haake, who had to wade through Gaelic, Navajo, and Irish folklore in addition to my terrible grammar.

Thank you to my agent, Matt Snow and the team at Paradigm Talent for your vision and support.

My family has been by my side through every victory, every book launch, every late night, every panic attack, every insecurity. They haven't changed the locks on me yet, and I am very grateful. I love you to the stars and back.

Sinder is about new beginnings, the shedding of old ideas, archaic traditions and mindsets. It is my hope that from the tumult and chaos, we all see a new world beginning to form. One where horror can stay firmly rooted in fiction. A waking world where we are kinder, more empathetic, gentler and accepting. Together, we can purge the old prejudices and open our hearts and minds to a more magical reality.